TRELL

NOTHING BUT THE TRUTH

TRELL

NOTHING BUT THE TRUTH

DICK LEHR

CANDLEWICK PRESS

Copyright © 2017 by Dick Lehr

"To Certain Intellectuals" from *The Collected Poems of Langston Hughes* by Langston Hughes, edited by Arnold Rampersad with David Roessel, Associate Editor, copyright © 1994 by the Estate of Langston Hughes. Used by permission of Alfred A. Knopf, an imprint of the Knopf Doubleday Publishing Group, a division of Penguin Random House LLC. All rights reserved.

"Angel" Words and Music by Chip Taylor, Steve Miller, Eddie Curtis and Ahmet Ertegun. Copyright © 2000 EMI Blackwood Music Inc., Sailor Music, Jim Rooster Music and Unichappell Music Inc. All Rights on behalf of EMI Blackwood Music Inc. Administered by Sony/ATV Music Publishing LLC, 424 Church Street, Suite 1200, Nashville, TN 37219. International Copyright Secured. All Rights Reserved — contains elements of "Angel of the Morning" (Taylor) and "The Joker" (Miller, Curtis and Ertegun). *Reprinted by permission of Hal Leonard LLC*

"Ready to Die" Words and Music by The Notorious B.I.G., Osten Harvey, Sean "P. Diddy" Combs, Barbara Mason, Ralph Middlebrooks, Walter Junie Morrison, Marshall Eugene Jones, Clarence Satchell and Leroy Bonner. Copyright © 1994 EMI April Music Inc., Justin Combs Publishing Company, Inc., Big Poppa Music and Embassy Music Corporation. All Rights on behalf of EMI April Music., Justin Combs Publishing Company, Inc. and Big Poppa Music Administered by Sony/ATV Music Publishing LLC, 424 Church Street, Suite 1200, Nashville, TN 37219. International Copyright Secured. All Rights Reserved — contains elements of "Yes, I'm Ready" (Barbara Mason). *Reprinted by permission of Hal Leonard LLC.* • "Ready to Die" by Barbara Mason, Gregory Webster, Le Roy Roosevelt Booner, Marshall Jones, Ralph Middlebrook, Walter Morrison, Clarence Satchell, Sean Combs, Osten Harvey, and Christopher Wallace. Copyright © 1993 by Embassy Music Corporation (BMI). International Copyright Secured. All Rights Reserved. Reprinted by Permission.

While every effort has been made to obtain permission to reprint copyright materials, there may be cases where we have been unable to trace a copyright holder. The publisher will be happy to correct any omission in future printings.

First paperback edition 2019

Originally published as *Trell,* Candlewick Press 2017

Library of Congress Catalog Card Number 2017953743
ISBN 978-0-7636-9275-9 (hardcover)
ISBN 978-1-5362-0490-2 (paperback)

19 20 21 22 23 24 BVG 10 9 8 7 6 5 4 3 2 1

Printed in Berryville, VA, U.S.A.

This book was typeset in Stone Print.

Candlewick Press
99 Dover Street
Somerville, Massachusetts 02144

visit us at www.candlewick.com

For Holly and Dana

CHAPTER 1
BIG VINNIE'S VAN

The moment the door swung open, I grabbed the chrome bar and pulled myself up into the bus. Right behind me, I could hear Ma hit the steps hard. She didn't need the bar. I looked back: she even skipped steps.

"Don't say it," Ma ordered the driver.

Big Vinnie ignored her. "Mornin' Glory!" he hollered.

Ma and I both knew Vinnie would say that. He always did. *Mornin' Glory!*—the words radiating from that big round sunshine of a smile.

The thing is, at the crack of dawn on a Saturday, I was not in the mood for his singsong voice. Or the "Vinnie-isms." That's what Ma and I called the things Vinnie said.

"How's the reindeer?" he said, snickering, as I hurried past him.

As in, "How's the rain, dear?" That's what I mean.

I took a seat by the window a few rows back, while Vinnie laughed like he always did, even if no one joined in. I think Big Vinnie imagines himself piloting Ms. Frizzle's Magic School Bus, taking passengers on some kind of otherworldly joyride. Otherworldly? Maybe. But joyride? No way. And if magic has anything to do with Big Vinnie's bus trips, it's more like the dark arts.

The truth is Big Vinnie had noticed a few years back that some of the mothers, wives, and girlfriends, and maybe their kids, from the neighborhoods of Roxbury and Mattapan were all needing to head out of the city on Saturday mornings, and Big Vinnie saw a way to make a buck.

He went and bought a mini school bus at an auction run by the city—a beat-up heap of yellow steel with more than two hundred thousand miles on it. Big Vinnie was handy, though, and he got the engine running okay, and he painted the body a sky blue. In cursive writing along one side he hand-painted *Vinnie's Van*, and right below drew a picture of a hula girl under a palm tree. I have no idea why Big Vinnie chose to add a hula girl, except he talked about one day, someday, going to Hawaii.

Big Vinnie's bus service has been running for six years now. Ma first heard about it from some of her friends at church— the AME Zion Church on the corner of Columbus Avenue and Northampton Street. Before that, when I was real little, every week Ma was either scrambling to find someone with a car that wasn't already filled or we'd rely on some combination of the T, the commuter train line, and regular buses. Big Vinnie sometimes tries to claim his venture is a public service, but that's crazy talk. He's no nonprofit. He is doing just fine, smilin' that round sunshine smile of his, with a waiting list of people wanting a ride.

My name is Trell, by the way, and I'm fourteen. Van Trell is my real name, but no one calls me that except the teachers at the new school I went to this year. No matter how many times I said my name is Trell, it was always, "Van Trell Taylor, would you please tell the class, blah blah blah." My ma's name is Shey, but really, it's Ma. Sometimes even her friends call her Ma.

When I dropped into my seat by the window, the morning sun was so blinding I could barely see. I heard Big Vinnie up front calling out again, "Morning Glory!" his laughter breaking from him like a big wave rolling across a body of water. The bus jerked forward, and a triple-decker outside the window on my left came between the slanted sun and me. Meaning I could open my eyes.

Just about everybody who usually takes Big Vinnie's bus ride was on board. Ma was already talking to Marlon Williams's mother, catching up on their week, with Ma asking if Marlon's great-aunt was feeling any better after the bad fall she'd taken down her cellar stairs. Terrance Jones's grandmother was in the front seat, and today she had brought along Terrance's three younger siblings. I overheard them talking about Terrance's birthday being next Tuesday. He was turning twenty-seven. My daddy's birthday was coming up, too, next month, in July. He'd be thirty-five.

The bus seated twenty passengers, and every seat was filled, with people like Ma and me, Marlon's mother, and Terrance's grandmother. We were like family because riding together these many months—years even—we'd all gotten to know one another pretty well. Where everyone lived, and who was who in their extended families, and certainly the reasons why we were Big Vinnie's regulars.

We were all taking the ninety-minute ride south of Boston to visit fathers and brothers and uncles in our lives—or, more accurately, missing from our lives. Walpole was our destination. It's the nickname for the state's maximum-security prison. It's where Marlon Williams is doing twelve for armed robbery. Where Terrance Jones is doing ten for drug dealing, or "possession with intent to distribute"—language I wish I didn't know.

My daddy? Romero Taylor?

Walpole is where he's in prison for murder.

Where he is sentenced for life.

Without the possibility for parole.

Except for one thing.

I know he didn't do it.

CHAPTER 2
VISITING HOURS

Even if Big Vinnie's Vinnie-isms are hard to take, one thing's for sure: I'm a lot more at home in his beat-up excuse for a bus than I am riding in the gleaming silver Mercedes-Benz minibus that my school owns. This year I started going to the Weld School, a fancy-Nancy private school I got myself into (and now maybe wish I hadn't). Ma and everybody else were so proud of me for getting myself out of Boston Public and setting my sights higher, for figuring out the Weld had a program for kids from Boston's poor neighborhoods, for getting an application together and submitting it by the school's deadline and then — surprise, surprise — for actually getting accepted, so long as I repeated the seventh grade.

It was my daddy who actually gave me the idea. I don't mean he knew about the Weld. But he got bussed to a public school in a

Boston suburb when he was a kid—before he started getting into trouble, that is. I decided I wanted to try to do something like that, too, and I felt pretty good about getting myself accepted. Except I'm not really feeling *accepted*. I'm lonely most of the time I'm there, and the bus ride is endless. It's summer break now, and I'm not sure I want to go back for eighth grade. This is one of the big things I need to figure out this summer—and soon.

I actually wanted to quit after the first week. I hated the bus ride, for one thing. I had to get up in the dark to catch the minibus the school sent around Roxbury and Mattapan to scoop up day students from the city. It was like an hour ride, and at first I thought I might sleep along the way. I sure was wrong. The ride was so bumpy, it made me think of Mattie Ross, the girl in my favorite book, *True Grit*. There are times where she's riding on horseback along the backcountry roads of Arkansas and Oklahoma, and it's just a whole lot of bumps, deep ruts, and constant starting and stopping. I certainly never got to school any more rested, and sometimes I had a headache or sore neck, too.

The bus wasn't the only bad thing. Or even the worst thing. It was the teachers trying too hard to seem so nice and supportive, but actually being totally creepy. My adviser, especially. The way the Weld works is new seventh-graders are supposed to meet with their adviser two mornings a week before classes. But because of my ridiculous commute, I usually got to school late, so I missed a lot of the meetings. Then one morning in early October, I got off the bus and my head and nose were all stuffed up. My eyes were swollen, maybe from allergies but probably just a cold, and Mr. Rowe, my adviser, caught up with me in the hallway of the middle-school building. I had missed our meeting earlier that week, and Mr. Rowe pulled me aside into an empty classroom. I was standing there rubbing my eyes, and I sneezed hard. Mr. Rowe studied me. He waited a second and then said that he had a question to ask.

"You're up all hours, aren't you?"

"What?"

"TV, video games, music—whatever," he said. "You're exhausted." Mr. Rowe fidgeted with his bow tie. He nodded. "I get it, Van Trell. I do. No one's home. Just you. No supervision. You're up all hours."

Mr. Rowe saw me making a face. Ma might work a lot and get home after dark, but she makes me turn out the lights at nine thirty. On the dot.

"Okay, okay," he said. "Maybe *someone* is home. But it's noisy, loud music. Party time. Alcohol, drugs—am I right? Is that why your eyes are puffy, Van Trell? You know, like second-hand smoke, from the marijuana?"

I couldn't believe it.

"You can tell me, Van Trell. It's okay. I'm here for you."

I was thinking, *Really? Here for me? You don't know anything, Mr. "I'm so hip" Rowe.* But I didn't say a word. Just as I'd hardly said a word to anybody during the first weeks of school. I think Mr. Rowe took my silence as a yes, because next he said, "We might want to explore how to go about making some changes on the home front." The meeting ended, and I hurried into class.

Besides making me mad, I was left feeling stranger than ever—and I was already feeling pretty strange, surrounded mostly by white kids. It wasn't the fact they were white that made it so weird. My neighborhood schools have plenty of white kids. The strange part was how rich they were. I'd never seen so many rich kids—coming to school in big black SUVs and Lincoln Navigators, sometimes with a driver. Living in gigantic mansions. We'd pass a bunch of them as we got to school in the morning. Houses with twenty rooms, thirty rooms, swimming pools, tennis courts. I didn't know how to talk to these kids, and I began feeling real self-conscious about where I was from. I mean, I couldn't imagine a kid from one of my classes seeing the two-family on Hutchings Street where Ma and I lived, and I didn't like that feeling. Then came times kids talked about colleges, and how their dads and moms went to Yale or Harvard or Stanford, places like that. I sure dodged those conversations, heading in the opposite direction before anyone could ask me about my daddy.

I basically went mute, and that's not me, not even close—usually you can't shut me up, and so I let Ma know how much I was hating the Weld. In November they held a special "Diversity Day," and when I got home, I told Ma it was pathetic. Because besides me, there were only a few other black and Asian kids at the school, and so I was like, *Really? Diversity Day?* They brought in a couple of speakers, but the talks were in the afternoon during sports, so it was like five people were in the room. If a tree falls in the forest and no one is there to hear it, does it make a sound? And that's when Ma stopped me. She was standing in the kitchen, hands on her slim hips and wearing that serious look I knew all too well. She made clear I had to finish what I started—and she meant a full school year. And I knew she was right, really.

Eventually there even came a moment when I began to make some sense of it, and it happened in my English class when we were reading this poem by Langston Hughes I ended up memorizing. It's called "To Certain Intellectuals," and it goes like this:

You are no friend of mine
For I am poor,
Black,
Ignorant and slow,—
Not your kind.
You yourself
Have told me so,—
No friend of mine.

Maybe it's a little harsh, but except for my English teacher, that's how I felt about Mr. Rowe and the other smarty-pants teachers who smiled down at me and gave me these earnest looks but never really wanted to know me. *You're up all hours, aren't you, living in the craziness of the inner city where everyone, young and old, runs wild?* Anyway, the poem helped me feel not so alone, and I tried my best to do my schoolwork while keeping to myself.

* * *

Big Vinnie slowed the bus as he approached Walpole, where a guard stationed in the entrance booth came into view. He was dressed in a green uniform, wore a gun on his belt, and waved Vinnie through. Vinnie drove the bus around the big circular driveway, passing the big main office building, made of stone and stained a dark gray after the more than hundred years since the granite blocks were first stacked into place. Next came the out-door space, extending for acres. It was closed in by not one but two rows of fencing topped with thick coils of barbed wire. Inside was a blacktop area where the men spent outside time. Some shot baskets, others lifted weights, and others just stood around. Farther back was the garden, where I could see some of the inmates working, and where Daddy liked to spend his outside time.

The sun was gone now, replaced by solid gray clouds that matched the color of the prison. Big Vinnie pulled up in front of the next building we came to. It was a three-story building called Cellblock C. It had prison cells in the rear, but in front was the prison hospital and the visitors' section. The way we had circled in was kind of like a slide show, with one part of the prison fol-lowed by the slide of another—the buildings in their dull gray-ness, the miles and miles of barbed wire, and the guards in green bearing arms. The images were stuck in my mind after all these years of weekly visits, always there even when I wasn't in Vinnie's bus pulling up on Saturdays, always there even when I didn't want to be thinking about it—and always leaving me a pit in my stomach.

The prison entry was burned into my memory the same way Daddy's official prison sheet was from the first time I saw it in Nora's files. Nora is my daddy's attorney; she's been fighting for him in court for a year now, and last year, when I was still thirteen, I happened to come across the single-page sheet in one of Nora's big manila legal folders. I was helping Nora at her law office. There wasn't much I could do at first, but I was able to organize files into alphabetical order, and it was while doing that that I came across a folder containing the form.

The official document had been filled out the day Daddy was taken away for good. (I was only a baby then, 1989 — one year old, to be exact.) The thing that caught my eye was Daddy's mug shot pasted on top of the page. It stopped me cold. Daddy was so young looking. He was only twenty-two, so of course he looked young. But it wasn't that. It was that I'd never seen him like *this* — two face shots, one looking straight ahead and the other in profile, and both photographs were grainy-looking, in black and white. In the one where he was looking straight into the camera, a tiny sign was pinned to his dark sweatshirt. In white block letters the sign read BOSTON POLICE. Underneath was a six-digit number — 195354. I recognized the number immediately as being Daddy's, the number that was always on the visitors list at the state prison and that was also stamped on all of the legal papers contained in Nora's files about his case. It was like Daddy no longer had a name, just a six-digit number. Then underneath the number was this date — 11-11-89 — which I also recognized. That was the day in 1989 — November 11 — when the jury unanimously decided Daddy had shot and killed the girl, and the judge sent him away to prison for life.

I could feel my heart beating faster as I gripped the sheet, studying it. Printed in bold on it were things like, *Name, Alias, Birthplace.* I read that Daddy was five foot six inches tall and that he weighed only 139 pounds. I knew that from lifting weights in prison and exercising he now weighed at least twenty-five more pounds than that. I read his parents' names (my grandparents): Joseph and Wanda. I read his alias was "Smut." I had never heard that before. Later when I got home I looked the word up in *Webster's.* Smut was a word meaning "a particle of dirt, a smudge." I walked into the kitchen holding the dictionary and asked Ma why Daddy would have a nickname like that. She laughed out loud. "I haven't heard your daddy called that in a long, long time." She said Daddy was called Smut when he was a little boy. Said his aunt had come up with it, because when Daddy was little he was always into everything, turning their apartment upside down and making a mess, and one time his momma and aunt came home to find Daddy in the kitchen, and the counter was covered in flour and sugar and broken eggshells. Daddy announced he was baking them a cake, and the two couldn't help but laugh, and his aunt started singing, "Oh, Romero, my little boy, you are always making smut, always making smut," and soon enough she was calling him Smut. Ma said it was a term of endearment, even if the word didn't seem so.

But as I read this information, I kept going back to Daddy's photo. His hair was cut in tight curls, and he wore a thin mustache that was kind of lame and looked like a teenager trying to grow facial hair. The form said his eyes were "maroon," which was odd, because they're as brown as hazelnuts. But it wasn't any of this that froze me in place. It was the look on Daddy's face. His eyes were hollow, and his mouth was slack. He was skinny then but looked heavy, slumping under the weight of something, some kind of invisible burden. In my whole life I'd never seen Daddy look so sad and lost, and it left me feeling like I might be sick.

Ma and I got off the bus, and in a single file behind Marlon Williams's mother, Terrance Jones's grandmother, and the rest who'd come this day, we slowly walked into the waiting area. The guards called it the Visitors Center, as if we were entering some kind of theme park, museum, or even a zoo. It always struck me as funny how people, especially the official-talking ones, play around with words, trying to fool us into maybe, just maybe, thinking something is not really what it is: harsh.

"Shey Taylor," a uniformed woman yelled from her chair behind a desk that was on a platform. "Van Trell Taylor." The woman had recognized us, and she signaled to another guard, who led us to the security checkpoint. Ma and I began the drill we knew by heart like we were the walking dead: take off shoes and place into bin with Ma's purse; step through a metal detector with its stop-and-go, red-and-green lights; and wait for the bin to emerge from an X-ray machine. Once we were cleared, the guard pointed across the room to a round table assigned to us.

The room was like a small school cafeteria, with its beige linoleum floor, sick-green tile on the lower part of the walls, and off-white paint on the upper half. The room was run-down — the linoleum was shredding, wall tiles were cracked and missing, and the paint was peeling off in long strips. The round tables and stools were made of stainless steel. The only good thing was the bank of windows along the far wall, so at least the outside light could shine in, except that today the sky just kept getting grayer and grayer.

Ma and I had a table by the window, and we sat down on the stools and waited. I thought about the mug shot in Daddy's folder. He certainly didn't look like that anymore. For one thing he was thirteen years older, and he was no longer trying to grow a mustache. He no longer had any hair either, because in prison he shaved his head. Daddy had quit high school his junior year, but in prison he'd earned his GED, and was now taking college courses through a program with Bunker Hill Community College. Daddy would get excited sometimes talking about what he was reading, whether it was the sociology course on urban justice or the course he took in American history. In fact, Daddy gave me some ideas on what I should read when I had to do a paper about the Civil Rights Act of 1964 for history class at the Weld. It was like we were working on the paper together, and that felt good. That's how Daddy was — not like in the mug shot but always seeming so upbeat, so happy to see us each and every week. I don't know how he did it.

Pretty soon the door on the far side opened. The duty guard entered, and behind him was Daddy. Right away I could see something was different. Daddy usually strode into the room, head high, smiling my way. But this time he was looking down, and he seemed to be shuffling, almost limping, across the floor.

"Hey, Shey-Shey." That's what Daddy called Ma. "Hey, Trell."

Daddy sat on his stool.

"Romie," Ma said. That's what she called Daddy. "Oh, Romie."

"I know. I know."

Daddy's lower lip was three times its normal size, all puffy and discolored. His left eye was practically swollen shut, all black-and-blue, and his left cheekbone was scratched, bruised, and also swollen. "I know," he said again. "I know."

Ma asked, "What happened?"

Daddy rubbed his chin. He didn't want to talk about it, but he also knew Ma wouldn't let them talk about anything else until he explained. "There was a new guy," he said, "young kid, busted selling weed. Nothing serious, really. He shouldn't even be put in a place like this."

Daddy took a deep breath. "The other guy, Lug—he's this dude from Brockton, sorriest guy I ever seen, unhappiest guy in the world, and meanest, too, a guy you keep a distance from. He starts giving the new kid a hard time, and I saw no reason for that."

"Oh, c'mon," Ma said. "You? Mr. Law and Order?"

Daddy gave Ma a look. "I know."

"So?" Ma said.

"I told Lug no reason to bully the new kid." Daddy paused. "We went."

It was a few minutes before anyone said anything. Now it was Ma's turn to take a deep breath. We all sat there, and then Ma spoke. "Nora says Trell is being a big help in the office, getting ready for next week."

Daddy looked up, happy the subject had changed, and he smiled, a crooked smile on account of his lower lip. Looking at Daddy's wounded head, it was like my head began to hurt, too. My parents started talking about the ruling from the court we were expecting on the big appeal Nora had filed during the winter in the state appeals court. In it Nora was trying to convince the court to reopen Daddy's case because the lawyer at his trial had been so incompetent. Daddy hadn't been able to pay for his own lawyer, so he was appointed a lawyer by the state, called a public defender. Nora says some public defenders are real good, but Daddy unfortunately didn't get one of them. Nora had discovered Daddy's trial lawyer was a drunk, which is kind of sad, really, if not for the fact he had Daddy's fate in his hands and was supposed to show the jury that no way was Daddy the one who shot the girl. Turns out the lawyer was drunk most of the time, and didn't ever do the basic things any defense lawyer would do, like talk to Daddy's friends who were with him when the girl was shot. Because you can't be two places at once. But the lawyer never told the jury about it. Unbelievable. Truly crazy. There was other legal stuff in Nora's motion, but this was the main one, something Nora called "ineffective assistance of counsel," which means his lawyer at the trial was so incompetent that it violated Daddy's right to a fair trial under the Sixth Amendment to the U.S. Constitution.

Daddy asked me a little about my summer, and that's when I noticed the duty guard heading toward us. This was the signal our hour was up, and I was shocked, because it didn't seem like an hour had gone by. I think it was because Daddy was so smashed up, and he seemed so down, which was unlike Daddy and strange to me. I must have spaced out. I looked over at the guard and saw it was my least favorite, a big beefy-looking guy who was never very nice. His name was Officer White.

"Time's up, Shey-Shey." Officer White hovered over the table.

"Shey," Daddy corrected. "Her name is Shey."

Officer White chuckled. "Sure," he said. Then he addressed Ma. "Whaddya think, Shey, about Romeo here? Lookin' good, you think?"

"Romero," Ma corrected. "His name is Romero."

"Romeo, Romero — what's the difference?"

Daddy grimaced from his wounds as he stood up to go. I moved close to Ma. We ignored Officer White, but the guard was not finished with us. Now he was looking at me. "Trell?" he said. "How old are you now?"

I looked at Daddy, then Ma, and then directly at Officer White.

"Fourteen," I answered.

Officer White nodded. He raised one of his meaty hands and began scratching his head. "That's what I was thinking. Exactly what I was thinking. You see, I was standing over there watching you today, thinking, ain't that sweet, the three of you together. And it dawned on me Trell was probably fourteen years old now. So, I just had to ask and, what do ya know, I was right. Trell Taylor's fourteen years old. Damn, how time flies."

Officer White paused before continuing. "I gotta say, Trell, you growin' up to look an awful lot like your momma, thin-like, and those pearly white teeth like hers that can light up a room with a smile takes up your whole face, and your skin, dark just like your daddy's, and your eyes like his, too, deep brown, big, and round."

It didn't sound like a compliment coming from him. I didn't say a word.

Officer White looked at my parents. "You two—I can imagine—must be real proud." He was nodding slowly, like he was deep in thought.

Then he asked, "You know what else I was thinking?"

None of us responded, but Officer White didn't care.

"I was thinking Trell's about the same age as Ruby."

Daddy's body stiffened.

"Romeo, you ever think about that?" Officer White's voice dropped down. "Your daughter and the little girl you killed—being so close in age?"

I was gonna explode—that's how I felt. Start screaming at

Officer White he was mean and to stop. Maybe even hit him. But before I moved an inch, Daddy stepped sideways in between the man and me. He knew how furious I was even before I knew it, and, with his back to Officer White, he gave me a hard look.

Officer White kept going. "Real tragedy, don't you think? Poor Ruby's parents never got to see their little girl on her fourteenth birthday."

Daddy didn't take his eyes off me. "Don't you dare, Trell," he whispered. "Don't you dare."

Next I felt Ma's hand on my shoulder. She steered me toward the door.

Our visiting hour was over.

"Trolls, bells, and candy canes," Daddy called to me through puffy lips.

I looked over my shoulder. My frown softened into a smile. It's what Daddy always said at the end of our visits. I don't remember when he started, but he's been saying it for as long as I can remember. Trolls, bells, and candy canes — silly stuff, really, but between him and me it was special, and it meant this: I love you.

CHAPTER 3
WHEN YOU COMIN' HOME?

The day was basically shot. Between waiting for everyone else to finish up and waiting for Big Vinnie to come get us, it was midafternoon before we headed back to Roxbury. Big Vinnie made a habit of going to Nickie's while his busload of riders were doing the prison visits. Nickie's was a pub a short drive away, and it was supposedly a popular pit stop for guards going to and coming off their shifts. One time I overheard Big Vinnie bragging that every Saturday, after dropping us off, he was at Nickie's door like clockwork in time for the opening bell, ten a.m. He seemed proud that the owner, a guy named Tony (there was no Nickie), had given him and four other regulars waiting at the door the nickname "the Starting Five." Like they were some kind of basketball team. Besides Big Vinnie, there was a guy named Ziggie, plus Paul, Pete, and Mary. Tony would let them in, and the Starting

Five would climb onto their barstools and enjoy the first pour of the day. Big Vinnie stayed through lunch and then came back in his van for us. Riding home to Boston, Marlon Williams's mother made sure to sit directly behind Big Vinnie, keeping a close eye on his every move.

Back home I went into my bedroom and stood in front of my bureau. I looked into the circular mirror balanced on top and leaning against the wall. I was thinking about what Mr. White had said. It was true: in the past year I had really grown a lot — like almost four inches — and I was now more than five feet tall, almost as tall as Ma, who was five foot three. I could easily be mistaken for fifteen or sixteen, that's for sure. It was also true I was built thin and bony like Ma. My aunt worried I was too skinny and was always trying to get me to eat more. But I ate plenty, and I think my thinness had more to do with the fact I'd grown so fast.

I tried smiling, and my mouth, the way I smiled, did look a lot like Ma's. I opened my eyes wide, and I could see what the guard meant when he said my eyes were big, round, and brown, like Daddy's, especially when I smiled. Like never before, I could see real traces of both Ma and Daddy in me, in an adult kind of way. It felt a little confusing, spotting the grown-up changes in my face. I was still a kid.

I looked at the photographs that circled the mirror. The one time each year that the prison let Ma take a picture of Daddy and me was on my birthday. We'd hold a little birthday party in the visiting room, just my parents and me, and before we left, Ma was allowed to snap a picture using one of those disposable cameras you can buy at CVS. I had arranged the birthday photographs clockwise around the mirror on my bureau, pinching the edge of each picture between the glass and the chipped wood frame.

The first couple of years, when I was still a baby, my daddy was cradling me, looking proud and smiling into the camera. But once I could stand on my own, the pose was always the same, with me leaning into Daddy's legs, my arms around him, and his arm around me.

Around the time I started to walk, I also started asking Daddy the same question at the end of our weekly visits. Every time, the same question, like if you put a word bubble next to me in every photo from when I was a toddler through elementary school, the question was the same, year after year.

"Daddy," I would ask, "when you comin' home?"

The photos were kind of like a calendar marking the years. First I stood at his hip, then his waist, and then his chest, and, last year, my head was tucked into his shoulder. In the beginning, I wore outfits that Ma got for me at Marshalls—little girly things, usually matching pink tops with leggings and with lots of frills. The older I got, the more I had a say in what I was going to wear. You can tell from looking at the pictures that I was trying to be fashion conscious, but, me being me, I could never quite pull it off. I'm basically always wearing sneakers, too, mainly because when I was little, I realized how much I liked running hard and running fast. I wear sneakers because I always want to be ready to run, to grab that good feeling that comes with doing it. To me, if a soft breeze comes up behind me, it's like someone has put their hand on my shoulder and is nudging me to get going, take off, and to run like the wind and to even become part of it. Anyway, the point is I might get dressed up, but when you look below my ankles and see my sneakers, it kind of bursts the fashion bubble. This past year is a good example. For my birthday I combed my hair out straight and tied it back in a bun, and I picked a nice black skirt with a layered, maroon-striped tank top. It all looked pretty cool. But then my feet were in orange-and-black tiger-striped Nike Windrunners—which I'd saved up for months to buy.

In the pictures I am smiling the big, toothy smile Officer White says reminds him of Ma, and that's because I'm as happy as I can be spending my birthday with Daddy. There's one picture, though, where something's not right. I'm hugging Daddy's waist, and he sure looks happy and proud to be with me, but you can tell I'm forcing the smile. I'm trying, but the look is halfhearted.

Mainly it's in my eyes. There's no spark, and instead you see sadness. It's from five years ago, when I was in third grade and I was turning nine. Daddy kept asking me, "What's wrong, Trell?" But I wouldn't tell him. I didn't want to ruin the birthday visit. He could tell, though, and he kept giving me looks, and so I'd make a pouty face back at him and shake my head, trying to be funny.

When I got home, though, I wrote him a letter. Ever since I

was little, I've written to him. In first grade when I learned the alphabet, the first thing I told Ma was I wanted to write to Daddy. So I wrote him a lot, and I made drawings with crayons for him, and I sent him cards on other holidays. He wrote me back, and sometimes his letters were basically little stories that he had made up, stories that always began, "This is a story about a princess named Trell."

This time I wrote him about what was bothering me. It was his case, and what people always said about him. For some reason right before my birthday that year there were stories on TV and in the newspaper mentioning him. I didn't really understand why, but different people were trying to get elected mayor and they kept bringing up Daddy's case when they were talking about safety in the city, the street gangs, and violence. The newspaper articles called Daddy a murderer, and I got really upset. I looked at the articles thinking all kinds of thoughts. I knew what they said was wrong, but there it was, in the paper. So I knew people were getting the wrong message. I didn't know what to do. I wanted to call the reporters and ask them "Why? How could you?" But how do you get them to print the right message?

The worst part, though, was in school. After the TV and newspaper stories, some kids gave me a hard time. Not my friends—they wouldn't say anything. But other kids said things. Especially one kid named Paul Parish. It's like meanness runs in his family. His uncle, Lamar "Thumper" Parish—well, everybody knows about Thumper Parish.

Thumper Parish is this scary, older guy—he's like around

Daddy's age—who rides around in a shiny Mercedes-Benz. He's huge, like over six feet, always wears dark glasses and dresses in a dark leather coat. He runs a gang, an outfit that moves drugs and guns, and it's like everyone freezes, like he's God or something, when he struts through the projects.

He's that big and bad, and he holes up with his family on Castlegate Road in his idea of a castle—an old Roxbury house built a long time ago, in the early 1900s, when the neighborhood was home to fancier people, so the homes were built with high ceilings and lots of pretty carved wood moldings. Thumper Parish turned the house into a fortress, behind a cement wall, with dogs roaming the grounds, and now him and some relatives live together under the same roof. It's where Paul Parish lives, and at school he acted like he was some kind of celebrity, but he was really just a mean little kid who watched the news on TV and bothered me with comments: "Your daddy's never getting out" and "He killed a little girl." Like it was a joke and he was just being funny. Well, I got mad and defended Daddy. I defended him with words. I didn't get into a fight. But I stormed over to Paul Parish and got in his face, and I guess I got to shouting because before I knew it, we were both taken to the principal's office.

I told Daddy about this in the letter I wrote after our little prison birthday party celebrating me being nine. The very next Saturday, Daddy sat me down and spent the whole visit talking to me about school. He told me he didn't want me to be getting into trouble. He even said maybe the boy Paul Parish actually liked me, and his meanness was opposite to how he truly felt. "No way," I said. The only good thing about Paul Parish I ever noticed was he seemed to take his schoolwork seriously, always raising his hand to ask a question or answer one. But *like* me? "That's crazy," I told Daddy. He tilted his head, and said, "Well, maybe so. But you have to just walk away, Trell." He told me no matter what anyone said about him or the legal case, I had to learn to just walk away. I promised him that I would try.

Daddy also explained why people kept talking about his case and why the newspapers were running stories with his name in them. He said politicians were using the case as a symbol for violence in the city. They were all trying to get elected mayor, and when they were giving speeches to voters about how tough they would be on street crime and how they were the best candidate to bring law and order to the city, it was easy for them to mention his case because a little girl had been murdered. It had become one of the most famous murder cases ever.

"Didn't you recognize one of their names?" Daddy asked. "In the newspaper stories, the one doing most of the talking about my case, like he was bragging or something?"

I shook my head.

"Frank Flanagan?"

I shook my head again.

"District Attorney Frank Flanagan," Daddy said, "the guy who came after me?"

"Ohhh," I said. Yep, I had heard Ma and Daddy mention his name—the man who had had Daddy arrested in 1988 and then got him convicted at the trial a year later. Daddy explained Frank Flanagan was running to get elected as mayor of Boston and was campaigning as the toughest of crime fighters.

I have to say, the things people said about Daddy hurt me and were hard to take, whether they came from Paul Parish in school or from the DA Frank Flanagan in the newspaper. Because I know my daddy would never harm a little girl. It would get so frustrating. But I felt better when Daddy was done talking to me about all of this, especially when he explained he was never giving up. He would find a way to fight his conviction no matter what all of the politicians said about him or what the whole city of Boston seemed to think about him as a result.

I hugged him good-bye. "Daddy, when you comin' home?"

"Trolls, bells, and candy canes," he said, smiling.

CHAPTER 4
NORA WALSH

The wheel of birthday photos on my mirror has only one with the three of us together—me, Daddy, and Ma. I'm standing between my parents. We're hugging each other, smiling, and because the picture is the only picture I have of the whole family, I consider it a treasure. The photo is from last year, when I turned thirteen.

It was taken by Nora Walsh. She wasn't our lawyer yet. In fact, her taking the picture was the first contact we had with her. But we didn't just get a family photo from that first meeting. The whole thing led to her becoming Daddy's lawyer. Here's how:

Ma and me were with Daddy having my birthday party at one of the prison tables when I noticed Daddy looking across the room. The visiting room was real crowded that Saturday, more crowded than usual. I'm not sure why, but it was jammed with small clusters of girlfriends and relatives, hunched over the small tables trying to get some kind of privacy even though privacy was impossible.

"Daddy, what you trying to see?" I finally asked.

Daddy pointed halfway across the room to a young woman seated at a table with an older prisoner. She was dressed in a gray pinstriped pantsuit and had a black canvas briefcase with her, and while she looked all put together in a slick, businesswoman kind of way, there was also something hard-looking about her. Her hair was cut pretty short and spiky, with a frosted silver tint, which I guess was her way of trying to look older, but it didn't work. Her face was too creamy-smooth and unwrinkled for that, so the hairdo ended up giving her an edgy look. Plus her lipstick was bright rose. It was like she was in a struggle, the business suit giving her some kind of professional look, but the hair and lipstick making it look like she couldn't wait to get home and change into blue jeans.

Daddy said her name was Nora Walsh. She's a lawyer, he said, here to meet one of her clients, the man seated with her. Daddy said the man had worked on the outside as an "enforcer" for a big-time outfit in Boston called the Winter Hill Gang.

"Like the Mafia," Daddy said, "except they're Irish, not Italian."

The enforcer was serving a life sentence for murder. He and Daddy were friendly, and the enforcer had told Daddy about Nora Walsh. How she'd paid her own way through Suffolk Law School. Just like she'd paid her way through an all-Catholic private high school, which was where the enforcer had come to know her. The enforcer's daughter had attended the same school, and the two girls were close friends. So when Nora Walsh graduated recently from Suffolk Law and then passed the bar exam, it was as a courtesy to the enforcer's family that she took him on as a client. "She's a fighter," the enforcer told Daddy.

Daddy said that after the enforcer told him this, he had started watching Nora Walsh whenever she came to the prison. Daddy learned that she might be new, but she quickly got herself a reputation. She worked for an old-time Boston criminal defense lawyer, and, being the rookie, she was given the firm's grunt work. That meant handling the disciplinary cases for inmates before a board made up of prison officials. They were called D-Board cases. Nothing glamorous, that's for sure, but Daddy said Nora defended prisoners before the D-Board as if she were appearing before the United States Supreme Court. Daddy heard stories how she was loud and gruff and impossible to intimidate. Daddy said her eyes even seemed to catch fire when she got mad at the board, and he said the enforcer told him the reason Nora was so tough was that she grew up poor in a housing project. Most people think only black people live in housing projects, but in Boston some projects are filled with poor white people, and Daddy told us Nora Walsh grew up in one of those. She was the third of six girls, all close in age, whose mother had divorced their father, a hopeless drunk, soon after the sixth was born.

"She never had it easy," Daddy said to Ma and me while looking over at Nora Walsh. "She's a fighter. It's what I need."

The enforcer began telling Daddy he should get Nora Walsh to be his lawyer, too. The two of them decided that while the enforcer was meeting with Nora Walsh during a Saturday visiting hour, my daddy would drift over.

"That's the plan," Daddy said. He stood up. "Trell," he said, "come with me."

Holding hands, Daddy and I walked across the room. I could see the enforcer talking quietly to Nora Walsh and tilting his head in our direction, so I knew he was explaining the situation the same way Daddy had just done. The enforcer got up and, as if on cue, excused himself. "I'm gonna get a candy bar," he said.

While the enforcer walked away toward the vending machine along the far wall, Daddy put out his hand. "My name is Romero Taylor," he said. "This is my daughter, Trell."

Nora Walsh studied Daddy first. Then she looked at me. I thought I saw a tiny smile on her face come and go quickly when her eye caught the new neon-yellow Reebok 500s that I had gotten for my thirteenth birthday.

"I'd like to talk to you about my case." Daddy's voice was wavering, and I realized he was nervous and pumped up, both at the same time.

Nora Walsh looked over in the direction of the two guards at the desk on an elevated platform at the front of the room. She looked back at Daddy and reminded him that Walpole Correctional Institute had strict rules about attorneys speaking to anyone other than the prisoner they'd signed in to see.

Daddy nodded. "I know, I know," he said, talking fast. He

asked her if she would come back to see him. Daddy was rushing his words.

"I didn't do it," he told Nora Walsh.

The guards had taken notice of the unauthorized encounter. One of them began walking over. We didn't have much time.

"What's this, Ms. Lawyer?" the guard asked firmly.

Daddy spoke first, and his voice was different now, no longer tense but casual and cool. "Oh, Officer, jeez, I was just asking this nice lady if she wouldn't mind taking a picture for us." Daddy nodded over to Ma back at the table with the disposable camera in her hands. Daddy told the guard we never had a picture of the three of us, that it was always just him and me because Ma was the one who had to take the picture. Daddy was hoping just this once we could get a family photo, it being my thirteenth, a milestone—I was a teenager now.

"I figured you definitely wouldn't want me to be asking one of the guys," Daddy said. "I figured no way. Then I spotted the lawyer."

"You shouldn't be figuring nothing," the guard interrupted.

"Sorry."

Daddy's apology hung there.

Nora Walsh said, "I have no problem with it."

The guard stood still, thinking. I looked around for Officer White. I didn't see him, which I took as a good sign.

Nora spoke again. "It's her birthday, Officer."

"Okay, okay," the guard said. "Be quick."

We were. Nora Walsh took the camera from Ma. The three

of us smiled and hugged, like it shows in the photograph on the mirror in my room, and Nora Walsh snapped the picture. It was when she was handing the camera back to my daddy that he held her gaze and whispered, "Please, come back?"

Nora Walsh pursed her lips. "Let me think about it."

She turned and walked away.

During the ride home afterward, Ma explained we had some work to do, and so on Monday after school, Ma was waiting for me outside our house. She marched me over to Blue Hill Avenue, where we caught the bus downtown. When we got off, she kept looking at a slip of paper she gripped in her fist, and she led me past a bunch of stores that included the famous Filene's Basement, where Ma always took me shopping ever since I was little and she bought me my first birthday dress there. We made our way up to Tremont Street across from the Boston Common and near the Park Street T station, where a dozen or more panhandlers shuffled around like zombies, unnoticed by the crowds of men and women dressed up in suits hurrying to get home. Ma stopped and looked up to check the number on an old office building against the one scribbled on the piece of paper.

"C'mon," she said.

The narrow brick building seemed invisible the way it stood, tired and old, between a pair of gleaming glass office towers. You could easily have walked right past it. Inside the empty lobby, littered with dust balls, candy, and empty cigarette packs, Ma looked at the office directory on the wall and then headed downstairs. I followed her, and we found the law office. There were no windows in the basement, and the air smelled stale. Inside the office an old lady with gray hair cut in a bowl shape sat at a desk with a cigarette hanging from her mouth. Her desk was piled with papers and files, and her ashtray overflowed with cigarette butts.

Ma asked for Nora Walsh.

"She's in court," the lady said. Then her telephone rang.

Ma led me back out into the hallway.

"Out here we can at least breathe."

We waited. I pulled out my homework, and then, after a little while, we heard footsteps on the cement stairs. We looked up. Nora Walsh marched out of the stairwell with a canvas briefcase hanging from one shoulder and a stack of manila folders in her arms. Ma walked toward her.

"Ms. Walsh?"

"Yes?"

"Shey Taylor, and this is Trell—from the prison the other day?"

"I know who you are."

"Romero was railroaded, Ms. Walsh."

The way Nora Walsh just stood there without making any movement reminded me of the prison guards, how they always stood stiff, with blank expressions, like statues.

Ma continued. "Trell was just three months old, Ms. Walsh. The three of us were upstairs in our apartment above the Humboldt Superette when police came. Ms. Walsh, Romero would never do anything like what they said."

"Listen," Nora Walsh finally said, "I've got thirty minutes to get a motion filed or my case is toast." She kicked open the office door and disappeared inside.

The next afternoon Ma and I returned to 178 Tremont Street. That's one thing about Ma—she's stubborn. The word *no* is not in her vocabulary. So we came back a second time. We were expecting to be told Nora Walsh was again over at the courthouse six blocks away. But the secretary surprised us. She said Nora Walsh was working at her desk. Except Nora was too busy to meet with us, the secretary said between drags on the cigarette that seemed attached to her lips.

The same thing happened to us Wednesday afternoon, and also on Thursday. The secretary told us each time that Nora Walsh was too busy for walk-ins off the street. On Friday I got smart. I brought along *True Grit,* and I was enjoying reading about Mattie Ross so much I forgot I was seated on a cold basement floor. Mattie's only fourteen, but she hunts down the man who killed her father. She gets a lawman to help her, a mean and crusty-faced cowboy with a name you never forget: Rooster Cogburn. The story gets scary at times. There's skeletons and snakes galore, for one thing. Mattie even loses part of her left arm. But I don't want to give too much away.

Ma brought along some reading, too. She leaned against one wall, looking at the test-prep book she'd been lugging around for a few months. The book covered rules and regulations for buying and selling property. Ma had a new idea she was going to get her real estate license, which Ma's friend Claudette thought was pretty funny. Not that Ma couldn't study and pass a test. But real estate in Roxbury? "Shey, my dear girl," Claudette had said, "who but a crazy person would ever want to buy into *our* neighborhood?"

We were both reading when the law firm's solid wood door suddenly swung open. The hard sound it made snapped me to attention. I climbed to my feet. Ma, still leaning against the wall, straightened up. Nora Walsh strode out into the hall. I stood next to Ma. Nora Walsh had her arms folded.

"Ms. Walsh," I blurted out, "you have to—"

Ma interrupted me. "Trell, stop."

Nora Walsh maintained that all-business look she had.

"You can go home," she said.

"Go home?" Ma said.

"I've got a ton of work," Nora Walsh said.

I couldn't keep quiet. "Go home? We can't go home, Ms. Walsh."

"Yes, you can," she said.

Then her blank face cracked—that tiny smile I'd seen at the prison when she spotted my running shoes. "I made an appointment. It's next Monday. I have business at the prison, but I've arranged to meet with Romero first."

"Thank you, Ms. Walsh, thank you!"

Nora Walsh turned to go back into her office.

"Ms. Walsh?" I said.

She stopped and looked back. "Yes?"

"My daddy? He didn't do it, Ms. Walsh. He's innocent."

Nora Walsh looked at me. "That's what they all say."

The next day, during our weekly Saturday visit, all we talked about was how Nora had agreed to see Daddy. Daddy wanted to keep us from getting carried away. "C'mon, it's just a meeting," he kept saying. "Who knows what's going to come of it?" Besides, he said, there's a chance the meeting would never even happen. Lawyers were always canceling for one reason or another, and the prisoners themselves at times couldn't keep an appointment, like if they got into trouble.

But Monday came, and Daddy got word to us afterward that he and Nora Walsh had met. Ma and I felt this big rush to race through the week. We couldn't wait to get to the prison when Saturday finally came to hear how things had gone. During the bus ride, I was more frustrated than usual with Big Vinnie's slow-poke ways and his Vinnie-isms.

And when we got to the visiting room, Daddy said he wanted to tell us the whole story, starting from the beginning. "Remember how nice it was on Monday?" he asked. It had been a dry and sunny spring day, and Daddy said sometimes on nice days the prison lets lawyers meet with their prisoner clients in the fenced-in courtyard off the visiting room. "We sat outside at that picnic table there," Daddy said, pointing to the table that was empty now. I tried imagining Daddy and Nora Walsh seated there as Daddy talked. "It felt good in the sun," he said.

Daddy said, "I didn't want to waste her time. I got right to the point." He said he asked Nora Walsh to take up his legal appeal, to be what Daddy called his appellate attorney.

Daddy said, "She shook her head, looked at me, and said, 'No way.'"

Daddy said he asked, "Why not, Ms. Walsh? Why not?"

She told Daddy, "First thing, my name is Nora. Stop calling me Ms. Walsh." She then told Daddy that challenging a murder conviction required an *experienced* appellate attorney, not one just out of law school. "The ink on my bar exam's barely dry," she said.

But Daddy pushed. He told Nora he'd heard from the enforcer about her battles with prison officials over the D-Board cases. That she was a woman elbowing her way around and not taking any guff from the guys who run the courts and the prisons, and that's exactly who he needed—a fighter.

Nora practically laughed out loud at Daddy. D-Board cases? She said the difference between an administrative hearing inside the prison and a murder appeal in the Superior Court was as big as the difference between sandlot baseball and the big leagues. "You get that?" she said. "I haven't done a trial yet—not even for a misdemeanor—never mind working up an appeal for a murder of this magnitude."

Daddy said, "I don't care about no experience. The thing is, you don't owe anybody anything." Daddy looked straight at Nora. "I'm doing life," he said. "Life! Without the possibility of parole! It's a death sentence," he said.

"Do me one favor, please," Daddy asked. "Read the transcript from my murder trial." He said if she read the transcript, she would learn a lot about him, some of it being not very nice—and pretty dark, actually. She would find out he was a high-school dropout who got caught up in cocaine and saw easy money dealing drugs in Roxbury. "I had this line I was known for," Daddy told her. "I'd be standin' on my corner and when someone came along my pitch was, 'If you pass me by, you won't get high.'"

He told her she would learn from the trial transcript how much he enjoyed buying nice things with the drug money, kept a wardrobe of new sneakers and Adidas running suits, and began shaping his Afro to look like actor Jim Kelly's bowl-shaped hairdo. "You know Jim 'the Dragon' Kelly?" he asked her. "Kung-fu dude with Bruce Lee in *Enter the Dragon* and *Black Samurai*? I wanted to be him, so bad. Two crazy-good movies."

She would also learn the 1980s was a different time, that Romero Taylor was a bit player in a bigger crazy thing going on around crack cocaine, not just in Boston but in New York and Detroit, and in any city, really, where instead of using fists to settle beefs everyone was starting to settle scores with handguns. "Got to be when a car backfired in Roxbury, people dropped to the sidewalk thinking they were being shot at," Daddy explained. "Families on their porches just doing their thing? They had to keep one eye rovin' up and down the street, ready to rush inside for cover if they spotted one of the gangbangers comin' down the lane."

But, Daddy insisted, if she dug into the transcript, she would also learn about a time before he gave in to the easy money and before he dropped out of school, a time when he was taking the bus every morning to school in Wayland, one of the wealthy "W towns" outside Boston — Wellesley and Weston being the other two. They and a bunch of other towns surrounding Boston were part of a program where kids from the city got a better chance by attending schools in better-off communities. It's like what the Weld School does, except the Weld is private and the town schools in Daddy's program were all public. My daddy's host family had a boy his age, and they were all really nice to him. Daddy would spend time after school at their house, eat over, and sometimes sleep over. He and his friend, when they were in the eighth grade, even got jobs together at a local Star Market as bag boys, and for a while Daddy was proud of returning home to the neighborhood with a paycheck.

But he also carried this feeling he didn't really fit in, a feeling that grew bigger as he did. Eventually, when he was fifteen, whatever was happening in Wayland, especially the minimum wage he earned at the supermarket, could not compete with the cash he saw on the streets of Roxbury. He began stealing cars and selling weed. He was making bad choices. But it was hard, so very, very hard, to resist the world that, just by chance, was his, compared to a world beyond that was not.

There was more, he told Nora Walsh. He and Ma may not have been married when I was born, but they always tried to be a family, the best they could be, even after his arrest. Daddy and Ma were even able to work it out so they could marry during his time at Walpole. The day they picked—February 11, 1990—happened to be the same day Nelson Mandela was released from prison in South Africa. So their wedding turned into a family story that brought a smile every time Daddy told it. Daddy was late for his Walpole wedding—kept Ma waiting in the visiting room—because he was glued to a TV in his cellblock tuned in to special news from across the ocean: Mandela, free at last, walking hand in hand with his wife, Winnie.

But most of all, if Nora Walsh studied the record, she would learn that while Roxbury was carved up into street gangs back in the 1980s, gangs with names like the Humboldt Raiders and the Castlegate Boys, the one thing my daddy Romero Taylor was *not* was a gangbanger and killer the way the government made him out to be. He might have been a drug dealer who tried to get along with everyone, and who loved the feeling of wads of cash in his pocket, but he was no way like Thumper Parish and some others who were born to be bad.

"Just do me that favor," Daddy said once more to Nora Walsh. "Just read the transcript, and after, if you think I'm guilty, I'll never bother you again."

Daddy stopped. He looked across at Ma and me. He took a deep breath. But no words came out. He took another breath. It was like torture.

"Daddy! Then what happened?"

Daddy smiled. "So that was on Monday. She left, said she was making no promises. Then yesterday I got a call in the cellblock. It was her. When I took hold of the receiver, my hand was actually shaking. Nora Walsh started out saying she first had a confession to make—which was to say the only reason she agreed to look over the transcript was to get you two to quit stalking her. She said she figured if she read the material, she could then say to us, 'Okay, I've read it, now that's it. Leave me alone.' But once she started reading, she said it didn't pass what she called her smell test. 'Something stinks' is what she said. 'I don't see how the jury came back with a guilty verdict on the basis of a bunch of kids saying they saw you at the scene. No gun, no forensics, nothing. Cops still haven't found the gun. It stinks.'

"I told her I sure do agree—it stinks, and always has."

So, Nora Walsh told Daddy she'd be his lawyer.

When Daddy finished, you'd think I'd be on my feet jumping up and down, the way I usually do when I am excited. But I wasn't. I don't know if I was in shock or what. But I just sat there feeling serious, letting the news sink in. Nora Walsh had agreed to be Daddy's lawyer. I saw time was running out on our visit, and suddenly a thought popped into my head. For the longest time I had said good-bye the same way, with a question: "Daddy, when you comin' home?" Well, this was the day one year ago—the day Nora Walsh became Daddy's lawyer—when that changed. When a little girl's question turned into a bigger girl's promise.

I said, "Daddy, I'm gonna get you outta here."

CHAPTER 5

CASE NO. 80-88

I've explained how Nora Walsh became Daddy's lawyer, which means at this point I'm pretty much caught up on everything important about Daddy's case. Except for one thing. And it's a pretty big thing. The reason Daddy was put in prison for the rest of his life. The murder of Ruby Graham.

Growing up, I never wanted to know too much. I knew that a little girl killed in 1988 was the reason Daddy was in Walpole for life. But that's about all. Then last year Nora came into the picture, and by September she'd cleared out her schedule to start working on the case. That's when I basically went to work for her—as an intern. I'd started at the Weld the same month, and the school requires students to do internships. It was Ma who came up with the idea, and Nora said she could use all the help she could get. Ma also liked the idea that she'd know where I was after school until she got home. The school was impressed—student legal intern—and approved it right away.

I began spending most of my free time at Nora's office. I'd do whatever Nora wanted, and the first thing was to help her organize the case documents, transcripts, and police reports called Form 26s that she considered pretty important. Form 26, she explained, was a report police had to write about any person they interviewed during an investigation—a witness, bystander, anyone. We set up a long table in one corner of her office. Nora began calling it the war room.

I liked helping out, making new files and writing labels on them. (It was while I was doing that stuff that I came across Daddy's "rap sheet" with the arrest photo.) Anyway, the more I hung around the law office, the more Nora gave me to do. I could tell she appreciated me being around, and it felt good to be doing something on the case. Made me feel proud and, in a funny way, closer to Daddy. After a while I began to feel like I was an expert on the files and was some kind of a junior attorney.

I'd watch Nora spend hours reading through the mountain of material, taking notes, scratching her head, and occasionally throwing a file against the wall. "I can't believe this! I can't believe this!" she'd scream. Then, after about a month, I arrived at the office one day after school, and Nora was leaning against the doorjamb as if she'd been waiting for me. She was acting all calm-like and had this serious expression. It felt like something was wrong, so I asked, "Is everything all right?"

"Of course," Nora said. "It's just . . ." Then she touched my shoulder gently. "Trell? Follow me."

Nora led me to a tiny couch and sat me down. "It's just that, now that I've gone through all the documents, I need to talk to you about why your daddy's in prison. I need you to know everything, so that nothing, absolutely nothing, will come as a surprise when we go to court and appeal your daddy's conviction."

My eyes began popping out of my head.

Nora pulled a manila folder stamped *80-88*. "You've seen this number on most of the files you've been organizing. It's the official number for his murder investigation." Nora looked me straight in the eye, and she said, "Trell, I'm going to tell you the story of your daddy killing a girl named Ruby Graham — the eightieth murder in 1988, and thus the homicide number 80-88."

Nora knew the way she said it was going to shock me.

"But my daddy didn't kill anybody!"

Nora took my hands into hers. I didn't even realize I'd jumped off the couch and clenched my hands into fists. Nora made me sit back down.

She said, "But the police and the district attorney say he did, and they got a jury to agree." Nora let go of my hands and settled into the couch. "I need you to know exactly how they managed to do that."

"Okay," I said. "Let's do it." And as Nora began talking, I held my breath like I was underwater or something. She started by explaining that the summer of 1988 was a wicked one in cities like Boston — record heat and lots of crime. Cocaine and other drugs, guns, and street-gang warfare were all out of control—making for an altogether rotten time to be in the city. I'd already heard something about this from my parents, because this was the same summer they were welcoming me into the world, on May 5, and with all the random violence and innocent people getting hurt, they'd told me how worried they were for my safety, even just going out for a stroll.

Nora said, "By the time August came around, the number of murders in the city was on pace to set a record." The way she was talking was the way someone telling a story talks, like a teacher to her class at circle time, or maybe like a lawyer to a jury during a trial. Start at the beginning. Set the stage. Introduce the main characters.

That summer, Nora said, a young couple named Romero Taylor and Shey Brown were living in Roxbury with their newborn baby, Trell, in a tiny one-bedroom apartment above a corner market on Humboldt Avenue. Romero Taylor was twenty-one years old, and while he held a job here and there—in the spring, for example, he'd worked the counter at the Au Bon Pain at Logan Airport—he mainly made money dealing drugs. Mostly marijuana but sometimes cocaine. He got "product" from any number of sources, and he was the sort of dealer known as "unaffiliated," meaning he worked alone and was not part of any organized drug-dealing operation. It was his easygoing manner that enabled him to freelance and get along in a Roxbury neighborhood that was like a tinderbox ready to explode, given all the turf battles. His girlfriend, Shey Brown, meanwhile, was a bit younger, just nineteen. Until their baby was born, she'd worked as a cashier at a Goodwill store in Dudley Square.

"Humboldt Avenue, where they were living, was no walk in the park. Not much better today, but back in 1988, the street was legend. Everybody in the city knew Humboldt Ave. I grew up in Brighton, a world away even if it was actually only three miles from Roxbury, but in my neighborhood we all knew about Humboldt. And what I knew, what every kid knew, was you didn't want to be going there, because of the shootings, the drugs, the gangs. It had a nickname, too."

"Heroin Alley," I said.

Nora seemed surprised. "You know that? Heroin Alley?"

I don't know why Nora thought I wouldn't know. I mean, I grew up in Roxbury, and where Ma and I live is only like a ten-minute walk away from Humboldt. So of course I'd heard stories about Humboldt Ave.

Nora continued. "Roxbury was carved up into a bunch of sections, each one controlled by gangs named after the street where their members lived. Like Humboldt Ave.— the gang there was the Humboldt Raiders. It was run by Tyrone Williams and his three cousins. The gang from Castlegate Road? It's called Castlegate Boys, and Castlegate has always been run by Lamar Parish."

"Thumper Parish," I said.

"Say again?"

"Thumper Parish. He's who you mean. I know about Thumper."

"You do?"

"His nephew—his name is Paul—is in my grade. I think he's a total jerk, by the way. Mean. I'm sure his uncle is the same, probably worse."

Nora was studying me, and I think she was beginning to realize I knew more than she thought. "Okay, then," she said. "Ruby Graham? 80-88?"

That's when I shook my head. "I don't know much about her." The neighborhood, I knew about. The murder, that was something else.

"Well, okay." Nora paused, like she was turning a page in her story to start a new chapter. "Ruby Graham was thirteen and lived with her family on a street off Humboldt. But that summer, her mother, with all the trouble, she'd sent Ruby to stay with relatives in North Carolina to keep her safe. Ruby was gone as soon as school got out in June, through July and during most of August. The Saturday night of August 20, 1988, was her first night home. She returned by bus, arriving in the morning. She spent the day with her mother and younger brother, and then after supper went out to see some of her girlfriends she'd missed all vacation.

"Lots of people in the neighborhoods were out, sitting on porches or yard chairs, trying to catch any hint of a breeze after another broiling-hot and muggy day that saw temperatures soar into the nineties. In some parts of the city, the fire department had opened hydrants so that kids could soak themselves. It was like Boston was one big fat candle melting away in the heat, and people were edgy.

"Ruby and her friends were gathered on a part of Humboldt Ave. with lots of shade, a grassy corner lot that was empty except for a squat brick substation owned by the light and power company where a large maple tree hung over the street like an umbrella. Ruby, so happy to see her friends after being away, was radiant—laughing and teasing some of the boys from the street who were hanging out. The heat wasn't a bother to her, and she was like a pick-me-up energy bar for the others, who stood around as she told stories about being on a farm down South.

"You see, Ruby had climbed atop the blue mailbox like it was a horse, and was sitting there, swinging her legs. She was the center of things, really, happy as happy could be, as the minutes passed by and got on toward dusk."

Nora stopped again. I could picture everything she was describing. I knew that corner lot, which wasn't grassy anymore but was littered with broken glass, rocks, and rubbish ever since the power company shut down the substation. I knew the maple tree she meant, and the blue mailbox was still there. I'd walked past it plenty of times over the years. I mailed my letters to my daddy in that box.

"Ruby wouldn't have known anything about the dispute that had been going on. How could she? She'd been away. Plus the latest trouble was not even forty-eight hours old. It had begun two nights before, when some Humboldt Raiders had ambushed two boys from Castlegate. Humboldt stole their cash and drugs, and during the altercation, one of the Castlegate boys was injured. To make matters worse, it turned out he was the boyfriend of Lamar Parish's sister. He was taken to Boston City Hospital with a deep knife wound in his gut. Lamar's sister became hysterical. The situation was red-hot the next couple of days, Lamar Parish and his Castlegate Boys wanting revenge.

"Ruby wouldn't have had a clue, as she sat on the blue mailbox. Maybe she noticed some of the Humboldt boys glancing around and looking over their shoulders while she entertained everyone with her summer stories. But probably not. Ruby was most likely just swinging her legs and happy to be home."

I began to feel queasy. Even if I did not know specifically what was coming next, I knew from growing up in Roxbury how things could change in a flash. How behind every tree, down every alley, in every stairwell or porch or rooftop, was the possibility of danger. It was a darkness that in an instant could swallow any light you had, and it could happen randomly and unexpectedly. You could be feeling good and carefree one moment, running for your life the next.

Nora said, "One of Ruby's girlfriends told police later that the sound of the first gunshot was like a firecracker. Initially no one was alarmed. But then came a second pop, and a third, and someone in the group screamed and began pointing to the lot behind them. A person wearing, of all things, a Halloween mask had come from behind the brick substation. He held a gun in one hand and was firing his weapon as he ran toward the group gathered on the corner.

"The kids began screaming and scattered. Some hit the ground and frantically crawled for cover behind cars and tree trunks, while others ran off every which way down the street. The shooter fired a few more times and then suddenly stopped. He turned and ran off. It was over in a matter of seconds. Kids lifted their heads off the ground, looked around, seeing if it was safe to get up."

Nora began shaking her head. "I don't know if it was because the gunman was running toward them as he fired his weapon, but for whatever reason, he couldn't shoot straight. His target had been the Raiders, but none of the boys from the gang were hit.

"Only one person was shot—the girl perched on the blue mailbox. Ruby Graham. Real quick, the others saw that Ruby was sprawled on the sidewalk, facedown. She wasn't moving. The kids shouted her name, and one girl ran off to get Ruby's mother. Blood pooled on the sidewalk near her head."

Nora stopped. She sat still for a moment. Then she stood up and walked over to the long table filled with boxes. She flipped through the files. I stayed on the couch, frozen in place. Nora pulled out a document, studied it, and returned to the couch.

"I was looking for the doctor's report." She sat back down next to me. "I wanted you to see it."

Nora put the report in front of me. It was two pages. She moved her finger down the document, scanning it until she found the part she was looking for. "Here," she said, pointing to a paragraph describing three bullet wounds. The words in the paragraph were hard to follow—big words and medical terminology. But I'll never forget the words describing the bullet that killed Ruby. The bullet penetrating her head, wrote the doctor, had "proved incompatible with life."

This was the worst story I'd ever heard. I covered my eyes.

CHAPTER 6
GUILTY: ROMERO TAYLOR

I didn't think I could take any more, but Nora was not done. She pulled out more stuff from the files — more original documents and some newspaper clippings. She pulled the main Boston Police Form 26 that officers responding to the scene had filed later that night. Using her finger, Nora moved from box to box on the form to show me the information the officers had typed in. The box for *Time of Incident* was filled in with "8:47 pm." The box for *Victim's Age* was filled in with "13," and Ruby Graham's occupation was listed as "Student." In addition to the section devoted to the victim, there was a section titled *Persons,* which meant suspects. The number 1 was typed into the box for *Number of Perpetrators,* and the answer "No" was typed into the box labeled *Can Suspect Be Identified at This Time?* In a bunch of boxes devoted to describing different things about a suspect, such as race, age, build, or weight, the same answer appeared: "Unknown." The only thing known about the shooter was contained in a box labeled *Special Characteristics (including Clothing)*. In this box, the officers had typed "Dark Adidas Running Suit & Halloween Mask." Police had little to go on, that much was clear.

Next, Nora came to a section where the officers briefly described the situation, which she read aloud. "Officers responded to a radio call for a child shot at 118 Humboldt Ave. On arrival, officers observed large crowd near corner and a young black female lying on the ground in front of mailbox bleeding from gunshot wound to the rear skull area. Victim's mother was at the scene at this time. Ambulance #5 with Conley and Drew responded and transported victim to Boston City Hospital, where victim was pronounced dead at 9:34 pm by Dr. Shah."

That was it, the official account of Ruby's killing in four sentences, and I could feel myself taking short breaths. Nora pointed to a list of names of other police who were there. "You see that?" Nora asked. "You see who showed up?"

I looked at the list under the heading *Responding to Scene* and saw that Boston Police Commissioner William Dewey, Police Superintendent Tom Evans, and three deputy police superintendents were there. "It's the entire top brass," Nora said, "and believe me, they were not working at that hour. They were having dinner, keeping cool someplace, and doing whatever they did with family or friends. But once this call came in, without a doubt they all responded. You know why?"

Nora pulled out a newspaper clipping and pointed to the

first paragraph of the news story about the shooting, which read, "A thirteen-year-old Roxbury girl was shot and killed last night while sitting on a blue mailbox, the youngest victim of street gang violence in the city's history." Nora kept poking her finger at that line of the story. "That's why," she said. "That's why the brass turned out. Every murder is horrible, of course, but this one, the killing of Ruby Graham, was beyond the pale, as if the violence in the city had crossed some kind of boundary line: Ruby was both an innocent bystander in a beef between two street gangs and also the *youngest* shooting victim ever. Her murder caused an uproar."

Nora then began flipping through a stack of newspaper clippings to prove her point. "Ruby became an instant symbol for all that was wrong that summer—the drugs, the guns, the gang wars and violence. The city was rocked by this kind of lawlessness." Nora showed me one headline in the *Boston Herald*. It read, "Win Drug War for Ruby!" and the story was about Ruby's funeral. "'Nearly one thousand mourners offered their tearful good-byes to thirteen-year-old Ruby Graham yesterday as outraged community leaders called for a renewed fight against the drug war that took her life.'" Nora shook her head. "People were scared," she said, "and they wanted action." She pointed to parts of the newspaper story where some city officials were calling for the deployment of the National Guard in Roxbury because things were so out of control and Boston police couldn't protect them.

"The National Guard—can you believe it? Soldiers in the streets of Boston?" Nora shook her head again. "The police were under a lot of pressure. Every day the story was all over TV and radio, and on the front pages of the newspaper—stories about the investigation and its lack of progress, and about the community growing almost hysterical, demanding justice. The situation got strange fast, and dangerous—a feeling in the city something like the Salem witch trials. The police seemed obsessed with making an arrest no matter what."

I knew what Nora meant when she mentioned the witch trials. We had studied them in history class. The whole thing was so creepy, the fact that settlers in the 1690s in Salem, Massachusetts, got so freaked out that actual witches might be around that they hanged a bunch of women and girls without any of them getting a fair trial. I learned that panic is a scary thing.

Nora pulled out another newspaper story tracking the investigation in the days after the murder. The headline read, "Police Net Closing In on Girl's Killer." The story opened: "An army of police working around the clock is closing in quickly on the killer of a 13-year-old girl who was hit by a stray bullet, officials said yesterday."

"See what I mean?" Nora said. "Pressure on police, the clock ticking." Nora put her hand on another newspaper in the pile and paused before pulling it out.

"Then there's this," she said, spreading open the paper and running her hand across the front page like she was smoothing a wrinkled sheet. The headline was the biggest yet on any of the papers Nora had shown me. "RUBY KILLER JAILED!" screamed the words in big block letters across the front page.

Nora grumbled something about how awful the media could be. "'Ruby *killer* jailed,'" she repeated. "What a headline. What about innocent until proven guilty?" Nora let the question hang there and then shrugged. "But no one seemed to care. The cops had caught the shooter. It was like the city breathed a big sigh of relief. People could sleep again at night."

I looked at the newspaper and saw a picture of Ruby's face next to the article. The photograph must have been taken at a birthday party when she was younger, because she didn't look thirteen. I could see the collar of a dress with a flowered print, and there was a bow in her hair. She was smiling brightly. She looked nice, this girl on the blue mailbox who had been shot and killed.

Next to the photograph was the news story that began, "Romero Taylor, a Roxbury gang member with a history of drug dealing, sits behind bars in the Charles Street Jail this morning, charged with the senseless killing of a 13-year-old girl on Humboldt Avenue a week ago." I could feel a chill race up my spine.

"But why?" I asked.

Nora said, "What?"

"Daddy. Why him?"

Nora said, "That's exactly what I need to explain next: Why Romero Taylor?"

In the days following the killing, she said, police canvassed the Roxbury neighborhood and tracked down kids who had been socializing on the street corner that night. Some of them told the cops that about an hour before the shooting, they'd seen Romero Taylor walk by. "No big deal, right? Your dad and mom—and you, just three months old—were living not even a block away, in the apartment above the store." But one of the kids said something that made the cops sit up and pay attention. "One kid said Romero Taylor was dressed in an Adidas running suit."

The police perked up. "Homicide detectives had already learned that the shooter was dressed in a black Adidas running suit. So when police heard your daddy wore Adidas, it was like some huge breakthrough. Like they'd discovered the gun with your daddy's fingerprints on it. Which, of course, they hadn't. Not even close. They never found the gun. But they treated the clothing info like that, and whammo! The focus was suddenly Romero Taylor. He was the prime suspect, a drug dealer who, the police theorized, had gone to settle a beef with Humboldt and by mistake killed a little girl. It was like the detectives had blinders on—from that moment, they only wanted to get Romero Taylor, put together a case against him."

Nora turned again to the front-page newspaper story about Daddy's arrest. "And they got their man—in just a few days!" She jammed her finger angrily at the story's middle paragraphs. "Here," she said. "Look at this, the talk at the big press conference announcing the arrest. Here, right here, where the district attorney—Frank Flanagan is his name—is speaking to reporters."

"He the one who ran for mayor a few years ago?" I asked.

"That's right—and he lost." Nora seemed glad about that. "You interested in politics?"

"Not really. It's just Daddy mentions his name sometimes."

"He's a piece of work, Frank Flanagan," Nora said, "always running for something. Heck, he just announced he's going to try a second time to get elected mayor." Nora did *not* seem glad about that. "Anyway, this shooting went down when Flanagan was first letting on he was power hungry—that he had his eyes on the mayor's office. So, after Ruby Graham was killed, he came out swinging, promising a quick arrest, selling himself as a crime fighter on a warpath who considers criminals maggots. That's his word—maggots. He talks openly about the pleasure he gets from 'hurting the people who hurt people.' Those are his words. In the story right here—look at the way he's boasting to the media about your daddy's arrest: 'We have many, many witnesses,' he's saying, 'who have identified Romero Taylor as the gunman who shot young Ruby Graham.'"

Nora moved her finger farther down the story. "This other quote is from Richard Boyle, the lead homicide detective on the case. He's the one who put the cuffs on your daddy." Nora read the paper: "'Taylor is a known drug dealer,' Boyle said during the press conference, 'and a member of the Castlegate Boys.'"

I was slumping farther into the couch.

Nora noticed. "You okay?"

"Not really," I said.

Nora gave me a hard look. I guess it was her lawyer look.

"You need to know this," she said. "I told you—and it gets worse, because next came the trial and the 'many, many witnesses' Frank Flanagan bragged about who were waiting to testify against your daddy. You see, they never recovered any physical proof—the gun, the mask, things like that—so Flanagan's case was built on testimony from kids, each saying something that pointed to your daddy. It's like a puzzle, with each kid providing a piece, and when you had all the pieces, it showed your daddy did it."

I was puzzled.

"Here's what I mean," Nora said. "The biggest pieces came from three kids Flanagan called to testify, all three being from the neighborhood. Their names are Juanda Tillery, Monique Catron, and Travis Golson.

"Juanda Tillery: She wasn't with Ruby and the other kids at the mailbox, but she testified that a little before the shooting, she had walked past Romero Taylor on the street. Not only that, but she also said he was wearing a black Adidas running suit. Juanda testified she knew Romero and that they began chatting. She said that another young man then came along and asked Romero if he wanted to go off and party with him. Juanda testified that Romero replied, 'Naw, I got some business.' Juanda said the man teased Romero, urging him to party instead, but that Romero shook him off and insisted in a real serious tone, 'Can't. I got to do this. It's business.'"

Nora stopped to take a breath. I think she wanted this to sink in.

"Then there was Monique Catron," Nora said. "Monique lived with her mother in an apartment on a side street off Humboldt. She testified that after hearing gunshots, she rushed to her front porch and saw a man hurry by, 'putting a gun inside his pants.' Monique then testified that when Detective Richard Boyle showed her photographs of nine different men and asked her if she could identify the man with the gun, she pointed to Romero Taylor. Monique told the jury, 'I'll never forget those eyes, because they was like staring right at me.'

"Last came Travis Golson," Nora said. "Travis testified that on the night Ruby Graham was shot, he'd seen Romero outside an apartment house a few blocks from the crime scene. Travis testified that Romero had a pistol on him. Travis also said he overheard Romero asking another man where he could find two of Humboldt's leaders. Travis further testified that he met up with Romero later that night, after the shooting, and that Romero was acting 'strange' and had 'ditched' the pistol."

Nora stopped there. "That's it—the key eyewitness testimony about your daddy before and after the shooting. When you put the pieces of the puzzle together, you have your daddy armed with a pistol asking for the whereabouts of the Humboldt Raiders while saying he's got some business to take care of; you've got him hurrying away from the crime scene stuffing a gun in his pants; and you've got him later acting nervous and telling someone he's ditched a weapon."

Nora said, "The jury took only an hour to find him guilty of murder."

It felt like there was no oxygen left in the room.

"It's bad," I said. Everything Nora said had sounded so real. Those kids—Juanda, Monique, and Travis—had really gone to court. Each had sworn to tell the truth, the whole truth, and nothing but the truth, and taken together, like pieces of a puzzle, the way Nora said, it sounded true. Had Daddy *maybe* done something terrible? The thought scared me. "It sounds really bad," I said.

CHAPTER 7
THE RULING

When Nora was done marching me through the murder of Ruby Graham and Daddy's conviction, I was in a deep funk. In all my life up to this point—all thirteen years of it—I'd never once thought Daddy was guilty, mainly because he told me he was *not* guilty, and so did Ma. But after hearing about the girl getting shot, and hearing about what kids like Juanda Tillery, Monique Catron, and Travis Golson had said, it sure sounded like Daddy did it. Just thinking this way made me feel kind of crazy.

I wasn't hungry at supper that night, even though Ma made one of my favorites, turkey tortilla pie, a recipe she'd found in a cookbook for kids. I wasn't in a talkative mood, either, even though dinnertime was when Ma and I usually went over how the day went. Mine stunk, that's for sure. Sometimes at the table we did "Thorns and Roses," sharing the worst and best thing that happened, but I didn't want to go there. The whole day seemed like one giant prickly pile of thorns.

After barely eating a thing and saying nothing, I drifted into the living room and plopped onto the couch while Ma cleaned up. Stacked in front of me on the coffee table were three books I had to read for the Weld—"independent reading" they called it. In the spring we'd had so much excitement: I'd gotten myself into private school, and Nora Walsh had become Daddy's lawyer. But at that moment, on the couch, I felt like a feather pillow that was flattened, all its feathers gone.

I stared at the books the Weld had assigned to seventh-graders. Ma had left them there for me. She'd bought them at a used bookstore we went to, the Book Rack, which luckily happened to have all three.

I looked at the titles. *The Catcher in the Rye* was one, *The Giver* another, and *To Kill a Mockingbird* was the third. From the summaries, I could see why the Weld picked *Catcher;* it was about a boy from a private boarding school. Jeez, like I cared. To me, the most interesting one looked to be *Mockingbird,* about a girl named Scout. Ordinarily I'd pounce and begin devouring it. I wasn't in the mood.

I noticed Ma leaning against the kitchen entry. She was drying her hands on a towel and looking at me. The way she was framed in the door, with her silhouette aglow from the kitchen light behind her, reminded me how pretty she was, and how young, too, compared to other mothers I'd seen during my visits to the Weld's campus.

"Nora called," Ma said. "Tough day?"

I nodded. Ma walked over and sat next to me.

"None of this is easy, Trell. None of it."

I leaned into her shoulder. "How do you do it, Ma?"

That's when Ma put her arm around me and talked for a while about her and Daddy, going back almost to the beginning, when they were together in their tiny apartment above the Humboldt Superette, excited to be having a baby. She knew about Daddy dealing drugs, but he was promising to stop. "He was one month into a class at the tech school to learn a trade. He wanted to be an electrician. But Ruby Graham was killed, and nothing was ever the same."

Then Ma started telling me things I never knew before. "You were still a toddler at the time," she said, "and it was maybe the lowest point in all of this.

"Daddy's very first legal appeal had been rejected by the court, and I never saw him so down. He lost all hope." During the next visit, she said Daddy insisted she move on and find someone else. "He demanded that I walk away from him, told me he didn't want me to come see him anymore. There was no reasoning with him." On the next visiting day, Ma said, he wouldn't even come out to see her. The prison visits stopped. Four months passed. Ma said, "I even went on a date, someone your aunt fixed me up with." My eyes widened. This was news to me.

Ma saw my reaction, and she chuckled. "Let's just say it did not go well." Ma looked at me. "The thing is, Trell, it wasn't like my feelings for your daddy had changed. It was circumstances that were different. I was a single mother, taking care of you, and when I looked around, I saw way too many broken homes. I wasn't going to let that happen to us. I mean our home *was* broken, with Daddy being in prison. But it was broken from the outside, not on the inside. Daddy loved me, and I loved him.

"Because your daddy wouldn't see me, I wrote all this down in a long letter. It was my letter of demand, I suppose, because I demanded he see me and stop all his nonsense. He did, and by the time I left the prison, we were back on track. We got married soon after, too — a promise is a promise. It's never easy, Trell, you know that yourself."

We sat still for a moment.

"Ma?"

"Yes, Trell?"

"The case against Daddy, what Nora told me, it looks so bad."

"I know."

"You ever have any doubts? About Daddy's innocence, I mean."

Ma gently took my face in her hands and looked at me. "No, Trell. I know him — my husband, your father. No way he would ever hurt anyone."

I felt better after talking to Ma, and I felt even better after I got to Nora's office the next afternoon. Nora told me the worst was over. "That's the government's case, what I've been telling you," she said, "and it's painful to hear, I know."

Then Nora said, "But I don't buy it."

She said she had this feeling after studying the case—an instinct is what she called it—that something was rotten. She said her doubts partly had to do with the prosecutor, meaning the lawyer who conducted the criminal trial for the government. "When it comes to justice, I don't trust Frank Flanagan."

She said there were things about the case she had noticed right away as she went through all of the documents and materials from the murder case:

Like Frank Flanagan telling reporters on the day Romero Taylor was arrested that he had "many, many witnesses" who incriminated him.

But Nora, after looking through the police documents, said police did not conduct their first interviews with Flanagan's three key witnesses—Juanda, Travis, and Monique—until *four months after* Daddy's arrest.

Like Mr. Richard Boyle, the main homicide detective, saying Romero Taylor was a member of the Castlegate Boys.

But when Nora came across the records from the police department's gang unit, which kept books that were kind of like photo albums and listed the members of the different gangs, Daddy was not listed as belonging to Castlegate *or to any street gang.*

Or this: even if Mr. Boyle was right, and Romero Taylor was Castlegate like he claimed, Nora said it made absolutely no sense.

"They say your daddy was part of Castlegate? But he and your Ma lived on Humboldt Ave., and there's no way that could happen. You can't have a Castlegate gang member living on Humboldt. The Humboldt Raiders wouldn't allow it. Your daddy, he'd be a dead man."

This made the most sense to me of all the points Nora was making. I lived here, and what Mr. Boyle was claiming showed he certainly did not.

Nora said it was going to take time, "like peeling an onion," and that's pretty much how we've spent the past year. Nora wading carefully through box after box of documents, poring over the material, and writing notes about things she came across that didn't make sense to her, notes that filled pages. Then she put the notes into separate folders. Her folders grew into a pile on the wooden table. October turned into November, which turned into December, and then came January of this year, when Nora said she had to start writing the appeal. She threw some legal terms at me I'd never heard before — writ of habeas corpus, for example, which Nora said was Latin for the document a lawyer files in court when they want a judge to review the legality of their client's imprisonment. Nora said it was probably easier to call what she was writing an "opus," or, more accurately, a motion for a new trial. But I actually liked the sound of habeas corpus.

"How's the habeas corpus comin'?" I'd ask Nora when I got to her office.

"It's coming," Nora would reply, "slowly." Because the writing took time, that's for sure. Nora was not getting paid for working on Daddy's case. We couldn't afford to. So Nora juggled the appeal with working on cases where she earned money. Plus,

Nora said, this was the first time she'd taken on a legal project like Daddy's. Sometimes she'd look at the pile of folders and say it looked like a big mass of clay, and she compared her challenge of writing a motion to a sculptor carving a sculpture from a clay slab.

"You get what I mean, Trell?" she'd say, rubbing her chin and staring at the pile of folders — the clay — atop the wooden table.

Her goal, she said, was to channel everything she was thinking about into the idea that Daddy's lawyer at his trial was a complete bust — which, like I said before, is called "ineffective assistance of counsel." I mean, this first lawyer didn't even bring up the fact that Daddy had an alibi — because when Ruby Graham was shot, Daddy was with some of his friends in an apartment a few blocks away. Anybody knows you can't be two places at once. But the lawyer did not get those friends to testify at the trial that Daddy was with them. How bad is that?

Finally, in February, Nora was finished. I got all excited in a way that surprised me, because, while that was a good thing for sure, it wasn't like anything had actually happened. Nora had gotten the legal paperwork all in order. That's it. But after nearly nine months, as I got closer to being fourteen, a part of me had begun feeling life would always be this way — Nora working on, but never finishing, the appeal.

So when Nora was done, and as I watched the pages spewing out of the printer in her office, I got this over-the-top feeling, as if someone had announced Daddy was being set free. It was crazy, I know, but I felt a joy. The joy felt big, and I wanted to share it, but I knew I couldn't. It had to be kept secret — at the Weld, I mean. Because during the year I'd never talked to anyone at my new school about Daddy's situation.

But apparently I wasn't too good at hiding the feeling. The next day, the same day Nora planned to bring the paperwork for the appeal to court, my math teacher was pacing back and forth holding a piece of chalk when she abruptly stopped in mid-sentence in front of my desk.

"Van Trell," she said.

I looked up at her. "Yes?"

"What's so amusing?"

"Amusing?"

"The smile. Ever since you sat down. You've been smiling."

I realized the problem right away. I never smiled when I was at the Weld. Never. Which meant even the slightest one was noticeable, a break in my everyday face. My math teacher had picked up on the crazy joy I was feeling inside. The joy I hadn't been able to hide. Quickly I made the smile go away.

"Nothing," I replied.

"Well, it seems like something. Why not share it with us?"

I repeated, "Nothing."

That afternoon after school, me, Nora, and Ma walked with a purpose to the clerk of court's office at Suffolk County Superior Court in downtown Boston, where Nora filed the writ of habeas corpus, all 249 pages of it.

Then came the wait.

* * *

February. March. April. May. June.

Waiting.

Ma and I kept up our visits on Saturdays, riding to the prison in Big Vinnie's Van, and we were waiting. Daddy got into a fight trying to protect a new inmate, and we were waiting. In May I turned fourteen, Daddy turned thirty-five in early July, and we were still waiting. We did our little birthday things in the visiting room, but it was like we were jittery or something. I could tell when I added the photo of Daddy and me to the photo wheel on my bedroom mirror. It was on our faces. The smiles are forced, distracted.

It was summer, and still we were waiting. I tossed and turned at night. Noise leaked into my bedroom now that my window was cracked open. I heard car engines revving, shouting, police and ambulance sirens, even the occasional *pop, pop, pop* of a gun. But I'd grown up with those sounds. They weren't what kept me awake. It was all the stuff on my mind. Like Daddy getting into fights. That sure worried me, even if part of me was proud he was sticking up for someone else. Or Officer White — the way he seemed to be trying to provoke Daddy so Daddy would get into trouble. Or the appeal — that was the Big Thing, because that's the legal thing Nora had been working on for so long, and now it has been five months since Nora submitted it to the court.

I was on pins and needles. In the daytime Ma went to her new job as an assistant manager of the CVS store in Dudley Square, and on her way she'd drop me off at the Orange Line T stop to take the subway downtown to Nora's office.

Each day I'd ask Nora, "Any word?" Not "Hello, Nora," or "How are you, Nora?" but, "Any word?" Nothing else seemed to matter, except waiting to get word from the court. "Not yet," Nora said. "Not yet." She tried to keep herself busy with her other cases, and I tried to keep busy helping her. But really there was not a whole lot to do, and we waited.

Then came the Wednesday morning the second week of July. Ma was rushing to get out of the apartment so she wouldn't be late for work when the phone rang.

"You need to come down here."

It was Nora.

"I have work," Ma said.

"No," Nora said. "Call in, tell them something. You need to come. Trell, too."

The front lobby of Nora's law office was empty when we arrived. We looked around and walked farther into the office. That's where we found Nora. She was lying on the couch with one arm covering her face. On the floor, sheets of paper were scattered about. It looked like she was passed out.

"Nora?" I said.

She turned her head. "Don't say it," she said.

I think she meant don't ask her, "Any word?" because before I could say anything, she said, "We got word."

I looked at Ma, and Ma looked at me. I felt dizzy. I turned to Nora as she began to lift herself up and turn to face us. But this was not the Nora I knew. Nora usually moved quickly, in sharp bursts. She was intense. This Nora moved slowly, as if in a trance, as if she weighed several hundred pounds and had to use every ounce of energy to sit up.

She slid off the couch onto the floor and, seated cross-legged, began shuffling the papers on the floor back together.

"It's not what we wanted," she said.

Ma and I, as if on cue, slumped to the floor, too. The three of us sat there, a pile of papers in the middle like some kind of campfire. Nora took a deep breath and flipped through the papers. "The judge denied the motion," she said. She found the page she was looking for and read, "'Romero Taylor, through his appeals attorney, has not demonstrated that his first attorney rendered ineffective assistance of counsel during his first-degree murder trial. I hereby conclude there is no reason to warrant the grant of a new trial.'"

No one said a word for what seemed like a year.

Nora looked up.

"I'm sorry," Nora said.

I had never seen Nora look like this—defeated. Ma put her head down, and I could tell she was trying to hold it together and not cry. I grabbed at the ruling. I was mad. "It doesn't make sense, Nora!" I shouted. "It doesn't make sense. What does the judge mean, 'There is no reason to grant a new trial'? Nora, you gave him reasons, lots of reasons."

"You're right, Trell. We presented a lot of reasons why the judge should overturn your daddy's conviction."

I stood up. "There's got to be something more we can do."

"I've done as much as I can—as a lawyer, I mean. We filed an appeal, and the judge said no."

Maybe it was because Nora saw how upset and angry I was, because she looked at me, and the regular look on her face began to return.

She said, "Because you're not lawyers, the thing you two probably don't realize is the way the legal system works: it almost always says no to people like us who think a jury was wrong. The legal system doesn't want to look back at cases that are completed. It doesn't want to reopen the past, because every day there are new crimes and new trials to deal with, and it needs to focus on new business if it hopes to stay afloat. That's what we're up against: a legal system that mainly wants to look ahead, not in the rearview mirror. It worships what it calls 'finality.'"

Nora flipped through the judge's ruling. "Here's what I mean." She cleared her throat, shook the paper so it was flat, and then read out loud in a deep voice to sound important, like a judge. "'We can't give new trials to everyone who establishes, after conviction, that they *might* be innocent. We would have no finality in the criminal justice system, and finality is important.'"

Nora looked up. "You follow this?" she asked.

"But it's not fair," I said. "Daddy's trial was not fair."

"I agree, Trell," Nora said. "But what I'm saying is the system makes it really, really hard to reopen a finished case like your daddy's. It wants finality."

"There's got to be something," I insisted.

We sat there in silence for a few minutes. Then Nora slapped the floor and popped up. "Maybe there is something."

I pulled Ma up.

Nora threw the judge's ruling onto the table, as if she were done with it. "We *are* right—the case is rotten, even if the judge doesn't agree. Maybe if we could get some help."

"What kind of help?" Ma asked.

"The press," Nora said. "We've been working pretty much on our own, in a vacuum. Basically, the only people who know about my motion are in this room, plus the judge. Of course, anybody can go to court and read the judge's ruling. It's a public record. But no one is doing that. No one is paying attention. Why? Because no one knows about it."

She looked at us and smiled. "What if we changed that?"

"How?" I asked.

"What if we got a reporter interested? What if a reporter knew what we know about your daddy's case—and what if the reporter was able to uncover some new evidence? What if the reporter wrote a story about this?"

I liked the idea.

"If people were to know what we know, that might put pressure on the police, the district attorney, the legal system— on all of them to take another look at the case. They might prefer finality, but with lots of publicity, they'd have to do something."

"I like this idea," I said, "a lot."

"Easier said than done, though," Nora said. "It's not like I can call up a reporter and assign them a story about your daddy.

I don't even know any reporters. But before you got here, I did make one phone call. I called a friend, another lawyer, who's mentioned in the newspapers all the time. I asked him if he could recommend someone good at digging into a case like ours."

"What did he say?"

"Well, first things first. Before we go down this road, I need to know you two are okay with it."

Ma was cool—anything to help Daddy, she said. Me too. I wasn't afraid of the truth. The problem had been all the lies. People at the Weld or anywhere else knowing the truth, I had no problem with that.

I asked, "What's the reporter's name?"

"Clemens Bittner," Nora said. "Works at the *Boston Globe.*"

CHAPTER 8

THE NEXT MOVE

Before we left Nora's office that morning, Nora called the *Boston Globe* and asked for the reporter named Clemens Bittner. I could tell right away that he didn't pick up. Nora left a message on his voice mail, a frown crossing her face as she put down the receiver.

"That is one grumpy dude," Nora said.

I asked what she meant.

"His voice," Nora said. "Not that I should complain. I'll never win any Miss Manners awards, but this guy — whoa." Nora imitated the reporter's phone voice for us. "Bitt-*ner*," she said, her voice dropping to a growl that sounded like rubbing rocks together. "Leave a message, if you want. No promises." Nora looked at us. "That was it. Click. Nothing like, 'I'm away from my desk.' Or, 'Leave me a message and I'll get back to you.' Nothing. Just a couple of grunts and the dial tone."

In my mind I pictured Clemens Bittner as a wrinkly, hundred-year-old man, his eyes barely open.

Later that day when Ma checked in, Nora said the reporter hadn't called her back. Nora tried again the next day. She tried again the day after that, and over the weekend, too. When I showed up to Nora's office on Monday, she shrugged. "Nothing," she said.

Another waiting game! This time waiting to see if a newspaper reporter would simply do the decent thing and return a telephone call. Waiting, waiting, and more waiting—it was driving me nuts!

"It is very strange," Nora said. "I don't know what to do."

I was standing in Nora's office, trying to think of something. My mind was blank. Then a question popped into my head: What would Mattie Ross do? Just like that: if Mattie were in my shoes—or my Nike 2000 runners, to be more specific—what would she do?

Nora asked, "What are you thinking?"

"I'm thinking we don't want to wait for Clemens Bittner to call us."

The next morning, I didn't go to Nora's office. I decided instead to take the T to the *Boston Globe*. If Clemens Bittner wasn't calling

Nora back, I would go and see him myself. That's what I'd figured Mattie would do. So that's what I should do, too.

For breakfast I ate a couple of peanut-butter-crunch sports bars. It's maybe the one *good* thing I learned during my year at the Weld School, from the track coach. She was always talking about eating a balanced diet and staying hydrated.

The day was sunny and already hot. When I left our apartment, I was wearing my knee-length running shorts with a short-sleeved green T-shirt, mint-colored socks, and, of course, my Nikes. I was taking a shortcut down Castlegate Road to the Orange Line station when someone called out.

"Yo, Trell!"

I turned to see who was yelling. I rolled my eyes. *Oh, no,* I thought.

"Trell! It's Paul. Paul Parish."

"I know who you are."

I hadn't seen Paul Parish for at least a year, and that was okay by me, because in school before I switched to the Weld, the only reason he ever talked to me was to mouth off.

Paul had closed the gate to his uncle Thumper's walled-in compound and was coming toward me. I looked past him over the fence at his uncle's fortress. The three-story Victorian was painted green with neon-orange trim, the same colors on the Jimi Hendrix T-shirt I'd seen for sale in the corner market. Mounted on each first-floor window were heavy black iron grills, like prison bars. Usually window grills were to keep anyone from breaking into some place, but on Thumper's I wasn't so sure. His bars were maybe to keep anyone from escaping.

At this early morning hour, all was quiet, in a creepy way.

"Hey, Trell," Paul said, catching his breath as he hustled over. He was wearing a white T-shirt over a pair of baggy, torn blue jeans that were too big and too long. The cuffs dragged on the sidewalk.

I didn't say anything.

"Long time," Paul said. He smiled.

I gave him a look.

"How you been?" he asked.

I turned and began to walk away, but he kept up with me.

"Really, Trell. How you been? You likin' that new school?"

I was expecting something mean to come out of his mouth, but nothing did. He smiled at me, a smile that seemed genuine, and he was standing there waiting for me to say something. It was like he wanted to have a real conversation. He said, "It's the Weld, something like that, right?"

"How'd you know?" I said.

"When you didn't come back to school, I asked around."

Before I could say anything, a shiny black Mercedes-Benz came sweeping in from around the corner, its tires screeching. The car braked sharply right in front of Paul's house. With its darkened windows, there was no way to see who was inside. But we could hear loud voices. The passenger door flew open, and out climbed Paul's uncle, Lamar "Thumper" Parish. Thumper walked around the front of the car. He was screaming at the driver the whole time, and he was jabbing the air with his finger like he was thrusting a knife.

My eyes widened. Thumper Parish, the way he moved, stirring up street dust like a cyclone, sure made a statement. He was tall and angular like a basketball player. The black nylon jacket he was wearing, with matching workout pants, was unzipped and flapping as he walked, revealing a flat and muscled stomach.

I couldn't make out exactly what Thumper was saying, except he was warning the driver he had better quit screwin' up, that he had one job and only one job, and there were no excuses. Thumper stopped beside the driver's-side window and pounded on the glass until the window rolled down. Thumper reached inside, grabbed the driver by the neck, and pulled hard. A pair of silver sunglasses, made of thick plastic, popped off the driver's face. The glasses rattled across the pavement.

Thumper pressed the driver's face down sideways against the open window, and the driver's eyes bulged. I could see the driver had a big, ugly, red scar running from above his left eye down onto his cheek. Thumper bent closer and began screaming into the driver's ear, "You understand me, bro? You got it? Do your job. Just do your job!"

Thumper stopped, as if he sensed he was being watched. He turned quickly and saw Paul and me. He dropped his hold on the driver and pushed him back inside the Mercedes.

"What *you* doin', Paulie?"

Paul did not reply. Thumper stood tall and straight, staring at us.

"Who you?" He meant me. Thumper tilted his head, like he was figuring something out. It made me a little nervous. He barked, "You Romero's kid?"

Like Paul, I didn't reply.

Thumper's face was twisted up, like a fist, and tired looking. His eyes were rimmed in red. His teeth were unnaturally white, like he'd gone to the dentist to have them worked on and polished.

Flashing those teeth, he stared at Paul. "Get inside," he ordered.

To me he said, "You, girl. Get outta here."

I could still feel my heart beating when I took a seat on the T, and it wasn't until I switched to the Red Line and got off at the newspaper's stop that I felt normal again. The newspaper was located on a street running along Dorchester Bay, which feeds into Boston Harbor, and I got there after about a five-minute walk. The front entrance was modern looking, made of big panes of glass framed in steel, and I entered through turnstile doors you push and go around in a circle. Filene's has the same kind of doors, and when I was little and shopped there with Ma, she always had to wait for me, her mouth tight in annoyance, as I just kept going around. It was the closest thing I had to an amusement park ride.

But this was no time to be doing that, so I just pushed my way into the lobby and let go of the door and watched it keep turning without me. Grown-ups were coming and going; the place seemed pretty busy, and behind a security desk I could see an escalator rising to a second floor. Seated at the front desk was a round-faced man wearing glasses, dressed in a navy-blue shirt with a badge on it.

"I'm here to see one of your reporters," I said. "Name is Clemens Bittner."

The man didn't look up from the newspaper he was reading, which I couldn't help notice was not the *Globe* but, instead, was the other paper in town, the *Herald*, a paper shaped differently from the *Globe*—a tabloid is what I'd heard people call it—and that *looked* different, too. The *Herald* always had huge headlines and big pictures on its front page, as if the world was ending every day. It was the *Herald*, by the way, that ran the headline I'll never forget after I came it across in Nora's files, the one about Daddy's arrest that said "RUBY KILLER JAILED."

I tried talking louder. "Bittner? Clemens Bittner?"

The security guard still didn't look at me, but this time he did nod in the direction of a telephone that sat at the edge of his desk. I stepped over to the phone and saw an employee directory of names and numbers next to it. When I dialed the one for Clemens Bittner, the phone began ringing—and ringing. Right away I began thinking I was going to get his voice mail the way Nora did, but then a real voice came on the line. Except it wasn't a man's voice.

"*Boston Globe* city room," said a woman in a businesslike but friendly way.

"I was calling for Clemens Bittner," I said.

"You have reached Mr. Bittner's line," she explained. "This is the switchboard at the message center in the newsroom. We pick up a reporter's call when they don't."

"Oh, okay," I said. "Is Mr. Bittner there?"

"Not at the moment."

I wasn't sure what to do next.

"Would you like me to put you through to his voice mail?"

She was at least trying to be helpful, not like the security guard.

"No, that's all right," I said.

"I could do that if you'd like," she said.

"The thing is, Mr. Bittner doesn't seem to ever return calls."

I thought I could hear the operator chuckle. She said, "It is true. He is not the best when it comes to following up."

I kind of liked talking to the operator. "Can I ask you something?"

"Of course, young lady."

Young lady? I guess my voice was a dead giveaway. If I was going to be taken seriously, like someone older, this was something I was going to have to work on. "Do you know when Mr. Bittner will be in?" I tried to make my voice sound deeper and older.

"That's not so easy to answer. Oh, hold on a minute."

The line went quiet, and then the operator came back. "Sorry about that. I had to take another call."

"When will Mr. Bittner be in?"

"Oh, yes. Hmmm. Ordinarily, that's a pretty straightforward

matter with most reporters. But Clemens, he's different." The operator paused and then continued, "What I can tell you is that he does not work days, so you won't be reaching him now."

"I'm not sure what that means."

"The day shift," she said. "We have reporters working shifts around the clock. Most of them work during the daytime, or the day shift. Clemens is different; he works nights, from midnight to eight a.m. We call it the graveyard shift."

"Graveyard? As in dead bodies?"

The operator chuckled again. "Yes, like that. Clemens works the graveyard shift."

I began thinking. "So, if that's when he works, if I call after midnight, I'll reach him?"

"Well, again, that's not so easy to say. In theory, yes— because Mr. Bittner is on the job then. But Mr. Bittner, he's very hard to reach, and if you've tried leaving him messages, I think you have an idea of what I mean."

"But I could call after midnight," I said, "and maybe get him?"

"Wouldn't that be past your bedtime?"

Before I could protest and tell her I was not some little girl, she said, "Okay, honey, I've got to go now, the board's lighting up."

Ma was asleep in her bedroom and had no idea about my plan to stay awake past midnight. I tried to keep busy reading magazines but actually dropped off to sleep. I awoke around one o'clock, startled. The lamp by my bed was still on, and I heard a police siren through my open window. I was sleepy, and it took me a second to remember what I was supposed to do. I felt some panic, like I'd missed something, even though the operator had told me the graveyard shift lasted from midnight to eight a.m. I picked up the cordless phone I'd sneaked into my room from the kitchen and dialed Clemens Bittner's number. It rang and rang, and, as I feared, it went to his voice mail. I heard the unfriendly mumbled message Nora always got.

I hung up. What was it with this guy? I called him again, and again got his voice mail. I hung up and dialed again. I could feel myself getting really annoyed as I listened to the ring, fully expecting my call to go again to voice mail.

Instead, a voice growled, "Yeah."

"Oh," I said.

I was shocked. Then I remembered about my voice, and dropped it down as low as I could as I said, "Is this Mr. Clemens Bittner?"

"This is Bittner. Who's asking?"

"My name is Trell Taylor."

"You the one been dialing my phone nonstop, giving me a headache?"

"Yes."

"Why would you do that?"

"I've been trying to reach you."

"Why?"

"Because I have a story for you."

Clemens Bittner grunted. That's all. Just a grunt. I took a deep breath and started telling him the things I'd rehearsed — about Daddy being in prison for murder, except he's innocent and didn't ever murder anybody. I told Clemens Bittner this was a really big story that he could work on and write for his newspaper. I tried to keep my voice deep as I spoke, but the more I talked about Daddy's situation, the more I got worked up and my voice rose to its normal high.

Clemens Bittner interrupted me. "What's his name?" he asked.

"You mean my daddy?"

"Whoever," he mumbled. "This guy, the one you say is innocent."

"Romero Taylor. It's a famous case."

"Never heard of him."

"It's been in your newspaper plenty of times," I said.

"I'm telling you the name doesn't ring a bell."

I didn't know what to say, and there was silence between us.

Then he said, "Who'd he kill?"

The question made my stomach turn. "He didn't kill anybody, Mr. Bittner."

Clemens Bittner repeated the question. "I'm askin' because maybe if the case is so famous, I'd recognize it that way."

"Ruby Graham," I said.

There was a long silence.

"You still there?" I asked.

"The girl on the blue mailbox."

His words came out flat and slowly. His voice had lost its crust.

"You know about her?"

"August 20, 1988."

"The day she died, yes. How'd you know that, Mr. Bittner?"

"I have my reasons" is all he said.

Then there was a quiet between us, so I continued.

"I was wanting you to write about my daddy. You see, the articles about him are all wrong. Somebody needs to write the truth, and the lawyer for my daddy says you're the one who could set the record straight."

"How old are you?"

It wasn't the question I was expecting. "What's the difference?"

"How do you know to talk like that—'set the record straight'?"

"I don't know. I read a lot. I've been helping my daddy's lawyer."

"Well, here's what I think: it's way too late for you to be up. Get to bed."

Then he hung up. I couldn't believe it. I just held the phone, hearing nothing but the dial tone.

CHAPTER 9
CLEMENS BITTNER

Because it was after midnight when I'd reached Mr. Clemens Bittner, and because I couldn't fall asleep right away, me being so mad, I slept in late the next morning. Ma worried maybe I was sick, but I told her I was just worn out and would be getting up soon enough to head downtown to Nora's office. That wasn't the whole truth, but I didn't want Ma knowing—at least not yet—what I'd been up to. So after she left for work, I lay in bed for a while thinking things over. I was feeling pretty frustrated about the past couple of days. I wasn't making much progress with Clemens Bittner, except for one thing. I had learned when he actually worked at the newspaper—midnight to eight a.m. I wasn't able to get him talking much on the telephone, but at least I knew his schedule. Maybe I could catch him leaving work.

But I'd decided that before I did anything, I first needed to know more about him. He was one strange guy — a newspaper reporter who avoided stories? Didn't like to talk? What was that about? So I looked at it like a homework project, and I spent the day at the Boston Public Library. I went to the reference room on the second floor, where they keep all of the Boston newspapers on microfilm, going back more than a hundred years. We learned about the library's microfilm room in history class at the Weld when the teacher, Mr. Thompson, went on and on about Boston being such an old city, as far as the United States is concerned, with lots of history and lots of ancient newspapers that attract historians from all over country who travel to here to use the library's microfilm in their research about events that happened a long, long time ago.

I wandered around looking for the *Boston Globe*, going up and down the rows of gray metal file cabinets filled with reels of microfilm. It took me a while, and I asked a nice man for some help, and he showed me the index to find articles by Clemens Bittner and also how to load a reel onto a reading machine. I noticed right away that it didn't seem like Clemens Bittner had done much work in a while. There weren't many recent stories by him in the index. Maybe a late-night story about a fire some-where in the city, or some other crime that I guessed must have happened in the middle of the night during the shift he worked. But nothing huge. Then, at last, I found something, a story going way back to 1985. It was a big story — actually, one long opening story followed by other stories he had written based on the first one. I have to say that once I began to read the package of stories, I couldn't stop. It was like reading a suspense book, and I think my mouth even gaped open in horror and amazement.

The story was about a terrible fire in a rooming house in Dorchester that started in the middle of a winter night. Eight people were killed, including five kids who were under the age of ten. It was the worst fatal fire in the history of Boston. Police and fire investigators said it was arson, meaning someone had started the fire on purpose. The fire department's experts said afterward that someone had thrown a Molotov cocktail through a window on the first floor. That's a bottle filled with gasoline and a rag sticking out of the neck of the bottle. When the rag was lit with a match, and when the bottle was thrown through the window, the gasoline inside exploded like a bomb. The fire spread fast, the red-hot flames snaking along the floors and up the walls and swallowing the building before anyone could escape.

It was so terrible, and so sad, and police soon arrested a man named Tony Rosario and charged him with setting the fire and killing the people. Police said Rosario was a thief who stole things to get money to buy drugs. They said he was addicted to heroin, and that he started the fire to get back at a man who lived in the apartment house and had cheated him out of some heroin he'd already paid for. Tony Rosario was convicted at trial and sentenced to life in prison without the possibility of parole. Which was the same kind of sentence Daddy got. Testifying at the trial were the fire department's fire experts and some people from the neighborhood who said they'd seen Tony Rosario pacing the street outside the building before the fire. The biggest thing, though, was the confession that police said Rosario had made after he was arrested.

It sure seemed like police and fire investigators had solved a horrible, horrible crime. But here's the interesting part. Clemens Bittner's story was not really about the fire and police catching Tony Rosario. That was like the background to Clemens Bittner's story. The fire, the deaths, and the trial—those things had happened ten years earlier, in 1975. When Clemens Bittner's story was published in 1985, Tony Rosario had been in prison for a decade. The interesting thing about the story I was reading was this: Clemens Bittner had uncovered new evidence showing that Tony Rosario was the wrong man. Clemens Bittner described the police interrogation of Tony Rosario like it was some kind of torture chamber, how Tony Rosario had been questioned for twenty-one hours without a break, and only when he finally signed a confession did the police stop the interrogation. Plus, Clemens Bittner reported that because Tony Rosario was addicted to heroin, and his body needed to have the drug to function, he began to suffer during the police questioning from not having heroin in his body. He began to sweat and moan and see things on the walls—at one point he screamed he saw giant spiders crawling toward him. He was hallucinating, but that didn't stop the police from questioning him, or from typing up a confession they made Tony Rosario sign. But, as the newspaper story said, Tony Rosario was nuts at this point and had no idea what he was signing.

The story also showed that police had pressured people to say they'd seen Tony Rosario before the fire. But, most of all, Clemens Bittner had interviewed scientists who were experts in what was called "fire science," and the scientists told him there was no way the fire at the rooming house had been started by a Molotov cocktail. The scientists said the fire department's fire experts in 1975 were plain wrong, and that new advances in science and technology proved the fire was caused by something else, perhaps an electric space heater that had malfunctioned.

The story in the *Boston Globe* blew my mind. It was huge, a big story on the front page that continued inside and ran across two pages with photographs. It was not your usual newspaper story, and the point of it was to show Tony Rosario was not guilty — and it was Clemens Bittner who had reinvestigated the case and come up with all of the new information. Now I understood why Nora Walsh had been given his name when she'd asked her lawyer friend for a newspaper reporter who knew how to dig into the past.

When I was done, I jumped up and asked the librarian for help printing a copy of the first story. We also made copies of other stories Clemens Bittner had written afterward about the Rosario case, as follow-ups to the first big one.

I was making my way back to the *Boston Globe* the very next day. It was early, and I was in a hurry because I wanted to reach the newspaper before eight a.m. I rode the T with grown-ups all dressed up for work, the men mostly in collared shirts and pressed slacks, maybe a summer suit, the women dressed in skirts and blouses. In a way, I'd dressed for work, too. I'd picked blue jean shorts with a cream-colored T-shirt. I'd pulled my hair back with a blue hair elastic, and changed the laces in my Nikes to a blue pair that matched everything else.

I hurried up the granite steps of the *Boston Globe* and was inside the front lobby just as the big clock on the wall hit eight. The stories I'd copied the day before were folded neatly inside a manila folder, which I had tucked inside a shoulder bag. The purple canvas bag with a white rope strap had been a gift from Ma at the start of the school year when I began going to the Weld.

I moved off to one side of the high-ceilinged room where I had a clear view of the escalator and the workers riding down it. My plan was to catch Clemens Bittner coming down the escalator. Except for one thing: I realized I didn't know what he looked like. I would be guessing. I decided that someone up all night might look it—a little tired. I decided that because he worked a graveyard shift, when basically no one was around, and also because of his wicked bad manners, that Clemens Bittner was not going to be a decked-out dude sporting the latest in men's fashion.

Pretty soon, though, I realized reporters, as a group, didn't seem to dress for success. I watched them crossing the lobby looking pretty casual. Even the women. They were neat and all, but not suited up like the women I watched getting off the T wearing heels and business outfits and hustling into skyscrapers to their office jobs at banks and law firms. Here at the *Boston Globe*, many of the men were wearing blue jeans, sneakers, and shirts untucked, with a book bag over their shoulder.

Guessing was going to be hard. I felt a little panicked. I began going up to the men coming off the escalator, the ones I thought *might* be Clemens Bittner, and asking, "Mr. Bittner?" I did this maybe three or four times. I guessed wrong each time. Each man looked at me, shook his head, and kept going. I wasn't sure what to do. Plus I'd drawn the attention of the round-faced security guard at the front desk who'd been so unhelpful before. He'd watched me going up to reporters and was now making a face like he'd eaten too many slices of pizza loaded with everything. He pushed himself up from his chair and wobbled across the lobby toward me.

"C'mon, c'mon," he grumbled. "What are you doin' here?"

"Waiting for Clemens Bittner."

He began shaking his head. "I can't have this." He stifled a burp.

"But I know he gets off work at eight a.m."

"You have to leave."

The guard put his hand on my shoulder. He wasn't rough about it, but he was trying to steer me away from the escalator, and when we both turned toward the front entrance, we stood face-to-face with a middle-aged woman carrying a hot-pink purse.

"Tommy O'Donahue," she said.

The guard was startled. "Oh," he said. "Hiya, Rose."

"God's gift to law enforcement," the woman named Rose commented.

The guard shifted uncomfortably.

Rose pressed on. "Why are you giving this young lady the shove?"

Rose was staring down the guard, her lips pursed. She was dressed in a pair of green cotton summer slacks, a matching blouse, and brown flats. Her brown hair was straight and cut short just above her ears. She looked fit and tidy.

"Well?" she pressed.

"She's bothering people coming off the escalator. I can't have that."

I spoke up. "I'm waiting for a reporter. He's getting off work."

Rose tilted her head as she studied me. "You wouldn't be the girl who was calling the other day for Clemens Bittner, would you?"

I was dumbfounded. "How'd you know?"

Rose smiled. "It's my job to recognize voices," she said.

She could tell I was confused, and continued. "I'm the telephone operator. When you called the newsroom the other day, we talked for a bit."

"Wow" was all I could think to say.

Rose's brow creased. I could tell she was thinking. "Let me guess," she said after a minute passed. "Clemens Bittner gets off work at eight a.m., and you're thinking you'll be able to run into him leaving the building?"

"That's right," I said.

Rose shook her head. "Clemens, I'm afraid, is long gone."

The security guard must have thought this was his opportunity. He nudged me and said, "Okay, that's it. Let's go." But Rose intervened. Maybe she saw the disappointment on my face after she'd said Clemens Bittner was gone.

"Hold on, Tommy," she said.

"Rose," the guard complained.

"No, Tommy. I'll take it from here."

The guard sighed, like a balloon losing air. Rose asked me my name.

"Van Trell Taylor," I answered. "But I go by Trell."

"I start my day with a cup of tea, Trell Taylor. Join me?"

Giving the guard a look and stepping away, I answered, "Sure."

Rose and I sat at a table in the newspaper's third-floor cafeteria that reminded me of a lunchroom you find in any public school—a linoleum tiled floor filled with square tables and chairs, a food line with a stack of trays at one end, and the kitchen workers on the other side either serving or cooking. Our table was near a bank of large plate-glass windows looking out the rear of the building onto its flat roof.

Rose sipped her tea. "Trell, tell me, where are you from?"

"Ma and me, we live in Roxbury."

Rose smiled. "I meant, originally. Your folks."

"Oh," I said. I had to think for a minute.

"What I mean is, my family's from County Cork."

"What's a county cork?"

Rose laughed. "County Cork is on the southern coast of Ireland, the largest county in Ireland."

"Oh."

Rose continued. "Both my parents came to Boston as children. Their families settled in South Boston. Everyone who came over seems to have settled there." Rose paused before continuing. "My parents met as teenagers and got married. My father worked thirty years for the T, as a lineman. My mother raised five kids. I live in the very house they raised us in, not even a mile from here. I walk to work."

I said, "Okay, I get it. Well, my ma's people are from Ohio, and I think my daddy's are from Georgia. But I've never been to either place. They moved to Roxbury when they were kids, and my parents met as teenagers, too."

"I guess we have something in common, then. The great Boston migration."

"Except we never stayed in one place. We've lived all over — all around Roxbury, I mean."

Rose smiled again. She sipped her tea. "Why are you trying so hard to find Clemens Bittner?"

"It's a pretty big story," I said.

Rose said she was not in any rush, so I explained everything to her about Daddy's case and him being in prison. "Our lawyer, her name is Nora Walsh, has tried legal appeals, but nothing's worked. I want Clemens Bittner to write a story showing that he's innocent."

Rose listened to every word, and then she sighed. "There certainly was a time when Clemens Bittner was the best investigative reporter in the city." She smiled, like she remembered something. "He can be so gentle in person, gentle as a cat, but it used to be, once he sank his teeth into a story, watch out. Other reporters joked he was like a heat-seeking missile for the truth. I think they were just envious."

"I saw the stories—it's no joke," I said. "The one about Tony Rosario, the man in prison for arson? Mr. Bittner wrote an amazing story."

"The Rosario case? How do you know about that? It was a big one."

"I went to the library and was looking up old newspapers on microfilm. It took me a while to find his stories. I had to go back a bunch of years, but I finally found them."

Rose was impressed. "You've done your homework."

"Stories like that are why I need Clemens Bittner."

"Except Clemens is not the person he used to be."

"What do you mean?"

"You've seen how he is," she said. "Unreachable."

I watched a sadness cross Rose's face.

"He's been that way for years," she said.

"But why?"

Rose folded her napkin. It was her turn to tell a story. "He had a son once," she began, "and when he was five years old, he was afflicted with Reye's syndrome."

I said I'd never heard of it.

"That's because it's very rare. But Clemens's son had contracted it—no one knows how, and no one knew at first he even had it. You see, the boy was home sick with the chicken pox, and he was being treated for that. Then he began to run a fever, so Clemens and his wife began giving him aspirin every few hours."

Rose paused and looked down into her lap. "It was what any parent would do, give their child aspirin to bring down a fever. But for someone with Reye's syndrome, aspirin is the worst thing you can give them. So, instead of improving, the boy's fever soared to 106 degrees. He became delirious. That's when Clemens and his wife realized something worse than chicken pox was going on. By the time they got him to Boston City Hospital, the boy was in a coma. His brain and liver had swelled, and the doctors said they could do nothing for him. Peter Clemens Bittner died in the emergency room. Everything happened so fast, in less than forty-eight hours."

"That's awful," I said.

"Fourteen years ago." Rose said. "August 20, 1988."

"Wait a minute," I interrupted. "You said August 20, 1988?"

"Yes—the day Peter Clemens Bittner died."

"It's the same day Ruby Graham was shot."

"Don't I know," Rose said. "It's why I'll never forget. On the one hand the city was in an uproar over the girl's shooting death—our newsroom was bedlam, with reporters racing around to cover the story, going to Humboldt Avenue, contacting Boston police, the district attorney, and the mayor. Meanwhile, Clemens Bittner walked around in a trance, like a ghost. He was never the same. Within a year, his marriage broke up, he moved into a one-bedroom apartment in Dorchester, and he began working the graveyard shift. It's a shadow he's never left. As I said before—unreachable."

It hit me. I told Rose how, after I mentioned Ruby Graham's name on the telephone, Clemens Bittner had known the exact day of her shooting. "August 20, 1988," he said. I'd been surprised at the time. But now I knew: Ruby Graham wasn't the only child who had died that day. There were two.

Rose and I sat in silence. I looked out the plate-glass windows onto the flat rear roof. The building's rooftop was used as a parking deck. Cars and a few pickup trucks drove up a ramp onto it. I saw people get out of cars and walk into the building.

"Rose, who parks there?" I asked.

Rose turned around in her chair to see what I was looking at. "Reporters," she said. "That's their lot. It's reserved for the reporters."

I had a new idea.

CHAPTER 10
TRELL AND CLEMENS

The next morning, I didn't bother with the front entrance. I hurried around the left side of the newspaper's redbrick building and followed the wide blacktop driveway past the paper's green delivery trucks with THE BOSTON GLOBE painted on each side. This end of the building held the printing presses, which were basically mountains of machinery you could see from the front because long windows allowed the public to watch the presses roll.

In back I spotted the ramp I had seen from the cafeteria. I was in a hurry because there had been a delay that morning on the Red Line. I'd wanted to be in position at the workers' entrance on the elevated deck by the end of Clemens Bittner's shift, but it was already twenty minutes past eight. I worried that, once again, I had missed him. I ran up the ramp.

The lot didn't have many cars. Rose had explained that newsrooms are not like most offices, where workers start their workday between six and eight in the morning. She said newsrooms didn't really get going until around nine-thirty or even ten o'clock. That's when reporters filed in, got their assignments, and spent the rest of the day chasing the news. Rose said they wouldn't actually start writing until late afternoon, which meant they tended to work well into the evening, until around eight p.m. or so. Obviously later than most jobs. Which was why, Rose said, reporters generally didn't begin their workdays until midmorning.

I also came better prepared. I'd asked Rose what Clemens Bittner looked like.

"He needs a haircut," she'd said. "I can tell you that much."

I kept my eyes on the rooftop entrance to the newsroom while scanning the parking deck. To see people leaving the building, I wanted to find a spot that was hidden. While I was looking around, something caught my eye. Off by itself in the far corner was an old, beat-up car. It looked like a cartoon car—painted a turtle green, with a rounded roof, rounded hips, and a rounded front end. I crossed the deck toward it and noticed someone was inside, in the driver's seat. The person was slumped forward. I saw, too, that the front window was rolled down. The car radio was blaring. I recognized the station, 96.9 FM, the station that played "All sixties rock, all the time." The DJ's deep, honey-coated voice was saying, "An amazing song, listeners, truly amazing: 'Our House,' a bona fide classic from one of the all-time great bands, Crosby, Stills, Nash & Young."

I tiptoed up from behind and spotted lettering stamped on the trunk's chrome handle spelling out the car's make and model: *Volvo 122.* I stopped at the driver's door.

The man inside was asleep, his arms draped over the steering wheel. He was snoring quietly. His back heaved with each breath. I couldn't see his face, because it was hidden beneath a curtain of long and mangy brown hair. Rose was right; he needed a haircut.

"Mr. Bittner?" I said.

The man did not move.

I reached into the car, nudged his left shoulder. "Mr. Bittner?"

The man jumped suddenly, and his arms flailed. He began talking nonsense, looking fiercely all around, while fumbling around for the car keys. "Outta my way," he shouted. "Outta my way." His head turned wildly, hair everywhere.

"I'm Trell Taylor, Mr. Bittner."

Clemens Bittner growled, looking straight ahead now.

"I've got to talk to you," I told him.

He turned on the ignition and revved the engine, which coughed a few times before kicking in. He noticed his door was still ajar and thrust it wide open to slam it shut. "Leave me alone," he shouted.

Papers sailed out of the car in a gust of wind that blew across the parking deck. I jumped out of the way and got a look inside; piles of old newspapers and empty coffee cups littered the car floor and filled the seats.

Clemens Bittner pulled the door shut. He turned and looked at me for the first time. His face was covered in whiskers; besides a haircut, he needed a shave. The shadow, the one Rose had told me about, crossed his forehead and eyes. But beneath the hardened lines, deep in his eyes, I could see a flicker of light.

"I'm outta here," he said, his voice still gruff but not so loud anymore.

The green Volvo roared off, heading straight for the down ramp. I was tempted to run after him. But even I can't outrun a car racing across an empty parking lot. I just watched him disappear.

Some of the papers from the car floated after him like paper airplanes, and that's when I realized I was standing on one. I picked up the sheet of paper. I recognized the logo across the top—a golden stick of lightning—from the electric bill Ma and I get every month from Boston Electric.

It was Clemens Bittner's monthly utility bill. I flipped it over and read the address: *Mr. Clemens Bittner, 11 Esmond Street, Apartment 2, Dorchester, MA.*

"Jeez," I said out loud. "I know where Esmond Street is."

To get to Esmond Street from where Ma and I lived, most folks would probably ride the Blue Hill Avenue bus. Not me. When I got home, I changed into my running shorts, put my papers and a water bottle into a light backpack, and started to jog the roughly two miles. Boston was still stuck in a heat wave, with temperatures each day hitting or going higher than ninety. But the heat wasn't so bad at the start of the day. Besides, it felt good to be running again. I'd gone a few days without a good workout, and once I was warmed up, I slipped into that feeling that comes with a smooth stride, a feeling like flying.

I knew where Esmond Street was because one of my aunts and her family used to live on the next street over. Esmond is a tough street, mainly due to George "G-man" Whigham. G-man is a drug dealer who lived there—or used to, until he was busted last year. For years he was Thumper Parish's main rival in Roxbury and Dorchester. Their gangs had fought all the time. Then Boston Police got onto G-man. The newspapers said an informant—a grown-up word for a tattletale—had tipped police off that G-man was about to receive a new shipment of cocaine. G-man's house was raided, and police found drugs, guns, and piles of ammunition.

The arrest had sure made Thumper Parish's day. He threw a block party on Castlegate Road the same weekend that news of the big bust was splashed across the front pages of all the newspapers. Everybody talked about the party for weeks after. Everybody also talked about how Thumper was more powerful than ever now that police had put away his competition.

I was remembering this stuff because I'd decided to run down Castlegate Road to get to Esmond Street. It was the fastest route, for one thing. I had another reason, though. Rose might have insisted that Clemens Bittner was a gentle guy, but who knew for sure? To me, he was a stranger—and kind of a crazy one, too, the way he flailed his arms and freaked out on the roof deck. Growing up in my neighborhood, you have to be smart about things, and

I was thinking I could use some company when I called on the newspaper guy living on Esmond.

I turned onto Castlegate Road hoping to get lucky, and sure enough, halfway down the street I spotted Paul Parish. Bingo. He was on a bike with a banana seat and high handlebars, popping wheelies. I pumped my fist. This was the luck I had had in mind—at least the first part. Now I needed to make the rest happen.

I strode up to Paul and began jogging in place.

"Hey," I said.

"Hey, you," Paul said back.

"How about you set the pace while I do my workout?"

"What's that mean?"

"Means you ride alongside me while I run."

"I don't know, Trell. Kinda too hot, don't you think?"

"C'mon. You could use a workout."

I started jogging, not sure he would follow me. But out of the corner of my eye, I saw him push off and pedal. *"Yes!"* I whispered, pumping my fist secretly at my side a second time.

Pulling up next to me, Paul shouted, "Where we goin'?"

"Just follow me."

I ran. Paul pedaled. It was hot out—Paul was right. We turned onto Esmond Street. I was concentrating on Clemens Bittner, and, as a distance runner, I was thinking positive—that sooner or later I was going to catch him. He could duck telephone calls, hang up on me, even roar off in his funny old Volvo, but he couldn't hide.

I saw the Volvo parked on the street; Clemens Bittner was home. I stopped next to the car. Paul kept going until he realized I wasn't with him, and then he hit his brakes.

He circled back. "What's up?"

"There's something I got to do," I said. My voice sounded serious. "Business right here."

"What business you got on Esmond?" He gave me a hard look of disapproval.

"Nothing like that, Paul. C'mon, you know better."

"Okay, okay. What then?"

"Just something. It's too complicated to explain right now. I got to see the person who lives here. You wait here, okay? I'll be out in a few minutes."

Paul rolled his eyes, as if he was realizing he'd been played.

"Please," I said.

"Yeah, yeah, okay," he said. "I need to stop anyways. You may be in shape. Not me."

I pulled the water bottle out of my bag and gave it to Paul. When he was done, I drank the rest.

"And, Paul, one more thing?"

"Yeah?"

"In ten minutes, if I don't come out, you need to come bang on the door."

The apartment was around to the side of the beat-up-looking triple-decker. Strips of cheap aluminum siding were peeled off its sides, and the original yellow color was turning a puke green because of a speckled green mold spreading from the ground up. Usually a triple-decker is divided into three apartments — one on each floor. But this one was carved into smaller units, two on each floor, and Clemens Bittner's was on the first floor. There was no name on his door, no doorbell, and no door knocker, just the number 2 nailed to the doorframe, and even that wasn't attached securely but was dangling at a slant.

It was after a second round of pounding that the door suddenly popped open. The shaggy-haired Clemens Bittner stood there, squinting in the morning light. Behind him, the apartment was as dark as a cave. He was barefoot and wearing baggy blue jeans and a white T-shirt. It took him a few seconds before his eyes got used to the brightness, and once they did, he gave me a look of recognition. His mouth dropped open.

"Unbelievable," he muttered.

"Trell Taylor," I said.

"Don't I know."

We both just stood there, not saying anything. The door was open, but he kept his hand on the knob. I worried he was going to slam the door shut, the way he had hung up the phone on me. I couldn't let that happen. I had to think fast, do something — and so, before he had a chance to close the door, I moved inside.

"Mind if I fill my water bottle?"

I was at the sink before he could do anything to stop me. I could hear him trying to summon a sound of fury from his chest, but I already had the tap water running. Filling my bottle wasn't easy, though, as I tried to angle it around the plates and glasses stacked randomly in the sink. I was feeling a little jittery—and felt glad I had Paul Parish hanging outside.

I looked around and saw immediately that Mr. Clemens Bittner's home was a total mess and totally small, basically one large room. In the kitchen area was a table with a couple of chairs, and there was a couch, side chair, and a coffee table in the living area. I saw a doorway on the other side of the room, and guessed it was to a bedroom. That's it. But from the looks of the couch, with sheets and pillows on it, it looked like Clemens Bittner slept there.

While I screwed the top back onto the water bottle, I also noticed a tiny framed picture sitting on the sill above the sink. I didn't recognize Clemens Bittner at first, because the man in the photograph was clean-shaven and the hair was different—still kind of long, but brushed back instead of stringy and all over. The woman in the photograph wore a gray sweatshirt with SUNY-ONEONTA printed on the front. She had shoulder-length hair that was a honey-blond color. She was pretty. Both Clemens Bittner and the woman were smiling, but the biggest and brightest smile belonged to the little boy between them. He was dressed in blue jeans with shoulder straps and a blue T-shirt, his arms hugging each parent. I could see a resemblance in his face, especially in the blue eyes, with his father.

It was a family photograph, from a happy time, and reminded me of the family photograph I keep at home on my bureau—the one and only family photo I own, taken last year on my thirteenth birthday at the prison. I turned around and saw Clemens Bittner standing in front of the couch, his hands on his hips, just watching me.

I wasn't sure what to say. I didn't have a plan. But I was thinking that if I kept moving, and talking, it lessened the chance of him getting mad at me. I looked around some more and realized that the apartment was kept awfully dark. Heavy shades covered the windows. I decided that trying to take charge might buy some time.

"You need light in here," I said.

"You think?"

I reached over the sink and pulled a shade up.

"Hey—what are you doing?" Clemens Bittner barked, his voice cold.

I pulled open a second shade.

"You really need to wash some dishes, too," I blurted out, trying to sound helpful.

I'd lasted a few minutes without getting thrown out. I stood at the sink. He stood at the couch. I wasn't sure what would happen next. Then Clemens Bittner dropped his hands to his sides in a relaxed way, and a piece of him thawed.

"Can't take no, can you?" he said.

"No," I said. "I mean, yes. I mean, yes, I can't take no."

He laughed quietly. "Stubborn, is what I mean."

"Yes."

"Determined," he said. "Persistent." He rubbed his chin and then continued. "I was teaching one time—a semester at

Emerson College in the fall. The class was basic newswriting for journalism majors. Newswriting 101. I told the kids right off that there were two traits they absolutely had to have if they were ever going to make it as reporters. I told them they might be way smart, and they might be terrific writers, but that if they didn't possess these two traits, well, forget about it."

Clemens Bittner looked at me, as if waiting.

"The two things," I said. "What are they?"

He smiled. "That's the first one," he said.

"What do you mean?"

"Curiosity," he said. "You were curious, so you asked. I'd tell those kids that reporters have to be curious—and not just plain curious, but insatiably curious, a hungry, starving kind of curious, curious about the world around them, about what makes the world tick. Because it's curiosity that propels a journalist to ask the tough questions that need asking."

I was all ears. "The second thing?"

"Stubbornness. Determination. Persistence. Reporters mostly are after information people try to keep from them. Reporters get the runaround. They get doors slammed in their faces. They don't get calls returned. They get hung up on. Reporters have to find ways around these obstacles. They have to persist. I could tell pretty quickly which kids had the right stuff for this line of work."

He stopped. "That was a long time ago, though."

I wasn't sure what to say next. So I changed the subject entirely and asked, "I was thinking, Mr. Bittner—what's a name like Clemens come from? I mean, the first time my lawyer mentioned your name, I was going, Clemens? Who gets called Clemens? What kind of name is that?"

The question hung in the air.

"Just curious," I said. I smiled at him.

He smiled, too, and then said, "Okay, reporter Trell Taylor, I'll explain. My father's favorite writer was Mark Twain. He owned every one of Twain's books, read everything Twain wrote."

"*Huck Finn,*" I said.

"Yep, along with *Tom Sawyer* and a bunch of other stories. Twain was a reporter before becoming a novelist, and his real name was Samuel Langhorne Clemens. So, in his honor, my father decided to name me Clemens."

I thought about that for a minute. "That's actually pretty cool," I said. Then I asked, "Your father? He write books like Mark Twain?"

"No," Clemens Bittner said. "But he was a reporter, for the *Hartford Courant* newspaper, in Connecticut. Mark Twain lived in Hartford in the 1870s, in a big house he built that was later turned into a museum. My father used to take me there a lot as a kid. I always thought it was shaped to look like a Mississippi steamboat—built so big and with so many porches surrounding it, like staterooms. The only thing missing was a paddle on one end." He stopped and chuckled to himself. "Reminds me. Twain's upstairs writing room, you wouldn't believe it—full of books, of course, but in the middle of the room was a giant billiard table.

I loved that. I pictured Mark Twain in there, writing and playing pool."

"Is that why you became a reporter? The pool table?"

He laughed. "Maybe so. But mainly from my father working on a paper." He stood away from the doorjamb. "But that was a long time ago." He ran his fingers through his hair and let out a loud sigh. "Okay, girl," he said. "You got me talking, but now it's time—"

I thought he was heading to open the front door, so I grabbed my bag on the table. I fumbled around inside and pulled out the photocopies of the newspaper stories about Tony Rosario. "I found these in the library," I said.

I held the sheets of paper up for Clemens Bittner to look at. "I know all about what you can do, and, like I said on the phone, I need you to write a story about my daddy's case."

Clemens Bittner stared at the stories, but did not move an inch to take them.

"That was a long time ago," was all he said. His voice was suddenly heavier.

"You keep saying that—a long time ago."

He averted his eyes and looked past me. "I'm semi-retired."

"Semi-retired?"

"Well, I work. You know that—nights. But, I, uhh, I am—"

"Unreachable?" I interrupted.

"What?"

"That's what Rose said. You're unreachable."

Clemens Bittner considered what I'd said. "I was actually

going to say I don't do that kind of work anymore. It requires everything you've got, nothing less."

"I know about your son, Peter." I blurted it out.

Clemens Bittner grimaced. I saw the shadow cross his face.

"Rose told me."

Clemens Bittner looked down at the floor.

I said, "It's so unfair."

"Maybe so," he said. Looking up, his eyes glazed over. "I always felt as a reporter I could do something for somebody. When something was wrong, I could investigate, write a story, and things could change. But this, all I know is this was different."

He sat down at the table. He moved gingerly, in slow motion, and it made him suddenly seem really ancient, as though he had transformed into an old man right before my eyes. I knew I needed to hurry. I was losing him, as if he were slipping into a coma.

"I understand what you're saying, Mr. Bittner." Then I raised my voice: "Like with Ruby Graham. No one could do anything to help her when she was brought into the emergency room."

He looked up. I continued, "Two children died that day, and nothing could be done for either one of them. It was horrible. But now there's another person, my daddy, and he's suffering from a fatal condition, too. It's called life in prison without the possibility of parole. But Daddy's situation is not hopeless. Something can be done. You can do something, Mr. Bittner, and write about his case. It's not too late to save the life of Romero Taylor.

"Mr. Bittner, will you help?"

CHAPTER 11

FIRST THINGS FIRST

I just stood there waiting for Clemens Bittner to say something, or at least do something. He didn't move, and I didn't either, our eyes locked in a kind of duel. I couldn't see past the dark shadows that circled his eyes to guess which way he might be leaning.

He started rubbing his chin.

"Quit the Mr. Bittner stuff," he said finally. "This isn't school."

The voice was flat, but I took what he said as a good sign.

"Okay," I said hesitantly. I tried out his name: "Clemens."

He walked across the room and opened the door. "Three days."

He signaled that it was time for me to leave.

"Then what?"

"Three days" is all he said.

Back outside, Paul Parish was next to his bike, practically jumping up and down. He said he was just about to do what I'd asked—come bang on the door. "What happened in there?" he asked.

"It's okay, Paul. It's okay."

I wouldn't tell him anything. I started my jog, and he climbed onto his bike. We headed back to our neighborhoods. I made a promise to fill him in when I could. He wasn't too happy about it, I could tell, but there wasn't any of that meanness about him, like before. He was different now. I think he liked the fact he had helped me out. Maybe Daddy was right: Paul liked me, always had, but was figuring out the right way to show it. We ended up at the corner store getting something to drink. We talked a bit about school and some of the teachers who drove us nuts, and then I took off. "See ya around," I said.

"Yeah, see ya around," he shouted after me.

I didn't even tell Ma about going to see Clemens Bittner. I wanted to wait until our visit to the prison on Saturday, when all three of us would be together in the visitors room.

Like I expected, when Saturday came, Daddy asked me about my week.

"Well, I have great news," I announced, and that's when I told them about me and the *Boston Globe* reporter.

"*WHAT?*" Ma said before I even finished. She was shrieking. "You were taking yourself to this newspaper instead of Nora's? Stayin' up all night makin' calls? Goin' by yourself to Esmond Street?"

"Ma," I said.

"I cannot have you runnin' all over the city," Ma said. "Esmond Street? C'mon, girl. Just last week a man got shot over there. What are you thinkin'?"

"But, Ma."

"Don't 'But, Ma' me," she snapped. "I got it hard as it is. I think you're at Nora's helping her out, and you're not! I can't have this, Trell. I can't be worryin' you're out somewhere."

Daddy leaned in. "Shey-Shey," he whispered. He tilted his head so Ma and I would notice that the commotion at our table had caught the interest of my favorite prison guard in the entire prison system.

Officer White strode up to us. "Everything okay here, Romeo?"

"Romero," Ma said. "His name is Romero." Ma was fuming. "How come, every time we're in here, we got to go through this nonsense?"

The guard smiled. "Ouch. Trouble in paradise, Shey-Shey?"

Before Daddy could say anything, I stood up. "Everything's fine, Officer White. Just fine." I wanted to stick my tongue out at him; instead I smiled the biggest fake smile I could. His eyes panned around the table, looking at the three of us. Ma and Daddy looked away instead of making eye contact. But I did. I looked right at the guard and kept smiling until he turned and left us alone.

"Ma," I pleaded, "this is what Nora said we need, a reporter."

There was fire in Ma's eyes.

"Shey-Shey," Daddy said. He took Ma's hand in his. "Trell's right," he continued. "I'm not happy the way she's gone about this, but Trell has managed to get to the guy. That's something. C'mon, baby, let's talk this through."

"I'm sorry, Ma," I said. "But Clemens Bittner wasn't returning Nora's calls, and someone had to do something. Because this is our last chance, right, to get help? It's what we want more than anything—getting Daddy home—and I figured I had the time. Everyone else is so busy. I figured if I could just talk to him and explain our situation..."

Ma was hard as a rock. I pleaded, "Ma, I think he's gonna help, I really do. And I can help him. It'll be like—like we're partners."

"Partners?" Ma said. She huffed.

"Yes," I said firmly. I was actually beginning to feel annoyed. It wasn't like I was a little girl anymore. I was fourteen. I knew my way around, took care myself, and, besides that, could run like the wind and outrun most anybody. I'd found Clemens Bittner after no one else had. "Ma, listen to me. It's summer. I got the time. Working with the reporter, trying to dig up information, it's a whole lot better than just hanging around Nora's office. This is our last chance, Ma. Nora said so."

Ma gave Daddy a look, and their eyes talked a language I couldn't follow, but then Daddy turned to me. "Listen, Trell," he began. "Definitely it's good news, havin' a reporter to maybe look into my case. But you cannot be keeping anything from Ma. Or Nora. They gotta know what you're doing. You hear me?"

"I do, Daddy."

Ma and Daddy traded looks again. Grudgingly, Ma gave him a nod.

"You gotta be careful, Trell," Daddy continued. "You gotta tell Ma and Nora everything."

"I will, Daddy."

"You gotta be safe," he said. "Her killer — Ruby's killer — he's still out there."

"We're going to get you out of prison, Daddy."

Clemens had said he needed three days, but he took only two. On Sunday morning, I was eating breakfast when I heard a tap-tap at the kitchen window. Ma jumped up from the table and knocked over her coffee.

I looked at the window. "Clemens?" I mumbled, cereal packed in my mouth. "Ma, it's Clemens."

Clemens was looking at us. He flicked his hand in a kind of quick wave and then hustled to the back door. I got up, unbolted the two locks, and let him into our kitchen. Ma had gone to the sink to put her empty cup in it. Her arms were stiffened against the counter, as if she was bracing herself. I could tell she was trying to keep her cool.

"Ma, this is Clemens Bittner, the reporter."

I stared at Clemens. He sure looked changed. For one thing, he'd shaved. The other thing was his hair. It wasn't any shorter, but he'd pulled it back into a ponytail, so at least it wasn't the mangy curtain I'd seen when he was sleeping in his Volvo. He was wearing blue jeans and a concert T-shirt from Crosby, Stills, Nash & Young.

"Ma?" I said.

She turned and looked at Clemens. "You can't do that. Not in this neighborhood. I freaked out for a second, and I don't like bein' freaked."

Clemens cleared his throat. "Sorry," he said. "I tried the doorbell."

"Broken," Ma said. "The doorbell is broken. I know it, landlord knows it, and still it stays broken. So be it. But you find the doorbell's broken, that means you try pounding on the front door. You don't come around back and tap on my window."

"Got it," Clemens said.

"Not in this neighborhood," Ma repeated. She gave Clemens a glare. "You should know better if you live on Esmond Street."

Clemens said the right thing. "I get it," he said. "Can't have that, Mrs. Taylor."

Ma made eye contact with Clemens. "That's the truth."

"I'm thinking it's good I came, then. So we could meet. In person."

Ma stuck her hand out. Clemens began to extend his. He was thinking Ma wanted to shake hands, but she waved him off.

"ID," she said. Her body was still stiff. "Show me your ID."

Clemens fumbled with his wallet until he found a plastic *Boston Globe* identification card. He handed it to Ma. She studied the photo, then looked at him. "Ponytail's definitely an improvement." She handed the card back.

Ma's arms relaxed, as did her voice. "Listen, Mr. Bittner—"

"Clemens," he interrupted. "Clemens."

"Okay," Ma said. "Clemens. I have not been happy with the way Trell got this going, but I can't argue with the results. If you're here to help, we need it."

"I'm here, ready to take a go at it, if that's what you mean," Clemens said.

"You said you needed three days," I said. "It's only two."

"Yeah, well, it went faster than I thought. I read the clips—"

"Clips?"

"The stories," Clemens said. "Lesson one in my reporting class: first thing you do on something like this is to read everything that's ever been written about it. So I had Lisa—she's the librarian at the *Globe*—I had Lisa pull the clips about Ruby's killing *and* your father's trial. That's what I've been doing—reading the clips."

"Oh," I said.

"I was also thinking we should meet with your lawyer—Nora?"

"Nora Walsh," Ma said.

Clemens continued. "Okay, Nora Walsh. Meet with her so I can check out her files."

Clemens seemed so different, like focused. I have to say I was semi-shocked.

"But before that," he said, "there's somebody I want Trell and me to see."

"Who?" I said.

"The lead homicide detective."

Before Clemens could say the name, I did. "Mr. Richard Boyle."

"Impressive," Clemens said.

As I'd done with everyone who'd had anything to do with Daddy's case, I'd memorized the name.

"I think we should see him," Clemens said.

"How come?" I asked.

"Because I know him," Clemens answered.

He looked at me and asked, "You free this morning?"

I looked over at Ma. "Yeaaah," I said, my voice rising. I was psyched. "Definitely."

Clemens said, "Richie's retired from the force, so we'll go to his place. He lives in Dorchester."

Ma asked, "How is it you know this man, this detective?"

"From stories I did," Clemens answered.

Clemens paused, and then he looked at us. He wore a serious expression. "I have to say that as I was reading the clips and saw Richie Boyle had worked this case—that he was one of the officers who actually arrested your father—well, it leaves me skeptical about your claims."

"What do you mean?" Ma said.

"I mean Richie Boyle helped me out on a lot of stories I wrote for the newspaper," Clemens said. "And it's my experience, he's one helluva cop."

"You mean you don't believe us?" I said.

"No, that's not what I'm saying," Clemens said. "I'm saying I know him, I'm saying he's a good cop, and I'm saying even if it's been a bunch of years since I've seen him, that retired Sergeant Detective Richie Boyle is a good place to start."

We left my apartment for Richie Boyle's place and were taking a route across Humboldt Ave. when it hit me to first show Clemens something about the actual crime scene.

We walked in silence. Clemens kept looking my way. I guess he could tell I was troubled by what he'd said about his cop buddy. Finally, he said, "What I was saying about Richie Boyle is that I have a track record with him. He's been helpful to me, as a source—someone giving me information from police files or pointing me to where I could uncover things."

I looked straight ahead, acting like I wasn't listening.

"Like the Tony Rosario case," he said.

That caught my attention. I slowed down. "He helped you with that?"

"He did," Clemens said. "He gave me records that were not supposed to be public. Like a full transcript of the interrogation of Tony Rosario, the one lasting twenty-one hours, where Rosario flipped out and, because of his heroin addiction, was in no shape whatsoever to make the confession the district attorney later used to convict him at his trial. Richie Boyle stuck his neck out; he gave me that file."

I frowned.

Clemens continued. "This is how it works, Trell. When a reporter develops a source like Richie Boyle, what the reporter is looking for is reliability. In other words, whether what the source says turns out to be legit. You follow me?"

I nodded.

"And, over time, I found Richie's information to be legit. He proved to be reliable. To a reporter, that's like having gold—in this case, a source inside the police who will leak you materials you need to write your stories. Plus, because he gave me stuff for a story showing Tony Rosario was innocent, I came to think Richie Boyle cares about doing the right thing. He actually cares about justice."

"Justice?" This wasn't helping me—putting Richie Boyle and justice in the same sentence. I frowned.

"Trell, listen. I'm trying to explain I have a history with Richie Boyle, okay? But at the same time, what's also important for you to know is this: a reporter goes where the story goes."

"What's that supposed to mean?" I asked.

"Keeps an open mind," Clemens said. "It's basic training, and it's a big deal—a reporter keeping an open mind while reporting each and every story."

I stopped at the blue mailbox. "Well, okay then, let's see."

Clemens had been so busy talking that he hadn't noticed where we were, and it took him a few seconds to realize that we were standing at the corner of Humboldt Ave. where Ruby Graham was shot.

I said, "I'm going to explain something that should get you wondering about police and *justice*—if you have an open mind."

Clemens stood silently and watched as I began performing a reenactment of the shooting. I put the people in position—Ruby Graham on the blue mailbox, her legs swinging; her friends hanging around, including the boys from the Humboldt Raiders; everyone relaxed and socializing, trying to cool down in the summer heat. I had everything from that night in my head, from reading Nora's documents. I'd memorized it all. It played and replayed like a movie. As I moved around, I narrated the action, kind of like a basketball game where an announcer does play-by-play.

"Then, from back there"—I pointed to a concealed side of the power company's redbrick substation—"from back there came the shooter. *POP. POP. POP.* Everyone screams; kids run in all directions; Ruby drops off the mailbox, shot dead in the head."

I realized I was breathing heavily and had worked up a sweat. I also noticed three boys, each dressed the same—baggy blues and gray hoodies, sleeves cut off at the shoulder on account of it being summer. They were walking in tandem, moving to a similar beat as if they were listening to the same music video in their heads. They slowed as they got closer to our corner. Three pairs of eyes, each deep in a hoodie cave, fixed on Clemens as if he were an alien from another planet.

I planted my feet and glared at them. "What you starin' at?"

"Law dog," the one in the middle snarled.

"Him?" I said, pointing at Clemens. "Gimme a break. He's no cop."

Clemens unfolded his arms and began to step forward. That's when I noticed the boy on the right more closely. I could see inside the hoodie and recognized the face.

"Paul?" I said. "That you in there?"

"Hey, Trell," Paul answered.

Neither one of us gave any sign we'd just seen each other a few days ago.

I looked around, surprised that boys from Thumper Parish's Castlegate turf were crossing Humboldt's turf. "What you boys doin' here?"

"Shortcut," Paul said. "From Dudley. Lazy, I guess."

"I guess so," I said. "Or maybe looking for trouble."

That got the three boys turning their heads, only to find that no one was around. Even so, they suddenly began acting nervous.

Paul moved first. "Which is why we got to keep goin'," he said, nudging the others. "Let's get."

The other two boys put their eyes back on Clemens but began

to follow behind Paul. They made sure not to go too fast, like they were in no hurry.

We watched as they left. Then Paul stopped and turned. "Hey, Trell," he yelled, "I was just thinkin'. Bunch of us are going to Water Country next week. Vinnie's takin' us up in the van. You wanna come?"

"Vinnie's Van?" I said. "How you swing that?"

"My uncle, he's payin' for it."

"Thumper?"

"He does stuff like that once in a while," Paul said.

"No, thanks," I said. I didn't want anything to do with Thumper Parish.

When the boys were gone, Clemens asked, "What was that all about?"

"You mean why they suddenly got jumpy?"

"Right."

"This is Humboldt—we're on Humboldt Ave. They're from Castlegate. The two don't mix—an oil and water thing. Or worse. They were takin' a chance cutting across Humboldt on their way home." I turned to look at Clemens. "But, actually, them doing that is perfect. It fits what I want to show you."

"I don't get it."

"I know." I turned and pointed down Humboldt Ave. "See the corner store over there?"

Clemens looked. "Yep." He read aloud the storefront sign. "Humboldt Superette."

"See above the sign, the second floor? The tiny apartment up there, a one-bedroom apartment, is where Daddy and Ma lived back then."

"Summer of '88?" Clemens said.

"Right. I was just three months old, and my parents lived there."

"Okay," Clemens said.

"So this is what I want you to be thinking about. The police — *your* police — have always said the shooting I just reenacted was gang war business. That the Castlegate Boys were looking to settle a drug beef with the Humboldt Raiders. Fighting over turf, who can sell drugs and where. And they said Daddy was a gunman for Castlegate — an enforcer — and that he came out firing from behind the building and shot poor Ruby Graham instead of his targets, the Humboldt Raiders."

"Yep," Clemens said. "That's how the case went down at trial."

"Except my daddy lived right over there. He lived *on* Humboldt Ave."

Clemens's head turned full circle — from me to the Humboldt Superette to the power company substation to the blue mailbox.

I said, "Makes no sense, street-wise. No sense at all."

I could see Clemens putting it together. "If Romero Taylor was a shooter for the Castlegate Boys, then what's he doing living on Humboldt Ave.?"

"That's what I'm saying," I said.

Clemens continued. "No way a member of Castlegate could

live safely on this street. It'd be a death wish. The Humboldt Raiders would never allow it. I see what you're saying. It makes no sense."

"Exactly." I looked Clemens in the eye. "So here's the thing: How come your big shot detective buddy Richie Boyle never put that together?"

Clemens looked at me and pulled on his ponytail. "Good question."

CHAPTER 12
RICHIE BOYLE

When he found us standing on his front stoop, Richie Boyle gave Clemens a bear hug. The ex-cop was wearing madras shorts, a sleeveless green Boston Celtics T-shirt, and a ratty pair of black flip-flops. For an old man, he was in great shape. Muscles rippled down his freckled arms as he held Clemens, and his neck was thick, like football players I'd seen on TV. Then he dropped Clemens, slapped his shoulder, and was all smiles, as if Clemens were an old buddy from high school he hadn't seen in years. But his mood went cold when Clemens introduced me.

"Last name Taylor?" Richie asked Clemens.

Clemens said, "Yep. Trell Taylor. Daughter of one Romero Taylor."

Richie looked cross-eyed. "What's this about?"

"Can we come in?" Clemens said.

I could hear voices inside his small dark house. They were loud, then quiet, then loud again. Like someone arguing. But after we followed Richie, I saw a police scanner in the middle of the living room. The noise was cops talking to one another on one of the police channels. I also saw why Richie was so fit looking. There was a chin-up bar in the entry to the kitchen, and the dining room was given over to a weight room, with barbells, free weights, and a hard rubber mat on the floor.

One thing really stood out—a giant, and I mean giant, framed photograph hanging in the middle of the living room wall. Nothing else was near it, and there was a plaque tacked underneath. The whole setup reminded me of a place of worship. The picture featured a row of white guys, some in police uniform, and smack in the middle stood Detective Richie Boyle, his arm around District Attorney Frank Flanagan. They were holding a red-bordered certificate, and the plaque beneath explained they'd received a commendation from the mayor for their public service in the apprehension of George "G-man" Whigham and his drug empire.

Overall, the place was immaculate. File boxes were stacked in rows along one whole side, cardboard boxes like the ones Nora uses in her law office. But these ones had BOSTON POLICE stamped on the side of them. When he'd retired, Richie Boyle must have taken cleaning out his desk at work to the extreme. It looked like he brought home every file from every single case he'd ever worked on.

"Unfinished business," Richie said when he caught us looking at all the stuff.

Richie filled a glass of cold water for Clemens at the kitchen sink, and only as an afterthought did he offer me one. Clemens said, "Speaking of unfinished business." Clemens drank the water in one long swallow.

Richie led us back into the tiny living room.

"Ruby Graham," Clemens said.

Richie Boyle wouldn't even look at me. Like I wasn't even there.

"Okay," Richie said. "Big case. One of the biggest ever."

"I'll cut to the chase," Clemens said. He asked about Daddy living on Humboldt Ave.

Richie rubbed his meaty fingers over his face as if he were bored. He exhaled deeply. "Yeah, yeah, yeah," he said. "I knew all about that."

I shot a look at Clemens, unable to hide my shock.

"Romero Taylor living above the Humboldt Superette but being a shooter for Castlegate? I knew all about that." Richie Boyle took another deep, bored breath. "So what?"

I couldn't sit still. "It makes no sense, that's what."

Richie turned from Clemens to glare at me. "Didn't change the evidence," he said emphatically.

Before I could stand up from the folding chair in Richie's tiny living room, Clemens's right hand reached across my lap to gently but firmly keep me in place. He lifted his hand and pointed to the police scanner that was blaring nonstop with cop talk. As if calling a time-out, Clemens changed the subject.

"Can't give it up, eh, Richie?" he said.

Richie stood and walked over to the scanner. "Keeps me entertained." He chuckled to himself. "Just last week, Clem, unbelievable." He began rubbing his hands together and opened a big smile, his bright-white teeth lined up neatly like the file boxes. "You hear about the shooting on Blue Hill Ave.? At the takeout joint—Wa-lukies, Wa-kukies? Some nutty name like that. Three guys walk in, shoot some dude at the counter holding his cheeseburger and fries. People flying for cover under tables. French fries flying, too, all over the place."

"Walaikums," Clemens said.

"What?" Richie said.

"Wa-lai-kums. The joint's name is Walaikums. Shooting was around midnight."

"So you know about it."

Clemens said, "I wrote the brief. I'm working the overnight now, and I wrote the news brief for the *Globe*. The victim—Teddy Evans, age twenty-three—was dead on arrival at Boston City."

"That's the one," Richie said. "Teddy Evans. Guess you could say he died hungry."

Richie was the only one who laughed.

"So, anyway, get this. The shooters jump in a car, take off. Police see 'em and follow. Other police join in, and suddenly you got this unbelievable chase, the shooters zigzagging their way through side streets, along Franklin Park. I'm listening to the entire thing on the radio. I'm on the edge of my seat. You have to understand, chases are usually over in a few minutes or less. Guy crashes into a pole or something. Police cut 'im off. But this thing just keeps going. The shooter at the wheel, man, must have been some kind of driver. So I'm listening—it's way better than anything you'll ever find on TV—and I realize the chase is heading my way. They're coming down Elm Street, just around the corner from me.

"I run out front. I'm standing in the yard. The sky is all lit up, maybe a dozen cruisers now, their cherry tops flashing. I've never seen anything like it. I see the shooters' car turn onto my street. I'm going, oh my Gawd! Here they come. The driver's got this wild look on his face, and the back window is rolling down. I'm thinking I better duck and dive, 'cause maybe they're gonna take a shot at me. But that's not it. They're throwin' something outta the car. Like a couple of rocks. If I was wearing a mitt, I coulda caught 'em—that's how close it was. I look down and on the ground. On each side of me is a pistol. They'd tossed their weapons.

"Unbelievable, right? They race past me in a flash, the shooters, and so do the police. The whole thing ends five minutes later in Mattapan, where they made a stupid turn and got trapped on a dead end, Woodruff Way.

"In the meantime, I run inside, grab a couple of evidence bags I keep just in case, and place the handguns in them."

Richie Boyle stopped there, his face glowing. "You shoulda seen the duty captain's face when I walked into District 5 carrying the murder weapons."

Richie looked at Clemens. "Unreal, huh?"

"Like the old days," Clemens said.

"Whaddya mean?"

Clemens said, "I don't know, sounds like something from the bad old days, the eighties. You know, when 'Crack was king'—all hell breakin'. Streets a war zone."

Richie's face went slack. "Gawd, hope not." His voice got serious. "That *was* hell, Clemens." Richie began rubbing his chin, his mind heading off in a different direction. "We weren't ready— that's the truth," Richie said. "Chief always saying it's a New York thing. He was in denial. Then crack hit us. Never seen street crews organized like that in Boston—binoculars, walkie-talkies, weapons like never before, pump shotguns, even Uzis. Pit bulls roaming their bunkers, a first line of security." Richie shook his head at the memories. "Bad things happened, bad things."

"Like Ruby Graham," Clemens said.

Richie shot Clemens a look. "Like Ruby Graham," he said. "Poor little girl. Flanagan and his people in the DA's office, along with us police—we were under so much pressure to cap the volcano. That's what the crack cocaine thing was, a volcano. It took us a while, but we took back the street."

Clemens said, "And from the ashes rose the likes of Lamar 'Thumper' Parish."

Richie let Clemens's remark go unchallenged. "Yeah, well,

maybe he's still out there. But we got most of 'em. We got the G-man." Richie pointed to the giant photograph hanging on the wall. "Remember him? George 'G-man' Whigham? He was a big deal. When he swaggered through the projects, it was like time stopped until he went through. Least we got him."

Richie paused, lost in a distant thought.

Clemens broke the silence. "Richie, what's with the front yard?"

"What? The lawn?" Richie gave us a crooked smile. "Everybody else on the street pours cement for a front yard doesn't mean I can't have a patch of grass? What the heck?"

"I'm not talking about that," Clemens said. "I'm talking about the monster sign you got planted smack in the middle of your little green acre."

Clemens meant the sign painted in red and blue letters on a white background: MENINO FOR MAYOR.

Clemens continued. "I'm surprised. I would have expected you'd be all in for Frank Flanagan. You were so tight, a crime-fighting tandem. That's how I remember it. I figure you'd want to help make sure he gets elected this time, right the wrong of his defeat four years ago."

"Well, things change."

For the second time since we'd been at Richie's, a silence took over. Then, just like before, Clemens broke it, and when he did I realized Clemens had had a plan all along, where, after a time-out and some small talk, he was looping back to the reason we were there. He was a reporter working an interview, I realized.

"It *is* kinda strange, Richie, don't you think?"

Richie looked at Clemens.

"That Romero Taylor would be a shooter for Thumper Parish's Castlegate, and he was living on Humboldt."

"Jeezus, Clemens, that again?"

"It is strange, Richie. Gets stranger, the fact Romero Taylor wasn't part of Castlegate, wasn't part of any gang, for that matter."

"May seem strange to you, but it wasn't to us," Richie said firmly. He was getting worked up. "We had evidence. *Evidence.* We learn the shooter was wearing an Adidas running suit. We learn running suits were Romero Taylor's everyday threads; he becomes a person of interest.

"We got witnesses come forward—and that's no easy thing, mind you, getting anyone in the neighborhood to stick their neck out to help police. God forbid that should ever happen. Maybe it's because the victim was so young—who knows. The point is they implicated Taylor. Bottom line: Taylor is our killer. End of story."

I watched Clemens studying Richie, and I watched Richie look away.

"Still," Clemens said.

"Still what?" Richie interrupted.

"Still doesn't explain what I was sayin' about Romero Taylor."

"Jeezus, Clemens," Richie said, his voice rising, agitated. "We had evidence, we made the case, we took it to the jury, and that no-good drug-dealing child killer was found guilty beyond a reasonable doubt. Jeezus, Clemens."

It took me every ounce of control not to interrupt.

Clemens said, "Your witnesses—seems convenient how they turned up."

"What?" Richie said.

"How it was months after the killing before they turned up—and just weeks before Romero Taylor's murder trial was starting. Seems convenient. How Frank Flanagan was able to roll out three witnesses in time for the trial."

"Like I said, it's rare we get any help from the neighborhood. It took time." Richie spoke the words slowly; he was gritting his teeth. He continued, "C'mon, Clemens, of all people, you know how it is. Human dirt like Romero Taylor? No conscience. Harms everything he touches. Even if this one wasn't his—and don't think for a second I'm suggesting that—but even if he wasn't the shooter on this one, I promise you he was on another."

Richie grew heated. "That's how it is, Clemens. You know that. With these guys, they're guilty with a capital G. If not for one crime, then it's another. So at the end of the day, everything evens out."

I finally had to say something. "What kind of crazy math is that?"

Richie Boyle and I traded looks. I thought he might explode at me. Instead it was like he saw me for the first time, and I wanted to make sure he saw exactly who I am, a fourteen-year-old teenager wanting the truth about why her father was in prison.

I said, "You sayin' police are fine putting someone in jail for something they didn't do, because if they didn't do that crime, they've done others — and that's okay? It all evens out?"

Richie didn't answer me. He looked down and began to rub his forehead using both hands. The veins on his temple were popping.

"Clemens," he said. "This is a long time ago. You sure you want to be doing this?"

"Is that a threat, Richie?" Clemens said.

"Threat? No. It's just I thought you were out of the game." Richie's voice was quiet now. "Like me — I thought you were done."

We left after that. Clemens and Richie Boyle went through the motions of saying good-bye. No bear hugs this time. Clemens and I walked in silence for about a block before I said, "You call him someone who cares about justice?"

"I know," Clemens said.

"Funny kind of justice, if you ask me."

"It's not what I expected."

Then Clemens looked at me. "Evidence," he said. "Now we're the ones who need evidence. New evidence. Evidence to show the evidence they used was wrong and unjust.

"We got heavy work to do," he said.

CHAPTER 13
NOWHERE TO BE FOUND

Right after breakfast the next morning, Ma and I took the bus downtown to Nora's office, and on the ride, I noticed that FLANAGAN FOR MAYOR signs were popping up all over the place.

Nora had called a meeting for her, us, and Clemens. "We need a strategy session," she told Ma on the phone. "To come up with a game plan."

When we got to her office, we found Nora standing in front of a dry-erase board she'd set up next to the table of documents from Daddy's case. The war room was growing. Nora, using a black marker, had made four columns on the board. One column was labeled *Alibi*. The other three were labeled:

Monique Catron
Juanda Tillery
Travis Golson

I recognized the names. The three kids Richie Boyle and the prosecutor Frank Flanagan had rolled out as witnesses against Daddy. Except they weren't kids anymore. If they were, like, thirteen, fourteen, or fifteen back when the trial happened in 1989, it meant they were in their late twenties now.

I looked around the office. Ma and I had arrived first.

"Someone's on time," Nora said, turning from the board to face us. She frowned. "Clemens Bittner?"

Ma and I both shrugged. But then we heard noise outside. Clemens kicked open the office door with his left foot. He entered balancing a takeout tray from Dunkin' Donuts. He was wearing blue-jean shorts, a sky-blue T-shirt, and sandals.

"Coffee? Donuts?" He put the tray down. "Nora Walsh: large coffee. With milk. Not cream. Not whole milk. Fat-free milk." He handed her one of the cups.

I was puzzled. "You two know each other?"

Nora and Clemens talked at once. "Yes. No. Not really. Kinda," they said.

Nora picked up one of the coffees. "I called him yesterday," Nora said. "He actually answered." She carefully lifted the lid on her coffee.

"Yeah, well, now that I'm back online, so to speak, new phone policy—when it rings, answer."

The way they were trading looks like a couple of kids, made me wonder how long they'd talked. It must have been long enough for them to break the ice, feel comfortable with each other.

Nora said, "We talked about the case. I told him I was glad he'd agreed to help."

"I told her about seeing Richie Boyle," Clemens said.

"And I said we needed a meeting."

"And I offered to handle refreshments."

Clemens smiled. Nora sipped the coffee and seemed satisfied with it.

"Thanks," she said. "Perfect."

"Shey? Trell?" Clemens said.

Ma took a coffee, passed on the donuts. I took a chocolate glazed. We stood in silence for a minute, sipping coffee and nibbling donuts. I watched Clemens look around the room, sizing up boxes of documents and the names on the board.

"Okay," Nora said. "Here's the deal—what we've got to do. We need to reinvestigate the evidence used at trial to convict Romero Taylor." Nora paused, took another sip, and looked over at Clemens. "Clemens knows something about this; it's what he did for the stories he wrote about Tony Rosario in the arson-murder case."

Clemens didn't say anything. He was just taking it all in.

Nora continued. "On the board I've written the names of the three star witnesses, along with a column for the alibi. We need to find those three kids—or, I should say, people. They're grown up now. We need to track them down and get them talking about what they saw back then and how they came to be witnesses. And we need to track down the kids Romero was with when Ruby Graham was shot, find out why they never came forward. Seeing they were his friends, Romero might be able to help on that." Nora shook her head hard. "Drives me nuts thinking Romero's lawyer never got his friends to give the alibi. Seems pretty simple. If Romero's with them, can't be shooting up Humboldt."

Nora was pacing in front of the document table. She stopped at the board.

Clemens spoke up. "Easier said than done."

"Say what?" Nora said.

"These people," Clemens said. "You try to find them?"

"I took a preliminary run at it," Nora said.

"Telephone book?" Clemens asked.

"Yep." Nora said.

"City directories?" Clemens asked.

I interrupted. "City what?"

Clemens looked my way. "Directories. They're these books that break the city down—by street addresses, occupancy, and telephone numbers. You can cross-reference your way into finding someone. Like if all you have is an old address for someone. You can look up the address, and the book will list the names of other people who lived at that same address, along with telephone numbers. Call all the numbers, talk to people, maybe it leads you to the person you're after. The point is, you play around in the directories, you can often track someone down."

"Tried that, too," Nora said. "Nothing. I even asked a private investigator—retired cop I know—to take a sniff. But it's not like I have a budget. He did a couple of quick checks for free, came back empty. Found not a one."

"8-Boy," Clemens said.

This time Nora, Ma, and I spoke at the same time. "What?"

"8-Boy," Clemens repeated. "It's Boston Police radio code. Means, 'nowhere to be found.' Like when police are searching for a suspect in a crime—however that might be, on foot, in their cruisers, knocking on doors, whatever. If they can't find the person, they report back to the radio dispatcher, '8-Boy.'"

Clemens said, "Police are always talking about how hard it is to find people deep in the neighborhoods. Roxbury, Dorchester—it's not like the suburbs, with the neat and tidy mailboxes out front of the single-family homes. Here it's rentals, people moving around all the time, kind of just disappearing. Hard to keep track."

Nora said, "That's what we got, then, for all three—Monique Catron, Juanda Tillery, Travis Golson. They're 8-Boy."

"Nowhere to be found," Clemens said.

"Which is why the meeting," Nora said. "You guys gotta find them."

I'd worn my running clothes to Nora's because after I wanted to do a workout—and I had this idea to make Clemens go along. I figured the way he lived cooped up in his dark cave of an apartment, the way he worked the newspaper's graveyard shift, he needed to get out, get some fresh air, get some exercise. So as we left Nora's office, I presented Clemens with a box containing a pair of New Balance running shoes. Fresh foam construction, skyline insoles, custom color: ocean blue.

"What's this?" he said.

I'd won the shoes for finishing first in the Roxbury YMCA's Memorial Day 5K. But they were a men's size 12. The organizers said all prizes were donated, and the only size they had was 12. Some woman said I could always give them to my father. I sure gave her a look. When I got home, mad they didn't have my size, I shoved the box all the way back in my closet. Then all this got started, and we got Clemens on board, and I figured at least now I might put the running shoes to good use.

I told Clemens my plan.

"I am not into sweat," he said.

Ma and I made him open the box. When he saw the brand-new shoes wrapped in tissue, I could tell he was wavering. We made him try them on. Clemens knew how much I was into running, and I think he appreciated the gift.

He caved. "What the heck?" he said.

Clemens drove us in his Volvo back to his place on Esmond Street so he could change. It gave us a chance to talk about the meeting at Nora's and the people search we faced. It would be like trying to find a needle in a haystack, Nora had told us.

"If I was looking for someone, I wouldn't ever use a telephone book or try one of those, what you call them? City directories," Ma said. "Wouldn't work. Not in my world."

"What, then?" Clemens said.

Ma said, "You ask around. Keep asking around until you get something."

Clemens gave Ma a big smile. "I feel like I'm in my news-writing class at Emerson. Like this is a teaching moment. Because there's no substitute for good ol'-fashioned shoe-leather reporting," Clemens said. "Hit the streets, wear out your shoe soles. That's exactly what you're talking about, Shey Taylor. Question is," he said, "Where to begin?"

Clemens came out of his bathroom wearing shorts made of thick gray cotton, the last thing anyone should wear on a workout run. His top was also cotton, a tattered maroon T-shirt with the word GUNNERY printed across the front.

"Gunnery?" I asked as we were leaving his apartment. "What's that?"

"Boarding school," Clemens said. "In Connecticut."

"What's it, some kind of military school?"

Clemens shook his head. "Everyone always says that. It's named after the guy who started the school, guy from the 1850s named Frederick Gunn. He was pretty famous, actually. And not just for being an educator. He was an abolitionist."

"Oh," I said. "You went there?"

"I did," Clemens said. "For a couple of years."

"You didn't finish?"

"No," he said.

"What happened?"

Clemens frowned. We were standing on this street corner. "What is this—Twenty Questions? Thought you were making me do a run."

"Just curious."

"Let's just say I wasn't serious enough, like I shoulda been. I missed my friends. Wasn't into this boarding school thing. Kinda juvenile, really. Like I wasn't ready to appreciate the situation. Anyway, I was asked to leave."

"*Asked* to leave?"

"That's what they call it when they're kicking you out. I was flunking everything. I went back to my public high school outside Hartford."

"Your parents mad?"

"Yeah, of course. Me? I was thrilled. Now I look back and wish I hadn't been such a jerk. It's basically worked out okay, but when I think of some of the great teachers they had, the small classes . . . Good stuff was going on. I missed out."

Whole thing reminded me a little bit of the Weld, and the decision I had to be making.

Ma had said she was fine waiting at Clemens's place. I told her we would be back in less than a half hour, but that was before I watched Clemens actually try to run.

Right away he fell behind. His shoulders slumped, and his head drooped—sure signs of fatigue. Ten minutes in, he looked a mess. His ponytail had come loose, and the worn-out Gunnery T-shirt was drenched in sweat. No serious runner would be caught dead wearing all cotton—and soaking wet, his clothes probably weighed two pounds heavier than when he started. They certainly didn't go with the new running shoes I'd given him. Total disconnect, clothes versus shoes.

"C'mon," I called to him. "You can do it."

Clemens didn't look up.

I stopped to wait.

From his apartment, we had crossed Blue Hill Avenue and cut into Franklin Park. I had a route mapped out in my head that would take us in a big loop around the golf course. Three miles max. But the way Clemens was gagging, I wasn't so sure.

Clemens shuffled to a halt.

"You really are out of shape," I said.

He leaned onto his knees, gasping.

"Clemens?"

I was worried he might puke.

He looked up, his eyes pleading. "Gimme a minute."

"Didn't you ever do a sport or anything at that school?"

"The Big G?" he said, gulping air. "Yeah. I played hockey."

"You any good?" It was hard to picture Clemens making it around the rink.

"Hey, watch it." Clemens got defensive. "I was a center iceman, a pretty good one, as a matter of fact." Clemens tried to smile, but he couldn't get past looking sickly. "Long time ago, though," he said.

Clemens finally stood up straight, and after a few more deep breaths, he no longer looked like he would pass out. We'd already taken a ten-minute break. I was completely cooled down.

"You ready to pick it up?" I said.

"Sure," Clemens said, "as long as we walk."

I grunted my disapproval, but there wasn't much I could do. We followed along the rim of the golf course, on Circuit Drive. Going in slow motion, I noticed things I wouldn't have if I'd been running hard around the park.

To our right was the Franklin Park Zoo. I spotted a bus emptying a load of little kids who were lining up to enter the kiddie zoo. I watched them giggle and laugh. It reminded me of my first school visit when I was in kindergarten. Most of the cages were empty then, messy and run-down. The few animals — a fox, some prairie dogs and sad-eyed sheep — seemed bored out of their minds.

Ma later told me that the zoo, which is like a hundred years old, was on the verge of shutting down. It didn't have any money or many visitors. Not a whole lot of families from the suburbs wanted to drive into the middle of Roxbury. But that's all different now. Soon after my first visit, some folks in the neighborhood got the ear of the mayor, who talked up the zoo as a city landmark in desperate need of attention. The mayor reminded everyone that Franklin Park itself was named after Benjamin Franklin. The zoo suddenly became the hot charity everyone supported. It got spruced up; exhibits were added, like the Giraffe Savannah, where three really tall giraffes live with a herd of zebras. The one I like the most is the new Tropical Forest, a large building with a dome. Inside is like an actual tropical forest. Gorillas, hippos, crocodiles, birds like vultures, bats and snakes—they all live there.

That's the good news. But if you live around here like I do, you know a different side of things. Because everything isn't what it seems. In the woods on the far side of the park, along Seaver Street, is where Kimberly Rae Barber was murdered about ten years ago. Kids from the Geneva Avenue gang did it. They'd been partying and had headed toward the park looking for a good time. They ran into Kimberly. She was just walking home from the Y on MLK Boulevard. It was bad. Like assault. Like strangling. For more than a month afterward, that whole corner of the park was off limits, sealed behind miles of yellow police tape.

Then a little farther down from where Clemens and I were headed, also off to the right, there's a tot lot. I heard squealing and shouting even from where we were, by the golf course. Like the zoo, the playground got a complete makeover a few years ago and was now real popular. New equipment, painted in bright candy colors. Its name? The Ruby Graham Tot Lot. Really. The sign doesn't tell the whole sad story of why a playground would be named after her. Like I said, you have to live around here to know that stuff. It just reads, "In Memory of Ruby Graham."

I didn't really want to be thinking about any dark things at the moment. Not during a workout. Not when I wanted to be free of everything except for the feeling I get while running. My head gets clear and I feel a lightness. So I turned my back to that side of Franklin Park, looking instead at the cluster of maple and elm trees, and the soccer fields beyond.

Clemens interrupted my thoughts. "You think I could do that?"

I think Clemens was looking for a way to keep his mind off running — and the pain that was fixed on his face.

He pointed to the golf course and the rolling fairways dotted with sand traps. Then he took a few air swings back and forth with an invisible golf club. "Probably get the hang of it pretty quick," he said.

"Never played golf," I said. "I don't know."

"Be easier on the body, for sure," he said. "Lot easier than this."

Clemens jogged in place and grimaced.

"You only need to get in shape."

Both of us spotted the golf ball leaping in our direction. Fast.

"Fore!" a voice shouted. "Fore!"

Clemens put his arms over his head and ducked. I did the same, even though I wasn't sure why. The golf ball trickled to a stop ten yards from us. It posed no danger. I stared at it nestled in the taller grass at the base of a tree.

Then I heard a voice call my name.

I looked up to see a golfer walking toward us, a man dressed in plaid shorts and a green pullover shirt. He was pulling a golf cart.

"Trell? That you?"

The man came closer and stopped next to his golf ball.

"It is you," the man said. "What a strange coincidence."

Strange? I thought. *What's so strange? I live around here.*

But I didn't say anything like that. Just like I barely said anything at the Weld.

"Hi, Mr. Rowe" is all I said.

Mr. Rowe stood there, hands on his hips, nodding. It was the same nod he gave me during our advising meetings before school started. Rubbing his chin, nodding.

"Well, okay," he said. The head nodded a few more beats. "What a surprise." The head still nodded. "Your summer? Good so far?"

"It's okay," I said.

"Okay." The head nodded some more.

Then, abruptly, the head stopped.

His forehead had creased. "Trell?" he said.

"Yes, Mr. Rowe."

"Trell, are you . . ." Mr. Rowe looked from me to Clemens and back again. "Trell, are you . . . safe?"

Clemens glared. "She's fine."

"I'm speaking to Trell," Mr. Rowe said.

I watched Mr. Rowe staring at Clemens, a sweaty, hulking man with long hair loosened from its ponytail so it was now half hiding his face. It was just like at school, I realized. Mr. Rowe seeing things differently from the way they were.

"Trell?" Mr. Rowe repeated.

"Everything is fine," I answered. "Fine."

The other golfers in Mr. Rowe's group began calling.

"Oggie!" one of them shouted. "C'mon, Oggie. Just pick up the goddamn ball. We're holding everyone up!"

Mr. Rowe waved to them. He stooped to pick up the golf ball. He looked back at us again, and he hesitated. "Okay, Trell, if that's it," he said. "But like I've said before, we're here for you. Don't forget that. We are here for you."

Mr. Rowe hustled across the fairway to join the others. We watched as he dropped a golf ball and chose a club from his bag. Mr. Rowe took a few practice swings and then wound up his body to take a real one. The ball took off toward the green, hooked sharply, and disappeared into some thick brush on the left. Mr. Rowe threw his club, and I watched it somersault across the fairway.

"Who was that?" Clemens asked.

"He's from the Weld. My adviser."

I told Clemens about the school as we watched the golfers walk farther along the course. I explained how Mr. Rowe always talked down to me, like he saw me as some stupid kid from Roxbury who either lived with drug dealers or had parents who partied all through the night. I told him how Mr. Rowe, taking pity, acted like he was a big help, when he actually made school worse.

I also told Clemens how halfway through the school year the biggest help I got was from the poem by Langston Hughes called "To Certain Intellectuals" that I read in English class, the only class I ended up liking. I said I thought the poem was about phonies like Mr. Rowe, people who think they are caring and open-minded but really are just stuck-up and prejudiced.

"The poem made me feel not so alone," I said.

I began to recite it for Clemens. "'You are no friend of mine. . . .'"

When Clemens joined in, I was in total shock.

Together, we recited,

"You are no friend of mine
For I am poor,
Black,
Ignorant and slow, —
Not your kind.
You yourself
Have told me so, —
No friend of mine."

"You know it?" I said.

"I wrote a term paper in college about Langston Hughes," Clemens said.

We walked in silence until Clemens howled with laughter.

"I was just thinking," he said. "*Oggie?* What's an Oggie?"

"His name," I said. "Ogden, I think. Ogden Rowe."

"Perfect name. For 'certain intellectuals,' I mean." Clemens scratched his head. "We had a few teachers like that at the Big G." He looked at me. "But they weren't all like that. Like I said, some were really good. You just had to find them."

We got back to jogging, finally. We resumed our route around the rim of the golf course. The heat wave had broken, and the air was dry. Felt more like a late spring day than late July. We didn't see Mr. Rowe again.

When Clemens opened the door to his apartment, he froze. Meaning that without any warning he was going to stop, I slammed into his backside.

"Whoa," Clemens said. "Whoa."

I peered around him and saw the reason for his surprise. The apartment had been tidied up. Newspapers, magazines, books — all stacked neatly on tables. Now you could actually see the floor, and it had been swept. The furniture was straightened, too.

Over by the sink, Ma was wiping down the countertop.

"Shey," Clemens said.

Ma finished before she turned to us. "Didn't take much, really. I've seen worse. It just needed a little bit of organizing, and a good sweep."

"You didn't have to," Clemens said.

"Yes, I did." Ma gave him a look. "Me and Trell be coming around here? Place has to be fit for humans."

I filled two glasses of water and handed one to Clemens.

"Took you a while?" Ma asked.

"Out of shape," Clemens admitted. "Pathetically out of shape."

I told Ma about bumping into Mr. Rowe.

"Reminds me, you got to start your summer reading," Ma said.

We emptied our glasses. I refilled mine.

Then Ma said, "While you were out, I got us some information."

"What do you mean, Ma?"

"Monique Catron," she said.

Clemens put his glass down. "That was fast."

"Ask around, told you that," she said. "Took me a few calls, actually." Ma looked at me and said, "Rachelle Williams, she knew something."

Clemens looked at Ma, then me. He was clueless.

"Marlon Williams's mother," I said. I explained about Vinnie's Van, and that Mrs. Williams was a regular on the ride to Walpole. "She's family now," I said. Then added, "Her son Marlon's doing twelve years for armed robbery."

Clemens began pacing, as if he was getting a second wind. "This is great news, Shey," he said. "Where is she?"

Ma stepped away from the sink and sat down at the tiny table in the kitchen. I could see she wasn't too excited.

"Monique is at New Calvary," she said. "The cemetery in Mattapan. Monique Catron is dead."

"Dead?" I gasped.

Ma nodded. "Long time ago, too: 1990 — a year after Daddy's trial."

"She was, like, only fourteen years old," I said. "That's what I read in Nora's file."

Ma said, "I know. Fourteen at the trial. Fifteen when she died." Ma said Rachelle Williams didn't know how Monique died. "Just that she was sick."

That's why Ma was not excited.

Clemens said, "This is not good. For us, I mean." The energy drained from his face. "That's the thing with cases like this. So much time has gone by. Witnesses are 8-Boy. Or worse, they die. It's uphill, all the way."

"There is one thing," Ma said.

"What?" I said.

"The girl's mother is still around. Rachelle told me she moved to Vassar Street, right off Washington Street, one of the triple-deckers. Number 22. Name is Lola Catron."

"Maybe she can help," I said. I was the one pacing now. "We should go."

CHAPTER 14
MONIQUE CATRON'S GHOST

Lola Catron didn't seem to want visitors. We pushed the doorbell for Apartment 3 a bunch of times before we heard her finally make her way down the stairs. Then she pulled up the curtain hanging loosely over the front-door window, saw us standing on the porch, and let the curtain drop.

"Go away," she said.

"Mrs. Catron," Clemens yelled. "We'd like to talk to you."

She peeked out again. She was dressed in a robe, and it was afternoon.

"I said, go away." She coughed, a hacking cough. "Go away."

Clemens and I looked at each other.

When Ruby Graham was shot, Lola Catron and her daughter, Monique, lived in an apartment on Homestead Street, right around the corner from the blue mailbox. During the trial,

Monique testified that after hearing gunfire, she ran to her front window. She testified she saw a man dressed in an Adidas running suit run past her apartment down Homestead. The man, she said, tucked a pistol into his waistband as he ran. The prosecutor, Frank Flanagan, then asked Monique if she saw that man in the courtroom. Monique pointed to my daddy, seated at the defense table with his lawyer. "You certain of that?" Frank Flanagan said. "Yes," Monique replied. "I'll never forget those eyes." Frank Flanagan nodded, smiled, and returned to his chair. "Thank you," he said. "No further questions."

I stared into the curtained window. "We can't go away, Mrs. Catron."

Mrs. Catron peered at us from one corner. Her eyes seemed stuck on Clemens. Her mouth was clamped shut, her jaw jutting out.

Without turning my head, I said, "Clemens, I have an idea."

"Okay," he said.

"You go back to the street. Give me a minute here."

"Huh?"

"Just give me a minute. You go wait on the sidewalk."

Clemens shrugged, turned, and backed off the front porch. Mrs. Catron's eyes stayed on him, following his every move.

"Mrs. Catron?" I said.

She looked at me. But not with the same hardness she had for Clemens.

"Can I talk to you?"

Mrs. Catron fiddled with the lock, then cracked open the door.

Nodding in Clemens's direction, I said, "He's not police."

"No?" Mrs. Catron said. She opened the door wider.

"No," I said.

Mrs. Catron sighed. She looked like the sigh was going to turn into another hacking cough, the way her chest heaved and her eyes widened, but nothing came out. She said, "I'm so tired of police."

"Me too, Mrs. Catron," I said. "Me too."

She opened the door wider.

I stepped into the entryway.

"His name is Clemens," I said. "He's not police. He's a friend. We want to talk to you about something."

"What might that be?"

"Something from the old neighborhood, Mrs. Catron."

She didn't say anything, just shook her head slowly as if whatever she was thinking pained her. She turned away and headed toward the stairs. She took the first step. I worried that was it, that she wasn't going to see us. But then her right hand flicked out from her side a few times. She was waving me to follow.

I waved to Clemens to come in.

We followed Lola Catron up three flights of stairs to her apartment. Slowly. When she stopped on the third-floor landing, I figured it was so she could catch her breath. But it was something else. She stepped carefully around a darkened area in the hallway. She pointed to the deep red stain in the wood floor.

"My son's blood," she said. "Died right here. Last year. Two bullets."

Mrs. Catron pushed open her door, shuffled across the room, and dropped into a couch. "Police have been too big a part of my life," she said.

We stepped over the bloodstain and followed her into the living room.

"Still sick to death," she said. Mrs. Catron got settled and looked at us. "Call me Miss Lola," she said.

We said we would.

She ran her fingers through her hair, which was wiry and gray and needed a good brushing. Her robe was floral, and she had thick padded slippers on her feet. On the table in front of her lay a pack of Winston cigarettes. The ashtray nearby overflowed with butts. The big-screen TV across the room was turned on to a day-time soap. Miss Lola used the remote to turn the volume down.

"Sick to death," Miss Lola continued.

I sat on the edge of an end chair, and Clemens sank into another. It was clear we were going to have to wait for Miss Lola, let her talk.

"The shooter chased my son, Robert, into the house and up the stairs. Can you believe that? Then right outside my front door. Bang. Bang. No place is safe anymore. Robert died on the landing." Miss Lola let loose a wail.

"Right . . . on . . . the . . . *landing.*"

She pulled a clump of tissues from the pocket of her robe and dabbed her eyes. "The police after—no way to treat a mother." Raided her apartment, she said, tore apart Robert's room, questioned her all night and into the next day. "Wouldn't leave me be," she said. "You'd think I done it."

Miss Lola pointed to the TV and said, "Later they wouldn't tell me nothing—it was on the news I learned about the arrest. Two boys from Geneva Avenue, belonged to a gang. Reporter on TV said Robert owed them money and wouldn't repay it. Police the reporter interviewed kept calling my boy Stinger. Like that was his name. But not to me it wasn't. He was Robert. My Robert."

Miss Lola reached for the pack of cigarettes. "Too much police in my life. Too much." She lit a cigarette. The cough started after the first puff.

Clemens waited until Miss Lola was breathing evenly.

"Sorry for your loss," he said. I nodded along with him.

"Still traumatized," Miss Lola said.

Clemens cleared his throat. "Well," he said. "Police is what we wanted to ask you about. Not about Robert, though. Longer ago than that—1988, to be exact. We want to ask you about the police and your daughter, Monique."

Miss Lola looked up toward the sky and moaned. I thought she might faint.

"I got so much pain as it is," she said. "Why Monique?"

Clemens continued. "Monique was a key witness in a murder trial."

"Don't need to remind me of that," Miss Lola said. Her look hardened. "I was there the whole time, right by my baby's side, doing the best I could to take care of her. Police, they had no right doing what they did, condition she was in. They wouldn't leave her alone. It's like they moved in, lived with us."

"That's what we're interested in—the police." Clemens sat forward in his chair, clasped his hands, and explained to Miss Lola that he was a reporter with the *Boston Globe*. He said he was following up on things he'd heard about the police and the way they handled witnesses in the Ruby Graham case. "We'd like to talk to you about what you remember, and we'd like to take some notes."

Clemens reached into his back pocket and pulled out not one but two slender spiral pads. Printed across each were the words *Reporter's Notebook*. He handed me one, along with a pen. I flipped mine open, and as Clemens began scribbling something into his, I looked at the blank page and wrote "Miss Lola" along with the date. It seemed like the right thing to do.

Miss Lola hesitated a moment, took a puff on her cigarette, and then crushed it out in the ashtray. "Well, I didn't see nothin'," she began. "I was inside my bedroom when it happened. Monique, she was in the living room, resting on the couch. Before you know it, they be on my steps. Police after the killing were like buck wild. Crazy. Banging on doors. Monique was in no condition for that."

I couldn't help but interrupt. "Miss Lola, you keep saying 'condition.'"

Out of the corner of my eye, I saw Clemens look at me. He gave me a little nod.

"What kind of condition?" I asked.

"She was not well." Miss Lola choked up. "My poor baby."

Gently, Clemens asked her to explain what was wrong with Monique.

Miss Lola collected herself. She said, "We were living at 72 Homestead, just Monique and me. Tiny apartment on the first floor. Robert, just a toddler at the time, was staying with my sister. To help me out, so I could work.

"That winter Monique began getting very severe headaches. They came out of nowhere. She was in pain. Constant pain. I'd have to sit up all night and hold her head in my arms. I was taking her to the doctor, but they didn't know what to make of it. Just give her some medicine. Then, in the spring, one day Monique collapses and falls flat on her face. She just lay there on the living room floor. I thought she was dead. The ambulance brought us to the emergency room at Boston City, and that's when we finally got the diagnosis."

"Which was?" Clemens asked.

Miss Lola stared off into space. "Cancer," she said.

I was scribbling as fast as I could in my notebook.

"Monique began doing treatments," Miss Lola said. "It's why she was resting on the couch when the girl was shot on the blue mailbox around the corner. Monique had just had another round of treatments. She was resting."

"So Monique was in treatment when Ruby Graham was shot?" Clemens said.

Miss Lola nodded.

"Did the police know your daughter had cancer?"

"Of course they knew," Miss Lola said. Her face hardened like before, agitated. "I told them she was ill. They didn't care. Cancer had nothing to do with her mouth."

"What do you mean?" I asked.

"Police were after her from day one to testify. Would not stop. She told them detectives first time they came around she'd gotten up from the couch and gone to the front window after the shooting started. Said she saw someone run past. Detectives wanted her to identify who it was. But Monique said she didn't know.

"That wasn't good enough. Detectives came back the next day, spread a bunch of police photos out on the table in the kitchen. They told Monique to pick out the face of the shooter. Monique tried her best. I know she did, even though her head ached and she was rubbing her temples the whole time.

"But Monique couldn't. Didn't get a good look, she said."

Clemens and I exchanged glances.

"Detectives were not happy," Miss Lola said.

Clemens asked, "You recall the detectives' names?"

Miss Lola shook her head. "If you said a name, maybe I'd remember."

"Boyle?" I said. "Detective Richie Boyle."

Miss Lola huffed. "Yeah. That's it. Boyle. He's the one always seemed so worked up and in a hurry, reminded me of a pot of water about to boil over. It's how I remembered his name."

"What happened after that?" Clemens said.

"Wouldn't leave us alone. Mr. Boyle and others kept coming around the apartment, harassing us. Like I said, after that shooting, police were running around the neighborhood wild, wanting to arrest somebody for shooting that girl. They even wanted me to see something I didn't see. Kept sayin', 'You were home— you got to have seen something.' Kept threatening to take me to court, subpoena me, if I didn't cooperate. But they backed off all that nonsense with me after they had Monique look at the photo array a second time."

"What happened the second time?"

"Detectives spread out the photos, like before. But this time a guy in a suit and tie had accompanied them. Kinda fat guy, acted like he was in charge."

"Name?" Clemens interrupted.

"I don't know," Miss Lola said. "It's hazy, so many years now. But I do remember Monique was scared. Police never let up after the first meeting. Followed us everywhere we went, saying, 'We got to talk. We got to talk.' My poor baby couldn't take it. She was ill. She was scared.

"So this second time, photos are on the table, and the man in the suit is pointing to one of the photos. It's Romero Taylor. The man's pushing my girl: 'C'mon Monique, you sure you don't recognize him? You sure?' he's saying. He won't stop, keeps askin' her that question, until suddenly he changes his tune. Now he says, 'That guy, he's the one, right? You can help us, Monique. He's the one?'

"Monique is under so much pressure. She nods yes. The guy

in the suit gets all excited, saying, 'Thatta girl, thatta girl.' He starts walking around the room, slapping the detectives, like he won the lottery. 'Look at those eyes,' he tells Monique as he starts waving the Romero Taylor photo. 'Never forget those eyes.'"

I put my pen down. "It's what Monique testified to at trial."

"Don't I know it," Miss Lola said. "I was there. Monique was a ghost by then. Pale. Worn down by the treatments. Barely anything left of her. She would have said anything that man wanted her to say. She was depleted.

"And six months later, my baby's gone. Fifteen years old. She'd been so scared, the way they harassed her. Wasn't cancer alone that killed her. Police did, far as I'm concerned."

It went quiet in the room. Miss Lola reached for the pack of cigarettes, lit another.

"Why now?" she asked. "This is so long ago. Why?"

I felt like it was my turn to speak up. "Romero Taylor is my daddy," I said.

This gave Miss Lola pause. She stopped pulling on a puff.

Clemens said, "We believe Romero Taylor was framed by the police and prosecutor. We need evidence, though. We need to find the witnesses used at the trial to convict him, talk to them. We started with Monique."

"Monique is dead," Miss Lola said.

The quiet came back. Miss Lola's face had turned hard again. She took a long puff. She turned to look right at me. "You seem like a very nice girl," Miss Lola began. "But I'm gonna be honest with you. Romero Taylor? He's dirt to me."

My body stiffened.

"One-stop drug store back then, that Romero Taylor. Real slick. Kids buyin' any kind of drug from him—hustlin' Romero Taylor with that line he was famous for: 'If you pass me by, you won't get high.' Thought he was some kind of street poet. But he was a poison peddler, nothing more. My nephew overdosed on something Romero sold him. My nephew nearly died. Spent three months in the hospital."

I realized my hand was frozen in place over my reporter's notebook.

Miss Lola continued. "Maybe you think they framed him, and maybe they did, but he almost killed my nephew, and he probably did kill some boy or girl with the poison he sold. So, you see, far as I'm concerned, he's right where he belongs, in prison."

"We heard that already," I said, the words coming out weakly. "From police. Richie Boyle. He was saying if my daddy's not good for the Ruby Graham murder, he probably killed someone else, so he's where he should be."

Miss Lola said, "Whaddya know. Seems me and the police agree on somethin'." She shook her head slowly. "Can't imagine ever saying that."

Miss Lola took a puff.

I closed my notebook. My body felt heavy.

"One more thing, Miss Lola?" Clemens said.

Miss Lola sighed deeply.

"The cancer?" Clemens said. "What kind?"

"Brain," Miss Lola said. "In her brain. Called cerebral—"

"Excuse me, Miss Lola," Clemens interrupted. "Trell," he said. "Can you get this?" It was like Clemens was shaking me awake. "Trell?"

I opened my notebook.

Miss Lola continued, "Cerebral astrocytoma. A-s-t-r-o-c-y-t-o-m-a. Not something you forget, the name of your daughter's killer.

"Now," she said, "I need rest. You need to go."

CHAPTER 15
SATURDAY DAD

I'm tellin' ya, the creep in the suit? Had to be Frank Flanagan. Had to be."

Clemens was standing in the middle of Nora's office, all fired up.

"Pressuring Monique the way he did," he continued. "Feeding her that line: 'I'll never forget those eyes.' Unbelievable."

Clemens began pacing. Nora stood next to the dry-erase board, stroking her chin. After leaving Lola Catron's apartment, we'd headed straight to the law office.

"This is great stuff," Clemens declared. "Great stuff."

"It's okay," Nora said. She tilted her head at the board. "But not great."

In the column on the dry-erase board marked *Monique,* Nora wrote the word DEAD in big letters.

Clemens said, "Whaddya mean? The girl testifies at the trial Romero Taylor ran past her moments after Ruby Graham's shot. Now we learn she was bullied into saying the guy with the gun was Romero. We learn she had no idea who the gunman was—*until* Richie Boyle and Frank Flanagan harass her, wave Romero's photo in her face, and plant her a line about 'those eyes' that sounds like something out of a Hollywood movie. Plus, we learn Monique Catron was sick. Not only sick, but *dying*? C'mon, this is great stuff for the story."

"Maybe for the story, but not so much for us in court," Nora said.

"C'mon! Whaddya talkin' about?" Clemens threw up his hands.

Nora said, "You can write pretty much what you want— thanks to the First Amendment. I get that."

"So?"

"In court it'll be different," Nora said. "We question Flanagan and the police about this, Flanagan will deny it ever happened. That's my prediction. He'll flat-out deny Monique was ever mistreated. Remember who he is, the esteemed Frank Flanagan, crime-fighting district attorney running for mayor. Most folks are inclined to believe someone in his position—and we don't have Monique to say otherwise. We don't have Monique Catron to tell a judge and describe, *firsthand*, the bullying, the pressure tactics, how she was scared back then into lying."

"Jeezus. What about Miss Lola?" Clemens said. "She was there."

172

"Right. We have Miss Lola," Nora said. "But what's that get us? Her word against Flanagan's. How's that gonna play? She's got no love for police. Makes that abundantly clear. She's not what English teachers call a 'reliable narrator.' Most folks would probably be inclined *not* to believe her."

"I believe her," Clemens said.

"Not saying I don't," Nora said. "I'm just saying that if we get Romero's case back into court, we need a lot more than Lola Catron facing off against the popular mayoral candidate Frank Flanagan. I'm saying it would be way more credible if instead of an angry, embittered, antipolice parent, we had Monique telling her own story."

"But Monique's dead," Clemens said.

"Yes, Monique is dead," Nora said. She saw that Clemens was deflated. "Listen, Lola's info helps. It shows we're on to something. We need more, is all."

Clemens plopped onto the couch.

While air rushed from Clemens's couch cushion, I turned my attention back to a thick manila file I'd pulled out of a box on the documents table. I'd been listening to everything Clemens and Nora were saying, but I'd gone directly to the war room looking for this particular file as soon as we'd arrived at Nora's office. I was seated on the floor against one wall with the file in my lap.

It held records of Daddy's criminal history.

The wooziness I'd felt when Miss Lola said those things about Daddy hadn't gone away. Coming from Richie Boyle was one thing, but coming from someone who lives in the neighborhood was another. Miss Lola made everything seem more real. Like describing her nephew, the one who nearly died on stuff Daddy sold him.

While she was talking, the old police photo of Daddy even popped into my head. The mug shot I'd come across last year when I was first organizing Nora's case files, taken when Daddy was twenty-two, showing him with a thin mustache and dark look that left me feeling so cold.

I'd stopped in my tracks when I first came across the photo. I did not want to look any further. Instead, I'd closed the file and put it in the box with other documents and police Form 26s. But after seeing Miss Lola, hearing her go after Daddy like she did, say Daddy is where he belongs, I felt I needed to dig deeper into the file for myself.

So I opened it up. The mug shot still sat atop a thick pile of police reports, Form 26s, and victim statements. Much of it was written using a kind of legal and police code, which by this time, and with Nora's help, I'd learned to translate.

One of the earliest charges was dated March 3, 1985, when Daddy was seventeen. He was charged with "Larceny of M/V; Poss Burg Tools; Dist. B-4." This meant he stole a car. I read the accompanying police report. It said Daddy, in the middle of the night, had used a screwdriver to break into a blue BMW parked outside a townhouse in the South End. It said he jump-started the car, drove away the wrong way down a one-way street, and was caught by a patrol car that happened to be around the corner.

The next case I read, Daddy was charged with "Poss. Cl. D.

W/I/D; Dist. B-2." Translation: possession of marijuana with intent to sell. The police report said Daddy, standing on the sidewalk on upper Blue Hill Avenue, had sold a little plastic bag of marijuana for forty dollars to a female police officer who was working undercover and dressed like a girl from the neighborhood. The report said Daddy was wearing a brand-new Adidas running suit with a gold chain necklace. He was standing on the street corner listening to a Walkman cassette player when he initiated the drug sale by saying to the officer walking toward him, "If you pass me by, you won't get high." That drug case was handled in the Dorchester District Court.

I next read that later the same year Daddy was charged with "Larc. Person; Assault, Simple; Dist. A-1." Translation: purse snatching. The police report said Daddy had knocked down a woman at noontime right in Pemberton Square, in downtown Boston, and grabbed her purse. The report said the woman, aged sixty-two, began screaming as Daddy ran away across the redbrick square, and that a Good Samaritan body-blocked him. Other bystanders then helped to tackle and hold on to Daddy until police arrived. The old lady suffered cuts and bruises on her legs. Pemberton Square is located right outside the Boston Municipal Court, and from the papers, it looked like Daddy had stolen the woman's purse right after leaving the courthouse, where he'd gone for a court hearing on one of his drug cases.

More papers in the file described other arrests over the next several years, for stealing cars, for break-ins, and for dealing drugs, including one involving Miss Lola's nephew, a teenager named Stephen Catron, who bought a tiny vial of cocaine laced with rat poison. Daddy served five months in the Deer Island House of Correction for that, according to the records in the file. But usually Daddy just got probation for his crimes and had managed to avoid any serious jail time.

Until the Ruby Graham murder case.

I got to the end of the file and sat still on the floor. Clemens and Nora were across the room near the board, discussing what to do next, but their fading voices seemed miles away. I couldn't hear what they were saying as I fell further into a funk. Fell deeper and deeper, through the floor, through the building's foundation, through the subway tunnel beneath, out into Boston Harbor and to the bottom of the sea, falling under the weight of this terrible information about Daddy. Daddy the drug dealer with his own clever slogan: "If you pass me by, you won't get high."

This felt so different from the awfulness I felt when Nora had first started working on Daddy's case and had made me go through the evidence that police and Frank Flanagan had used to convict Daddy of murder. Even though that evidence looked so bad, I knew—and always had—that Daddy didn't do that. He was framed. But this crime file was different. It was real. Daddy was a drug dealer. Going through it, I began to understand why Miss Lola had said such angry things about Romero Taylor the drug dealer. The harm he'd done—he wasn't someone anyone should like.

* * *

Saturday morning, I wouldn't get up. I was stuck in the funk. I heard Ma rushing around in her bedroom, then in the kitchen, getting ready to go.

"C'mon, girl!" she yelled. "Five minutes, the van's gonna be here."

I stayed in bed. Didn't say a word. Ma appeared at my door.

"What is wrong with you, Trell? Vinnie is not going to wait on us."

"I'm not going," I said.

"What?"

"Not going."

"You've never not gone. You're the one always rushing me." Ma stood there, studying me. "You okay? Somethin' happen?"

I was silent.

"Daddy's expectin' us, Trell. Give him the update how things are going."

I turned away to the wall.

"I don't have time for this," Ma said. She was frustrated. "Vinnie leaves without me and nobody gonna be with Daddy." She turned to leave. "This is *not* over." She gave me the strangest, most disbelieving look I'd ever seen on her face.

I heard her pull the front door shut. The apartment went quiet. I turned back and faced the pile of books on my night table. I had no interest in any of them.

Ma was riding alone in Vinnie's Van to see Daddy at Walpole. Thinking about Daddy, part of me felt like crying. But nothing came. I tried to picture him, but the only image that filled my mind was the grainy police mug shot from that file.

The funk. Not much feeling inside the funk, just a spooky kind of emptiness. Like I was lost.

I must have drifted off for a few minutes, because the next thing I heard was a pounding on the front door. I found Clemens standing on the stoop, bouncing on the balls of his feet. He was dressed in baggy shorts, the T-shirt from his old school the Gunnery, and the running shoes I'd given him. His green Volvo was idling in the road.

"I was about to go for a run and your mother called," he said.

He saw me looking him over, from top to bottom, from ponytail to running shoes. "Yeah, yeah," he said, "I was going for a jog. After our outing—I won't even call it a workout—I decided I gotta do something about being so pathetically out of shape."

I still hadn't said a word.

"What's the deal? Your mother was upset, said you wouldn't go to Walpole. We're making progress here, Trell. Why aren't you on Vinnie's Van with your mother?"

I looked to each side of Clemens, then past him, but not at him. I noticed that in the empty lot down the street, a new big sign had gone up saying FLANAGAN FOR MAYOR. It made me realize signs for Frank Flanagan were everywhere now. I looked up and saw a clear blue sky, and thought it would be a good day for a run, a really long one. Finally I looked at Clemens, who was still rocking on his toes, and said, "That file."

He squinted at me. "File? What file?"

I told Clemens about digging deep into Daddy's crime file while he and Nora were talking. "I'd never really read it, but Miss Lola, after she said those things, I had to." I told Clemens I felt all mixed up. I told him I couldn't get the picture of Daddy in the mug shot out of my head. "Daddy, he hurt a lot of people. Things you *do* go to prison for."

Clemens nodded, then rubbed his chin. "Okay, okay." He looked at his car. "We still got plenty of time to make visiting hours. Get in the car."

I hesitated.

"Trell, you gotta talk to your dad on this one. Not me. Him. Let's go."

Deep down I knew Clemens was right. I changed, pulled the front door shut, and trudged down the steps. Clemens had done some cleaning up in his car, gotten rid of the stacks of old newspapers. There was room for a passenger now. He shifted the gear stick, and the old Volvo made a grinding sound as it pulled away from the curb.

We were approaching the intersection when a shiny black Mercedes-Benz turned onto my street. The car slowed way down, and the front window opened as it crawled by. The man behind the wheel turned toward us. His face was tough and bony. He lowered his sunglasses to give us a hard glare. It was like in slo-mo.

I felt a chill run up my back and into my neck.

"Thumper," I whispered.

When the Mercedes was nearly past, Thumper Parish turned

away and floored the accelerator. The engine roared, and the car took off, practically popping a wheelie.

"What was that about?" I said.

"Dunno," Clemens said, looking in the rearview mirror as Thumper disappeared. "Probably not a coincidence, though."

When we got to Walpole there was still thirty minutes left for visitors. Clemens had made the drive a lot faster than Big Vinnie ever could in his wobbly, rocking minibus. He dropped me off and said he'd wait. I signed in, walked through the security checkpoint, and entered the visiting room. Ma and Daddy were sitting by the windows. They both looked up.

Ma stood when I reached them. "I'll give you two some time," she said.

"Okay, Shey-Shey," Daddy said. "Next week."

I felt nervous all over. I sat, but kept my head down.

Daddy started. "What's wrong, girl?" he said.

My hands were clenched into fists in my lap.

"Trell?"

I looked up. "It's just . . ." I began. "It's just that I seen it. For the first time."

"What do you mean?"

The words came out fast. "I seen it, Daddy. I seen *it*."

"Seen what?"

"That file. The one in Nora's office that starts screaming at you when you start reading all the information inside it: screaming through the reports and forms and police reports that Romero Taylor is not a nice person. That's he's not innocent."

Daddy was startled. "What?"

"The *big* file," I said. "The one with everything before Ruby Graham."

Daddy shifted in his seat. He straightened up. He didn't say anything for what seemed like a long time, and then he said, "You're perfect?"

Daddy's tone surprised me. It was firm. Made me look up and at him.

"You're perfect?" he repeated. His eyes were fixed on me, steady. The tone in his voice stayed neutral. He rested his hands on the table. He seemed so calm.

"No, I'm not, but I would never . . ." The records began flashing in my mind, like pages flipping in a book. "Steal a car. Or sell pot in plastic bags to undercover police." I charged ahead. "I would never knock down some old lady, steal her purse!

"You should have seen Miss Lola." My voice got loud. "You should have been there, Daddy. Heard her tell me how back then you thought you were so cool, with your own hook: 'If you pass me by.' Miss Lola's nephew. He almost died, Daddy, because of you."

I felt like crying, but couldn't.

Daddy stayed calm. "I did some terrible things," he said.

"But how could you? How could you?"

"Listen, Van Trell."

Daddy never called me that.

"Look at me."

I did.

"You never made a mistake?" The question hung there. Daddy continued, "Remember a few years ago? You were nine, I think, and Ma took you shopping to Filene's Basement for some school clothes. Remember? You wandered into the sports store nearby. Picked up a shiny mesh visor off a display table, put it on your head, and walked right out of the store. Remember?"

I couldn't believe Daddy remembered. Not that it wasn't a big deal. It was. Ma was out of her mind at the time. Made me return the visor and for the next month made me come right home after school and sit tight. No playing with friends. Like I was in prison. But Daddy, being in prison, only heard about it afterward.

"Why you steal that visor?" Daddy said.

I didn't answer even though I knew why. I'd stolen it for three reasons: the running visor shaded my eyes, the top was open to catch a constant breeze, and the new mesh design was quick-drying. There was another reason, too. More style than technical—I loved its color, a lime green I hadn't seen anywhere. So I stole it, which was a huge mistake, and I got into big trouble afterward. But I didn't know what that had to do with anything, and I didn't know how Daddy even remembered it, him not being around when it happened.

"There's a big difference between a cap and cocaine," I snapped back.

Daddy nodded. "No argument there," he said. "No argument. But here's the thing, Trell. You wanted the visor, is why you stole it. Well, I wanted my gear, clothes I liked, anything so long as it had a label. Ralph Lauren. Izod. Shirts. Jeans, an Adidas running suit, brand-new Adidas sneakers, whatever. I had no education, no real job, and easy money came from the drugs. So I did it. I was a drug dealer, Trell. I did the crimes you read about in the file, and then some.

"But here's the thing—what I done was a mistake. Terrible mistake. I know that now. I'm not gonna run from it. I sold drugs, and hurt people doing it. I'm sorry I did, and I'm gonna have to live with it the rest of my life. But I never killed little Ruby Graham. You know that, Trell. I never killed her."

"Oh, Daddy," I said. "I know *that*. I'm not talking about her."

I don't know exactly where the words came from, but it was like the funk and mixed-up feelings from reading about crimes Daddy actually had committed sorted themselves out into some kind of order where suddenly I could explain why I was so mad. "It's not Ruby Graham," I said. "It's not her. I know you didn't do that. It's you leaving me and Ma. That's what I mean. Not being with us. Because maybe that doesn't happen if you never did the crimes before. If you hadn't made a name for yourself as some big-shot drug dealer stylin' your way around the neighborhood, maybe you don't become the person police are looking for when Ruby Graham is shot on Humboldt. And if that doesn't happen, maybe you stay home. For Ma. For me. Instead of being a Saturday Dad, you'd be a stay-at-home, everyday Dad. If you hadn't done all those other things, maybe that's how it would have been."

I was out of breath, like when I run a split. I welled up. I could feel things building. The tears that had been stuck the last couple of days began trickling out. I leaned into Daddy's arms. "I wanted you home." Daddy held me for a few minutes. Didn't say a word. I opened my eyes and saw the guards at the door were stirring. The clock on the wall said there were just a few minutes left.

"I get it, and I'm sorry," Daddy said. "It's good you told me this. You been cheated, and I'm sorriest about that." Daddy held me at arm's length. "You grown up so fast." He wiped the corner of his eye, then shook like he was trying to clear his head. "We don't have much time," he said. "Ma caught me up. Told me about Monique Catron. How Nora thinks the new information is only okay."

I nodded. "Me and Clemens are going to be looking now for the other girl."

"Juanda Tillery."

"Yeah, her."

"Before you leave," Daddy said. He pulled a slip of paper from his back pocket. "For you and Clemens — the address for one of the kids I was with that night."

I opened the slip. In Daddy's handwriting it read:

Tracey Dailey
11 Geneva Avenue

Daddy said, "I been asking around for where she lives. Asking people in here to ask people. Asking anybody who might know her or someone in her family. Finally got this, from one of the guys works in the kitchen. Tracey's his second cousin. She's one of the kids I was with when Ruby got shot."

"You, Tracey, and two more friends, right?"

Daddy smiled. "You know the file, Trell, that's for sure. I asked around on the others, too. But no one's heard anything for years. Seems they left Boston a long time ago. My guess is South Carolina somewhere. It's where they all had family. So it's a dead end on them. But Tracey, we find her, maybe she can help."

The bell went off. The guards, led by Officer White, started moving through the big room, ushering visitors toward the exit.

I put the slip away. "Daddy, I'm gonna get you outta here."

"Trolls, bells, and candy canes," he said. "Just like always."

It didn't make any sense for Ma to ride home separately in Vinnie's Van when Clemens had driven, so we headed home together in the green Volvo. Ma was relieved Daddy and I had been able to talk, and she thanked Clemens for bringing me.

"No sweat," Clemens said. He tugged at his T-shirt. "Saved me from a *real* sweat."

No one laughed at the lame joke.

And I said, "Still plenty of time for a run."

Ma raised her hands. "Oh, Trell," she said. "I completely forgot — that boy Paul called for you yesterday, when you were at Nora's. Something about Water Country."

Monday was the day Paul Parish said he was going to the water park in New Hampshire with a bunch of kids in Vinnie's

Van—paid for by his uncle Thumper. I couldn't help thinking it'd be fun, especially with the weather forecast saying Monday was going to be clear and sunny. But Thumper Parish?

The rest of the ride, Clemens and Ma talked about Lola Catron and about the next move—tracking down Juanda Tillery, another of the young witnesses from Daddy's trial. I mentioned Daddy had given me a lead for Tracey Dailey. "He thinks she's living somewhere over on Geneva Avenue."

"This is good," Clemens said. "We're startin' to cook."

Clemens began tapping the steering wheel. "I was also thinking—the cancer Miss Lola told us about. Cancer that killed Monique. Trell, what kind she say it was?"

I pulled out the notebook Clemens had given me and flipped pages until I found the right one. "Cerebral," I said. "Not sure I can pronounce the rest." I broke it down and tried. "Cerebral astro-cy-toma."

Ma said, "Never heard of that. What is it?"

"We should find out," Clemens said.

CHAPTER 16
TUNNEL OF TERROR

The line snaked around the base of the iron staircase, then up six flights to an elevated platform where the ride started. Paul and I had been moving in it for about twenty-five minutes. Way down below, kids shrieked as they exploded out from the other end of the tube ride and splashed into the water. I was getting impatient. I don't like lines. I don't like waiting. I like moving. But Paul just kept telling me, "You'll see, Trell. You'll see. I'm telling ya, it's worth the wait."

We were lugging a two-person tube like everyone else and were nearing the top. The higher we got, the better the view, so that made waiting a little bit easier. I could see across the water park and for miles beyond. I could see the highway that Clemens took to get us here. He'd seen I was torn about turning down

Paul's invitation. So Clemens decided to drive me. He'd even talked Nora into taking a half day off to come along. I could see both of them in the wave pool on the other side of the park. I know Water Country brags it has the largest wave pool in all of New England—holding something like seven hundred gallons of water. But I don't get the thrill in just bobbing around. I'd rather be racing a million miles an hour down one of the slides. Clemens and Nora seemed happy enough, though. They bobbed and talked. I was thinking it wasn't only about the case. Okay by me.

It was sunny and plenty hot, and I was glad we'd come. I could see Vinnie's Van in the parking lot. The lot was packed with cars. Paul had ridden up with about twenty kids from home. They'd gotten here just before we did. And they were pretty easy to spot, a bunch of black kids in a sea of white. Some were floating down the lazy river. Others were in line for Shoot and Screamer. Those are amazing fast, but over in a few seconds. The Double Geronimo was popular, too. The line was pretty long. It's maybe the steepest body slide, and scary. But after Paul and I saw each other and he got over the surprise of meeting, he insisted that we had to ride Dr. Von Dark's Tunnel of Terror.

I also spotted Vinnie. He wasn't inside the park cooling off somewhere but had stayed put in the parking lot. Wasn't the water park type, I guess. He was leaning against his van, smoking a cigarette, and he wasn't alone. He was talking to someone.

"That your uncle?" I said. "With Vinnie?"

Paul shook his head. "No, no. Wouldn't waste his time."

"Didn't think so." I squinted, curious. Then it came to me.

The guy with the scar on his cheek you couldn't miss a mile away. The red scar that ran like a river down one side of his face, the guy whose silver sunglasses had popped off after Thumper slammed his face against the open window of the Mercedes.

I said, "Isn't that the guy your uncle whaled on outside your house?"

"The one," Paul said. "My uncle made him come, keep an eye on things."

"Chaperone?"

"I guess. I dunno really. My uncle's always orderin' the guy to do something, but then starts givin' him grief, always yelling at him. The guy's a mess."

"Strange."

"Totally. I mean my uncle, he seems to hate the guy, but then does everything to keep him nearby. The guy lives with us."

"In your house?"

"Kinda. He's in a shack out back, actually," Paul said. "Go figure. My uncle wants the guy close. Only thing he'll tell me is the guy's been with him a long time, longer than most everybody else he's got. Says the guy was in a bad way. But the way he yells at him, you'd never know he cares. Whole thing's pretty weird."

"Definitely weird."

"One thing, I think the guy's hooked on something. Not that I see him much, but when I do he's, like, jittery and scratching his arms. But maybe the guy's just scared, worried my uncle's gonna pound on him. I dunno. Hey, we're gettin' close," Paul said. "You ready?"

We'd reached the top platform and maybe only a dozen kids were still ahead of us. Near the mouth of the tunnel slide, a park worker helped riders drop their two-person tube into a big whirling tidal pool.

Paul said, "Trell, there's something I been wantin' to ask."

"What's that?"

Paul looked away as he spoke. "The Weld. The school you go to."

"Yeah?"

"You think I could get in?"

The question surprised me. Even though I remembered Paul seemed serious in school, I never would have guessed him to be wondering about making a big change like that. I've been thinking all summer I might want to get out of the Weld, and Paul's thinking about maybe wanting to get in?

The way my eyes popped out, Paul could see his question had shocked me. He said, "I know, Trell. It's crazy. Me? I'm not smart, not the way you are."

"No, no," I said quickly. I didn't want him thinking I thought he was stupid or something. It was just such a stunner. I said, "Don't say that."

My thoughts raced around as I tried to come up with something more, and when the words finally came out, they sounded like a version of what Clemens had told me about his time at the Gunnery school. "They've got really small classes at the Weld, which is good for learning, and some really cool teachers." I was thinking about my English teacher, Harry Goldgar, who had us read a lot of Langston Hughes's poems. Paul's question was making me remember the reason I had pushed myself to get in. So I wanted to be encouraging. The bad stuff, like my adviser Mr. Rowe, could come later.

"I don't see why you couldn't," I said. "I'll help, if you want."

Paul smiled. "I got to do something to get out, and when I saw you got in there, I dunno, it got me to thinking. I even learned the Weld, it has rooms for kids to live in, and I hate being at my uncle's Castlegate. More like a gated castle, you ask me. It's like I'm a prisoner."

The park worker was waving and yelling at us to hurry up.

"We gotta go!" Paul shouted.

We plopped our tube into the churning whirlpool and jumped in. We got a quick shove and took off, swept away into the darkened mouth of Dr. Von Dark's Tunnel of Terror. Inside was pitch-black, and I could hear kids in front of us screaming. I couldn't see a thing, only feel water splashing all around as we pitched from side to side. The tube turned sharply and descended suddenly. My stomach dropped. We took another sharp turn. I screamed my lungs out.

"Hold on!" Paul yelled.

His hand grabbed hold of my forearm.

I liked how it felt.

We rode a bunch more water rides, and then I told Paul I had to go. That was the deal with Nora. She'd take a half day off and come with Clemens and me if we promised to get back to Boston early in the afternoon.

I told Paul he was right. "Dr. Von Dark was the best."

"Told you," Paul said.

"Okay," I said. "Soon."

"Soon," he said.

I began to hurry away.

"Hey," he said. "The Weld?"

"The Weld," I said.

I found Clemens and Nora near the changing rooms at the front entrance dressed and ready to go. Clemens was pacing. The three of us walked quickly to the car. I spotted Vinnie and waved across the lot to him. He straightened up and waved back.

"Mornin' Glory!" he shouted.

I made a face. "It's afternoon, Vinnie." I shook my head. The man with him—Thumper's guy—didn't say a thing. Just stood there and watched us walking to Clemens's Volvo. I did notice him scratching his arms, though. Like Paul said.

Clemens was acting hyper, and when we got in the car, he explained why. While he was changing out of his bathing suit, he'd gotten a call from the doctor he'd been trying to reach about Monique Catron.

"She got back to me finally," Clemens said, "and you gotta listen to this." He explained that the doctor was a neuro-oncologist, which meant her specialty was brain cancers. "I told her about Monique, and she told me it was *extremely* rare for someone

Monique's age to have cerebral astrocytoma. Usually people who have it are much, much older."

"Okay," Nora said. "How's that help?"

"It doesn't. I'm getting to that."

Clemens seemed annoyed, like he was getting into one of his "teaching moments" and wanted to take his time. He said cerebral astrocytoma was a primary brain tumor. "Meaning it grows in the brain itself and doesn't travel from the brain to other parts of the body. Plus, people can have it for a long time and be asymptomatic. Meaning they don't act sick, even though they have this awful thing growing in their brain.

"But we already know Monique had symptoms. She collapsed, for friggin' sakes. Had crippling headaches months before Ruby Graham was shot."

"Okay?" Nora said. "And?"

Clemens shot her a look. "Okay. Here's the thing: cerebral astrocytoma affects cognitive function."

Even though I knew what *cognitive* meant I said, "Please, Clemens. Talk normal."

"Perception! Memory!" Clemens was practically shouting. "People with cerebral astrocytoma, they're screwed up when it comes to what they see and what they remember. You get it? Frank Flanagan relied on a girl as a major witness who was dying from brain cancer—a cancer that messes up a person's ability to see and to remember."

Clemens looked at Nora. "Talk about an unreliable narrator."

Clemens drove, and we were quiet as the information sank in.

I said, "Why'd the jury believe Monique if she had a cancer like that?"

"Because the jury didn't know," Nora said. "That's the point. The police, they knew Monique was ill, but they never told anyone. If they had, and if the jury at your daddy's trial had learned about Monique's brain cancer, it would have ruined Monique's credibility. No one would have believed her testimony about Romero Taylor. This is just the kind of *new* evidence we've needed."

It was like there was some kind of special energy in the car. Invisible, but I could feel it. Clemens was in a hurry and drove fast. He said he wanted to drop me off at my house and head downtown to the state Office of Vital Records before they closed for the day. "Monique's death certificate will be at Vital Records," he said. "We need a copy of that. It will list her official cause of death."

"Why?" I said. "We already know the cause of death. Miss Lola told us."

Clemens pulled up to the curb outside my apartment. He looked back at me. "Okay, lesson time: Journalism 101. We call it the principle of verification."

"Principle of verification?" I asked, like a student who maybe hadn't had time to do the reading but still didn't want to miss anything.

"Confirm every piece of information you're gonna put in the newspaper story—or Nora's legal motion to use in court. Sure, Miss Lola told us, but much better than her word is the actual death certificate showing that brain cancer killed Monique. No way to cross-examine an official document like that. It's the best proof."

Clemens revved the Volvo. He told Nora he'd drop her off at the subway.

"Later," he said to me as I scampered out, and he was gone.

I felt left behind. Ma was at work, wouldn't be home for a couple of hours. Nora was being a lawyer back at her office. Clemens was being a reporter racing to a state office, getting verification. Me? I was wandering around my living room. Bored. I thought about Paul and the Weld School, and went digging around my closet for the school catalog and some other stuff I'd saved that I could give to him. Next I tried reading, which usually works for me, but didn't this time. I couldn't sit still. The buzz I felt on the ride home, the idea we were really getting somewhere, was too distracting. Then I remembered Tracey Dailey and the note Daddy had given me. I pulled the folded slip of paper from my back pocket.

Tracey Dailey
11 Geneva Avenue

Geneva wasn't too far. Not far at all. In fact, it was just a couple of blocks north of where Clemens lived, on Esmond Street. I could get there and back before Ma got home.

I was out the door before even finishing the thought. I didn't run because I didn't want to get all sweaty. But I was doing a kind of walk-run.

I felt no hesitation until I was about halfway there. Geneva is in the middle what Ma calls a "hot spot." She means trouble. It's got lots of crime. Lots of rundown houses and empty lots piled high with trash, construction debris, and junk cars. Ma says friends from church who live there say they do not even let their kids play outside. Sometimes you hear a city official or neighborhood activist complaining and calling for improvements and more police, but nothing changes. In June, just when I was getting out of school, Ma showed me a newspaper article. Outside a club on Geneva, there'd practically been a riot on a Saturday night. It started when some guy was stabbed in the butt and taken away by ambulance, and when police got there, a whole bunch of kids were shoving each other. Fights broke out. Kids threw bottles. Police began arresting everyone, including two men caught slashing the tires of a police cruiser. "See?" Ma kept saying as she showed me the article. "See? It's hopeless."

This went through my mind as I reached Geneva, and it gave me a hesitation. But really only for a second. I wasn't going to freeze, not when one of the people who could vouch for Daddy the night Ruby Graham was killed was living on Geneva.

Tracey Dailey's house at 11 Geneva sure fit in. One side was missing entire rows of shingles, and another side didn't have any, just plywood sheathing. From the shingles that were left, it looked like the house was a gray color. The glass in the big window on the first floor was cracked. Garbage was strewn around the front yard, an old stove sat sideways, and a refrigerator with no door was half-buried in dirt. I headed up the stairs to the front porch, careful to step over spaces where boards were missing.

Two black metal mailboxes were mounted to the right of the door, one for each apartment. Pieces of paper with names handwritten on each were taped to the boxes. Tracey Dailey was on the one for the second floor. Next to the boxes was a doorbell, which surprised me. I pushed it, and it buzzed. That surprised me, too.

Nothing happened. I pushed the buzzer again. I heard noise upstairs, the sound of a window rattling open. Someone yelled, "Who that be?"

I leaned over the porch railing so the woman up there could see me. The railing was loose, so I was careful not to fall through.

"What you want?" the woman called.

"Tracey Dailey?" I asked. "Are you Tracey Dailey?"

"What you want?" she repeated. Her head tilted, like she was put out.

"Can I talk to you?"

"What about?"

I looked around. "Romero Taylor," I said, not wanting to shout.

The woman's head straightened. Her eyes woke up, looked hard at me.

"He's my daddy," I said.

The woman shut the window. She didn't slam it, which I took as a good sign. Seconds later, the front door opened. Tracey

Dailey was wearing a baggy white T-shirt. I couldn't tell if she had shorts on underneath. She held a cigarette. She was tall and skinny. Her tight curly hair was brown, and freckles filled the skin on her cheeks.

"C'mon," she said.

I followed her upstairs and into her apartment. She led me into the kitchen, where it looked like a dish hadn't been washed in months. She motioned me to sit at the table while she filled a cup with coffee.

"You Romero and Shey-Shey's girl?" she said.

"Trell," I said. "Actually, Van Trell, but everyone calls me Trell."

Tracey nodded and sipped her coffee. "I remember when you was born." She kept nodding as she spoke, looking me up and down. "Your daddy showin' you off all over the neighborhood after you come home." Then Tracey looked away. "Didn't see you after that, though. Not after Ruby was killed, an' everything changed."

I heard footsteps in the hall, and another woman drifted into the kitchen.

"This is Boo," Tracey said. "My roommate."

The two looked about the same age. Boo's skin glowed.

"Boo," Tracey said, "meet Trell Taylor. You know, Romero? Shey?"

Boo's eyes widened. I said hello and tried smiling. She studied me. "Yeah, I do see it, I do," Boo said. "In the smile, it's Shey. Those eyes, Romero."

Tracey said, "Boo and me, we been together forever." Then Tracey asked, "You want something? Coffee? Something to drink?"

I realized my throat was dry as sand. "Water?"

Boo washed out a juice glass at the sink, filled it, and handed it to me.

I drank it whole.

"So, I don't think sellin' Girl Scout Cookies is the reason you're here," Tracey said.

That was my opening. I started explaining everything as best I could, the main point being that I was working with a lawyer and a newspaper reporter on getting my daddy out of prison. "It's like we're reinvestigating the case," I said, trying not to go on for too long. "We know he didn't shoot Ruby Graham."

Tracey and Boo traded looks. Boo said, "That's the truth."

Tracey put down the cigarette and closed her eyes. She sighed deeply. Sighed a second time. When she opened her eyes, they had a faraway look in them. She said, "I'll never forget, when they first grabbed Romero, I was like, Romero *Taylor*?"

Tracey had gone back in time, back to the late summer of 1988. "I knew, Boo knew, a lot of people knew, no way Romero could be the shooter."

"No way," Boo added.

Tracey said, "He was with us on Sonoma Street when Ruby Graham was shot. That's the first thing, probably the main thing—he can't be shootin' no gun when he was with us at the same time.

"But that's not the all of it," Tracey said. "When they arrested Romero, what they said, police and that prosecutor—Frank something, the guy who's running for mayor—go on TV and call Romero Taylor a tough-guy killer for the Castlegate Boys. I couldn't believe it."

"What do you mean?" I said.

"Romero was never the gangsta type, with the guns and everything." Tracey looked at me. "Your daddy, he was into his own little hustle—the drugs. That's all."

Boo nodded along.

"He just wanted a way to get his gear, stay high," Tracey said.

"I heard about that," I interrupted. "Daddy, last time I visited, told me."

"Money in his pocket, stylin' around in new gear, and gettin' high—that was Romero," Tracey said. "Gun-totin' killer? Police had it all wrong."

Boo listened, then laughed softly.

"What?" Tracey said, looking at Boo.

Boo smiled, saying, "You remember Romero used to like wearing baggy gym shorts with striped sweat socks pulled all the way up to his knee, when most guys keep 'em rolled down to their ankles?"

Tracey smiled, too. "That's it. That's him." She practically laughed out loud at the thought. "Your daddy, Trell, acting like he always had to be cutting a fashion statement when he was out there sellin'. He was never no gang member."

Tracey and Boo fell silent. I let them be with the picture of

Daddy in gym shorts and knee socks in their minds' eye. It was kind of ridiculous to me, too. But I wasn't about to let things end there, not after hearing so much information that was helpful to Daddy. I asked, "Tracey, how come you never said anything? Never told police? Never testified?"

The question erased the smiles from their faces. I was worried Tracey was going to get mad, start yelling at me, but that didn't happen. Instead, her face turned serious, almost sad looking. She looked at her roommate. "Boo?"

Boo sat down at the kitchen table with us. She said, "What you gotta understand, Trell, is people are scared of police."

I sat there. Didn't say a word. I was thinking, *That's it?*

Boo looked at me. I guess she could tell she had to explain more. She coughed, cleared her throat. "People were doin' their thing," she said, "and no one wanted to be involved with cops."

She paused.

"Don't you see?" she asked.

"Not really," I said.

Tracey said, "She means people were hustling."

Boo nodded. "Yeah."

Tracey continued. "Because everyone in the 'hood—and I mean *everyone*—wanted to be flyin'. Crack cocaine comin' in from NYC? The real hating started with the crack. Smokin' it. Shootin' it. Snortin' it. Didn't matter which way you did it, so long as you were flyin'. It got ugly real fast. Turf. Big money. The gangs."

"That's right," Boo said. "That's what I mean. We were

always runnin' *from* police, never *to* them." Boo rubbed her forehead, as if the memories pained her. "When Ruby Graham was killed, the heat really come down hard. Police were everywhere. In our faces. And we all had something goin', something to hide. Wanted to keep our heads down. Couldn't think about helpin' Romero."

"Couldn't think *clearly* to do right, is how it was," Tracey said.

I think Tracey was trying to say she was sorry. I noticed a gentleness in her eyes that I took to be regret. She unfolded her arms and rested her head in her hands, and it was then that I saw the scars and needle tracks up and down her forearms. Hundreds of marks the size of tiny pinpricks. Tracey looked up and caught me staring. "Crack queen is what they called someone like me," Tracey said. "I liked it in my arm. Boo, she liked it in a pipe. Everyone had a way they liked. It's why you didn't want to get caught talkin' to police," she said.

Probably the reason we were able to hear the noise was because the kitchen had gone so very silent. Boo was the first to notice. She leaned forward in her chair to hear better. We all strained to listen. There was a tapping sound coming from downstairs, then a sound like something scratching on metal. Tapping, then scratching. Then a pushing sound—quietly. Someone didn't want to be heard.

I had no idea what it could be. Tracey stood up and tiptoed to the window over the kitchen sink. She suddenly turned around and rushed toward me.

"You gotta go!"

Her hands were on my shoulders, pushing me to my feet. The chair knocked over as she pushed me across the kitchen toward the rear hall. Boo, meanwhile, had hurried over to the window. "Oh, no. Oh, no!" she began chanting.

Given the racket we were making, whoever was downstairs must have decided trying to be quiet didn't matter anymore. Because the next sound was the first-floor front door exploding open, glass and wood shattering in the entry.

"Hurry, hurry," Tracey said, ushering me back.

Then came a second explosion: the sound of footsteps pounding up the front stairs, along with the voice: "WHERE IS SHE?" The first sound was followed by an angry tirade: "Don't think I know what's goin' on? Snoopin' around, asking questions? DAMMIT, I got eyes and ears everywhere."

The voice was cold to the bone.

"Hurry," Tracey commanded, pushing me toward the back stairs. It had gotten dark out while we'd been talking, and the hallway, without any lights that worked, was darker than outside. I could barely see. My mind began spinning. Who was it climbing the stairs, yelling like that? What the heck did he want? Me? Why me?

"WHERE IS SHE?" the voice roared, sounding closer and louder.

I was scared. The hallway was a tunnel of terror.

Tracey pushed open a door at the far end.

"Down the stairs, Trell," she ordered. "The door opens to the driveway. Right there is a hole in the fence. Use it. It'll put you in the next yard. Then you run. Run, and keep running. Now, go. Hurry!"

I quick-stepped down the stairs, running my hands along the walls to keep from stumbling in the dark. I pushed open the door and crashed into a garbage can that was in my way. I broke the fall with my hands but could feel the skin scraping off. I got up and rubbed my hands. They stung. I looked around and spotted the hole in the fence Tracey had mentioned. I turned to go there, and as I did I got a look down the driveway to the street, and that's when I saw it. The car parked at the top of the driveway — the black Mercedes, engine growling and ready to roar.

Thumper Parish!

I squeezed through the hole and ran. I started one way, then the other, and then made myself think about where to go. Clemens's house was closest, so I ran toward Esmond. Down one street, through a lot, and then across another street. Within a few minutes, I was there. I fidgeted around beneath a piece of flagstone where Clemens kept a spare key and unlocked the door. I burst inside, slammed the door behind me, and locked it. My chest heaved. I gasped for air. I'd run less than a half mile but felt like I'd finished the Boston Marathon. I paced around in circles, then fell onto the couch. It was quiet, except for the pounding of my heart. I was shaking. I hugged a cushion. Held on for what seemed like hours.

CHAPTER 17

OVER THE HUMP

My eyes popped open. I could still hear Mattie Ross crying for help, but her voice was fading quickly. In my mind I could see her, down in the dark pit, stuck on a crevice. Surrounded by skeletons. Worse, the rattlesnakes. They hissed. Moved closer to her. I was watching from the surface, helpless. Feeling panicked, my mind racing. Where was Rooster Cogburn? Where was he? He was supposed to save her.

Then Mattie was gone. I breathed hard, awake now, and my forehead was wet. I wondered if the sweat from escaping Tracey Dailey's had just stayed with me during my nightmare about Mattie from *True Grit*. My body felt stiff. I hadn't moved an inch on the couch.

The room was pitch-black, except for a tiny light near the kitchen sink. I had no idea what time it was. I began hearing another voice, and it belonged to Clemens. He was standing by the sink, talking quietly into the phone. He was talking to Ma.

I pretended to be asleep.

"No, I don't think you need to come over," Clemens said. "Really. She's fine. I know. I know how upset you must be. But let's let her sleep. In the morning, we'll deal, get to the bottom of what happened, where she's been. Really, she's okay."

Clemens was running his fingers through his hair, pacing.

"Okay," he said. "I promise. I'll call first thing in the morning."

I stayed asleep. Didn't move an inch. Clemens gently put the phone down. He slumped into a kitchen chair. He sat still. The apartment was totally quiet. I realized I was holding my breath. Elbows on his knees, Clemens leaned forward, buried his face in his hands. He made a muffled sound. His shoulders shook.

I sat up, and a bed sheet I hadn't noticed slipped off my back.

"Clemens?" I said.

Clemens froze.

"Were you crying?" I asked.

Clemens lifted his head. I could see moisture around his eyes glistening in the dim kitchen light.

He sighed deeply. "I wake you?"

"You crying?" I said again.

Clemens rubbed his thighs, stood up and came over. He sat down on the coffee table across from me. He shook his head, and his hair twirled, like string.

"Hey, Trell," he said.

I studied him. "You were crying."

Clemens half smiled, an awkward, almost sheepish smile. "I don't know, Trell." He nodded. "Yeah," he said, "maybe a little bit."

Clemens took his third giant breath and made a loud half growl, half groan, like he was trying to get something out of his system. He looked at me and said, "They just came. I got off the phone with your ma, and the tears just came. Trell, we were worried."

Clemens was wound up, and he started talking about what he'd been through the past few hours and the feelings he'd had that spun him all around. He said after he was handed a copy of Monique's death certificate at the State Office of Vital Statistics, he stood there just staring at it. "Then *bingo!*—I knew we had nailed down something big to help prove your daddy's innocence. I practically ran out of the office, in a hurry to show Nora, you, and your ma. It was like I was flying across the parking lot. I got into my car and let out a shout, and that's when I recognized it. The way I *used* to feel when I'd uncovered a crucial piece of information. It's a terrific feeling, a big-time high, and, like fuel, it keeps you going so you can push for more, knowing that now you're really on to something important.

"Trell, I'd lost all of that. Hadn't known that feeling in years. It was history, and I was done. But driving back to Nora's office, I got the rush. And it caught me off guard at first, and then I realized something else. I realized it was because of you these past weeks. Working with you on your daddy's story."

Clemens stopped to catch his breath.

"But that's a good thing," I said. "Right?"

Clemens's eyes widened.

"Not if someone gets hurt."

He glared at me. Then he looked away. His voice choked up.

"Then your ma calls Nora's, looking for you. She was certain you'd be with us. But you weren't. We told your ma you were supposed to be at home—that's where I'd dropped you off. Now we all got frantic. Nora stayed at the office in case you showed up, your ma stayed put at home, and I started driving around, searching for you. Driving all over the neighborhood, and that amazing rush I'd just been feeling was completely gone. The pendulum swung the other way. I'm in a panic instead. Freaked out that something's gone terribly wrong, that maybe something has happened to you. I recognized *that* feeling, too, Trell. When you lose someone important."

I knew he was thinking about his son, Peter. I felt bad.

I said, "But I'm okay."

"I see that now," Clemens said. "But your ma. Nora. Me. We were crazy worried. Trell, where have you been? What the heck were you thinking?"

I told him about going over to Tracey Dailey's place. Right away I could see Clemens was not happy. His face tightened into knots. I kept trying to emphasize the good part. The fact that Tracey and Boo—I told him about Boo—were with Daddy when Ruby Graham was shot. "They *verified* Daddy's alibi. It's more good information."

Then I got to the part about Thumper Parish.

"I guess he knows we're going around, asking questions," I said.

"You think?" Clemens said impatiently.

"Why does he care?"

"I don't know," Clemens said sharply. "I don't know." Clemens was upset. "But what I do know is we're in over our heads. We have no business—*you* have no business—getting mixed up with Thumper Parish."

"But—" I said.

Clemens was shaking his head. "No buts. It's gotten too risky."

"No," I said.

Clemens looked at me hard.

I tried to get myself calm, collect my thoughts. It wasn't like the whole Thumper thing hadn't been scary. It was. And it was real. Not like my nightmare with the snakes and skeletons. But Tracey Dailey was real, too, and so was the alibi. I felt shaky, but when Clemens began to waver, something else inside me took over.

I said, "I'm sorry I went over there alone. I'm sorry about that, but there's no way we can stop. Not now, Clemens."

Clemens sat still and let me make my argument.

"We got the alibi," I said. "Tracey and Boo will help us when the time comes. I really think that. We got proof about Monique

Catron, that no jury in its right mind would believe her testimony if they had known she had brain cancer and her memory was messed up."

Clemens still didn't say a word.

"C'mon, Clemens," I said. "We're into a big story. We only need to get to the other two witnesses that Frank Flanagan used to convict Daddy. Keep going. Find Juanda Tillery and Travis Golson. We can do it."

Then it came to me. "We gotta be persistent," I said. "It's what you said, the day we first talked. You said a reporter had to be two things: curious and persistent. You think I forgot? You said a reporter's got to overcome obstacles. Persist."

I could see in Clemens's face that I was making some headway.

"Journalism 101," I said. "Reporter's got to be determined. Persistent."

I gave him the goofiest smile I could.

"Maybe add one more thing: careful," he said.

I waited.

"Do I get an A?"

Clemens huffed. He pointed to a clock. "It's the middle of the night." He began walking toward his bedroom. "Let's sleep on it. Talk in the morning."

I must have slept like a rock the rest of the night. When I awoke, Clemens was already up, seated at the table with a cup of coffee.

The sun shone through the big kitchen window, the one that used to be covered until I pulled its shade open the first time I was in the apartment. Since then, I don't think Clemens had pulled it shut once.

"What time is it?" I asked, stretching my arms over my head.

"Top of the mornin'," Clemens said.

"Stop," I said. I was thinking he sounded like Big Vinnie and his "Mornin' Glory."

Clemens smiled but didn't look my way. He had his laptop open and was staring at the screen while his fingers pecked away on the keyboard.

"It's almost nine," he said.

"Wow." I hadn't slept that late ever.

"Your ma should be here any minute."

I wandered over. To Clemens's left was a copy of the morning *Boston Globe*. To his right, some papers were spread out. The newspaper's front page caught my eye. It featured a photograph of Frank Flanagan at a campaign rally. He was cheering at the audience, with his fists raised above his head. To me, he didn't look like a nice man. But it was obvious plenty of other people thought differently. The news story next to the photograph was headlined: "Flanagan Leads in Mayoral Primary."

Out of the corner of his eye, Clemens noticed me studying the article. "That's our guy," he said, not looking up from the keyboard.

I read the beginning of the story.

"Says here a new poll puts Frank Flanagan out front in the primary."

"Way out front," Clemens said. "He's the next mayor, looks like."

"But what about the November election?"

"Look at the poll numbers," Clemens said. "If he wins the primary with the kind of margin the polls are showing, it's over. November will be a mere formality. Right now, it's Frank Flanagan's race to lose."

"That's depressing."

I looked across the keyboard to the sprawl of papers and notes.

"What are you doing?"

"Oh," Clemens said. He stopped typing and finally looked at me. "Getting some notes down. Working out some thoughts. I figured it's about that time."

"Time for what?"

"To start roughin' it out." He paused. "We're getting to critical mass."

I made a face, told him he had to explain what that meant.

"Last night, what you said, about Monique, about the alibi," he said. "It made me assess where we're at. Don't get me wrong. We're not done. We still have Juanda Tillery. Travis Golson. Still plenty to do. But I learned a long time ago that on a story like this one, it's never too early to start roughin' it out."

He could tell by my frown I was still puzzled.

"Like the story of mine you told me you read—the one

about Tony Rosario and the fatal fire, where I showed he didn't do it. It's not like I waited until the last minute — the night before publication — to whip up a story from all the information I'd gotten over the weeks and months before. No way. If I'd waited until the end to organize everything, a lot of which was complicated, it would have felt like being dumped in the middle of a forest with no way out."

I was starting to get it.

"So, with these kinds of projects, when you reach a certain point —"

"Critical mass?" I interrupted.

Clemens nodded. "Exactly. Critical mass — when you realize you have enough information to base a story on. You want to take that and start roughing out an outline." Clemens paused and scratched his head. "Maybe look at it this way: our story is like a house. But you can't build a house without a floor plan, and that's what I'm doing now, with what we've got so far. Going over everything, writing memos, jotting notes. Basically designing a floor plan for the story that will come once we finish our reporting."

I was fully awake now.

Clemens turned his attention back to his papers and resumed typing. "Your notebook handy?" he asked. "I want you to check if you got some quotes I missed when we were with Miss Lola. When she was describing Monique picking out your daddy from the photo array police had put in front of her."

I felt my back pocket where I kept my reporter's notebook. But it wasn't there. I worried I'd lost it running from Tracey

Dailey's. I rushed to the couch and fumbled around the cushions. Then I spotted it, underneath the tangled sheet.

"Got it," I said. I began flipping through it and summarizing my notes.

"Miss Lola, she was describing the pressure they were putting on her daughter to pick out Daddy's photo." I skimmed a little farther. "Wait, here, this is the part, what I think you want. Miss Lola was saying the guy in the suit got real excited when Monique finally did what he wanted — pick out Daddy — and he starts cheerin', 'Thatta girl! Thatta girl!' She was saying the guy began slapping the detectives' backs, acting like he'd won the lottery or something."

Clemens typed fast. "That's it," he said. "That's good."

We worked side by side until there was a knock at the door.

It was Ma.

Clemens let her in, and Ma blew past him. She was steaming mad. She plopped her bag down on Clemens's coffee table. I braced for the storm. Even closed my eyes.

But then it didn't come. Ma was furious. Just not at me.

"Nora called," she announced. She was walking in circles. "She got a call last night from the prison — regarding Romero."

My stomach turned. "Ma, what?"

"Daddy's in solitary," Ma said. Her jaw was clenched. There was fierceness about her I wasn't used to seeing. "They went after him."

Ma pounded the table with her fist.

"They?" I said. "Who's 'they'?"

Clemens said, "Start at the beginning, Shey. What happened?"

Ma gathered herself. "It was early evening," she said, "and Daddy was in the dining hall, sweeping the floor. The room's basically empty, kitchen crew gone. Daddy's been doing this job seems forever. He likes it, the quiet and all.

"Suddenly the overhead lights start going off. Flick, flick, flick, one row at a time. It gets dark. Daddy's looking across the room, spots two guys in the shadows moving quickly his way. He can't tell who they are, or what's up, but he knows it's trouble when one whispers his name and says, 'Got something for ya, Romero Taylor. Message from Thumper Parish.' The two start rushin' at Daddy."

I nearly screamed.

Ma put her hands on her hips. "Thing about your daddy, he knows how to take care of himself. He starts swingin' the big broom like a sword, keeping the two men away. Meantime he starts kicking chairs over, banging on the tables, making the biggest, loudest ruckus he can to draw the guards' attention."

"Is Daddy okay?"

Ma nodded. "Yes, he's okay, Trell, he's okay. Nora said he got a few bruises and cuts, but guards came and broke it up before it got past bein' a scuffle. The thing is, they threw Daddy in solitary. Four weeks. No visits."

"No visits?"

"No visits."

The three of us stood there. I was thinking about Thumper

Parish. Thinking Thumper Parish was starting to turn up everywhere.

Ma was thinking about Thumper, too.

"Thumper don't seem to want us looking into Daddy's case," she said.

Clemens gave me a look, and that's when I spoke up, told Ma about Tracey Dailey and Thumper's surprise arrival at her apartment over on Geneva Ave. I didn't try to sugarcoat it like I did with Clemens, tell her it was great Tracey vouched for Daddy's alibi. Just told her in a straightforward way.

Ma listened. Didn't move an inch. I couldn't tell what was going on with her. I figured it was not good. Thumper ordering two guys to make a move on Daddy. Thumper at Tracey's. You add it up, I figured Clemens and I were finished. Thumper here. Thumper there. Thumper everywhere. I heard those rattlesnakes from my dream again, hissing in my head. It was true; this had all gotten pretty scary, and I could understand it, Ma saying we were gonna have to quit.

"Can't do this," Ma said.

When she said that, I figured I'd guessed right. We were done. But I was wrong.

"Thumper Parish can't do this," she continued. "He can't scare us off." The words came out of Ma so matter-of-fact, her eyes hard, like steel.

"I don't know why he don't want us pokin' around," she said. "Don't care. Your daddy, he's the one I care about. And it's gone on long enough. He don't belong in solitary, don't belong in prison—and you two been gettin' the proof. No stoppin' now," she said.

It was resolved. I felt thrilled and scared at the same time. I looked over at Clemens. He was nodding gently. He'd been quiet during Ma's talking. Had to. He knew this was Ma's call. But Clemens was no longer the guy I'd found slumped over asleep in his car that morning in the parking lot of the newspaper. We were working up a critical mass.

Ma wasn't finished, though. She turned on me. "YOU," she shouted. "You do not do any more—whatcha call it, reporting— ALONE. You two stick together."

It was an easy promise to make.

The three of us let out huge breaths, acting strangely giddy, like we all knew we'd gotten over some kind of hump together. We could get back to work.

"I have something else," Ma announced. She made a big show of reaching into her bag, rummaging around, and pulling out—a reporter's notebook!

"Ma!" I said, shocked.

"What?" She gave me a look. "You the only one who gets to have one?"

"No, but I—"

Clemens said, "I gave it to her. You never know."

"That's right. Never know," Ma said mockingly. She opened the notebook. "Let's see. Juanda Tillery." Ma made a show of licking her finger, flipping through the notebook. "My girls at church, they got back to me. They came up with where Juanda Tillery is livin'."

Clemens pumped a fist. "Unbelievable," he said. He shook his head, impressed with Ma's detective work. "I wish I'd known years ago about your church crew. They coulda helped me plenty. Who would think they got better street intel than police?"

"Yeah," Ma said. "But that's the good news."

"What else?" I said.

"Still nothing on Travis Golson," she said. "The girls, they tried everything. Got no clue as to where he's at, or if he's at anywhere. He's their mystery man. Stumped."

Clemens took it in, grimacing. "And he's the big one," he said. "The big piece in the puzzle Frank Flanagan put together for the trial. Travis testifying he saw Romero before the shooting, carrying a pistol and saying he had business to take care of. Testifying he saw Romero after Ruby Graham was shot, acting hyper and saying he had to ditch the gun. That was the icing on Flanagan's cake."

Clemens rubbed his chin. "We get to Travis, he recants, says none of that was true, it's game over. Flanagan's case against Romero collapses into a pile of lies." The more he spoke, the more intense Clemens became. "Shey, can the church girls keep at it? Keep shaking the trees?"

"Of course," she said.

"We need Travis," he said.

Ma tore the sheet of paper from her notebook and handed it to Clemens.

Clemens looked at the address, then handed the paper to me.

I read Juanda Tillery's address: 22 West Selden Street.

"You know where that is?" he asked.

I nodded. "Lower Roxbury, in Mattapan."

Clemens shut his laptop, put it to sleep.

"Let's go," he said.

CHAPTER 18

THE STREET TALKS

It had become obvious to me that Clemens was totally locked in. Chasing after a story and pursuing the truth. Like the dog that grabs ahold of someone's cuff and won't let go, no matter what. I saw the intensity after I woke up on his couch, and if I had any doubts, I witnessed it for certain once we hopped into his Volvo and were headed to Mattapan to track down Juanda Tillery.

Because instead of driving straight down Blue Hill Avenue toward Mattapan, he took a quick left onto Columbia Road and headed into Dorchester.

"Slight detour," he announced before I even had a chance to ask why.

I asked anyway. "What's up?"

"You'll see," he said. "It'll be quick."

Three minutes later, Clemens was backing into a space near a Dumpster in the far corner of the Burger King parking lot on Dorchester Avenue. He'd picked a space right next to a gray Chevy Impala. Inside the Chevy sat a man wearing a Red Sox hat, his snow-white hair bordering the edge of the cap.

"Only take a minute," Clemens said.

Clemens jumped out of our car and into the passenger seat of the Chevy. The two men shook hands. The mystery man then reached beneath his seat, pulled out a thick manila envelope, and handed it to Clemens. They shared a laugh. The man patted Clemens on the back as Clemens climbed out.

"See ya, Jack Snow," the man yelled. He pulled away.

"Get out of here," Clemens shouted after him, smiling. He got back into the Volvo.

"What was that?" I asked.

"That, my cub reporter Trell Taylor, was a handoff." Clemens smacked the envelope with his hand. "Handoff of what? you might ask. Well, in this envelope are copies of *all* the police reports from the night of the shooting. Every single one. Police that night, anyone who responded to the blue mailbox, they each had to write an incident report accounting for their whereabouts, what they did, what they saw. Every cop had to write one. They're called Form 26 reports."

"Nora already has them. I filed a bunch myself."

"Maybe she does," Clemens said. "But maybe not *all* of 'em."

"How so?"

"Nora got the ones the police gave her. It's what they're

required to do—give lawyers copies of Form 26 reports *relevant* to a case. It has to do with fairness. Nora or any other defense attorney can't do their job if they don't know why police arrested their client. And that information is in the Form 26 reports. The thing is—and here's the catch—it's police who decide which reports to give up. They may have to turn over reports, but only the ones they decide are *relevant* to the case. If police decide a report is not relevant? They sit on it, keep it under wraps."

I began to see where this was going. "So, maybe, just maybe, they don't turn over everything? Maybe there's some information police don't want to let out, so they decide it's *not* relevant and don't release it?"

"Exactly. I'm not saying that's what happened here, but we don't know. It's our job to see if there are any reports from the police files that weren't in the stack they gave Nora. Because maybe, just maybe, police held some back. It's a hunch, but reporters always have to be playing hunches, even if they're long shots. It's part of being skeptical, never taking anything for granted and—"

"Verification," I said, finishing his lesson.

"Right. Trouble is, police aren't about to let us walk in off the street to pull every single Form 26 report pertaining to the Ruby Graham murder so we can inspect them. We need help inside the PD on the down low."

Clemens dropped the envelope into my lap. "Enter the man in the Red Sox cap," he said. "So now let's you and me swing by Nora's office, give her the envelope, and while we're in Mattapan, she can match the Form 26s she was given last year against those we just got from the police's own files, thanks to the generosity of Ronan Conley."

"Ronan Conley?"

"The man in the cap," Clemens said. "Ronan works in the police department's Division of Records and Audits. His cousin and I played Bantam hockey together. Anyway, his cousin is how I met Ronan, and Ronan's been a big help here and there over the years, providing internal police records. Someone's rap sheet, a probation file, or, like now, a complete set of the Form 26s in the Ruby Graham investigation."

"I thought Detective Richie Boyle was your big source—Truth-and-Justice Richie Boyle. Remember all that?"

Clemens shot me a look. "Do I detect a hint of sarcasm?"

I nodded yes. "More than a hint."

"Noted," Clemens said. "Thing is, to get these records, I couldn't ask Richie. Not after what happened when we were at his house. Besides, a reporter can never have too many sources. That's where Ronan comes in. I called him last week."

I thought about Clemens reaching out to Ronan and I hadn't even known. He was working every angle, anything he could think of, totally focused.

"One more thing," I said.

"Shoot."

"Why'd he call you Jack Snow? When you got out of his car he laughed and said, 'See ya, Jack Snow.'"

"Oh, that." Clemens grinned. "It's my code name."

"Huh?"

"I know, sounds like a spy movie. But when I first asked Ronan for help, he didn't want anyone knowing. He'd get fired if he ever got caught slipping records to a reporter. So to keep things secret, we came up with a code name. We picked Jack Snow because Ronan's hair has been the color of snow since he was a kid.

"So whenever I needed to contact him, I'd call his office and leave a message that Jack Snow had called. Ronan would see the message and know right away it was me. When he was alone, he'd call me back, and we were in business.

"That's why he was having a good laugh—it's been years since he got a message from Jack Snow. Ronan thought it was a hoax, it had been so long. But he figured what the heck, and called back. I'm glad he did." Clemens pulled out of the Burger King lot. "Really has been a long time I've been out of action."

We drove to Nora's office downtown, ran the envelope with the Form 26 reports into her office, and got back to locating Juanda Tillery. We took Blue Hill Avenue south toward Mattapan. The sun glared hot in our faces, and we had the windows rolled down. Clemens's old Volvo had air conditioning, but it was broken. We drove past Franklin Park on our right, past the nail salons, gas stations, auto-body garages, takeout restaurants, convenience stores, and storefront churches that lined the street. Looking out the window, I got to thinking about Daddy, and what it must be like for him to be in solitary. No window. No contact with any-one, except when a food tray came. I shut my eyes to see what it might feel like, so dark.

I got to thinking we would drive down Blue Hill Avenue together when he came home. He could see how different it is today from before he went away. I know a lot has changed, because when I was little, most of the storefronts that Clemens and I passed had been boarded up with plywood. People used to call Blue Hill Avenue "Plywood Avenue." But now there were lots of new shops.

Maybe Daddy and me, driving down Blue Hill, could stop and get a foot-long hot dog and soft ice cream at Simco's — one place that was definitely there before Daddy went to prison. Simco's is like a famous landmark, sitting near the railroad bridge on Blue Hill Avenue just before you get to Mattapan Square. Ma once told me that Simco's first opened in the 1930s, during the Great Depression. It's got the best hot dogs ever. People go to Simco's from all over.

We crested a small hill and the big neon Simco's sign came into view.

"Hungry?" Clemens asked. "We could stop, grab a hot dog, some chili?"

Clemens slowed. There was a line at Simco's window, people putting in their food orders. I saw old people and young people, mothers and sons, fathers and daughters. I watched the families and thought I would wait. I would wait until I could have a hot dog at Simco's with Daddy after he got home.

I told Clemens I wasn't hungry. He drove on.

"Clemens?" I said.

"Yeah."

"You know how you said we're getting to critical mass?"

"Yeah."

"Well, I was thinking. I know *we know* Daddy didn't do it, but I was thinking, if Daddy didn't do it, who did kill Ruby Graham?"

"The million-dollar question," Clemens said. "But to be honest, it's a question we don't have to answer."

"What do you mean?"

"Our story, is what I mean," he said. "The point of our story is to show that Romero Taylor was not the shooter. It's not to figure out who did kill Ruby Graham. Just like in the Tony Rosario story, where I was able to show he did not start the fire killing those people. Didn't have to find out who the arsonist was."

"Sure gets you wondering, though."

"Of course," he said. "But it's the police, their job, to find the real killer."

I frowned. "Supposed to be their job, and supposed to be done right."

I showed Clemens where to make a left turn onto Babson Street, and, after a few more turns, I pointed out West Selden Street. People call Boston a city of neighborhoods, and West Selden is what they have in mind. It's a street lined with sidewalks, trees, and houses with real yards. Most of the houses looked like they could use a fresh coat of paint or a roof repaired. Still, it's definitely a step up from Esmond Street, where Clemens lives, or Vassar, where Miss Lola is. Or Hutchings, where Ma and I live. People on West Selden actually own. Ma talks about some-day owning our own house, so I know that counts for something.

We were halfway up the brick front stairs at 22 West Selden when a dog began barking ferociously from inside the house. Clemens and I looked at each other. I rang the doorbell even though I didn't need to, not with the dog going nuts.

Someone came to the door but didn't open it. "Who's there?" a voice shouted from inside. It was a man's voice, sounding deep and sluggish.

"We're looking for Juanda Tillery," I said.

"Not home," the voice shouted over the dog.

"Can we come in?"

"Go away," the voice commanded.

Clemens took a try. He told the man who he was—a reporter—and that we were working on a story about the Ruby Graham case. "We'd like to talk to Juanda," he shouted. "It'll just take a few minutes to explain, if you'll just open the door."

"Go away," is all the voice said.

The barking never let up. At least we knew we were at the right house. But it was clear the man behind the door was not going to open it. "What do we do?" I asked. Clemens shrugged. He reached for his wallet and took out a business card. I didn't even know he carried business cards. It had the newspaper's name on it, then his name and his office telephone number.

Clemens could tell I was surprised. "They can come in handy—once in a while," he said. Clemens took out a pen and scribbled his home phone number on it. Then he wrote a message: "Juanda Tillery, please call, and I can explain." Clemens wedged the card in between the front door and the doorjamb. The dog barked more.

"C'mon," Clemens said. "Let's go. I'll make us a sandwich."

We made it back to Clemens's apartment in less than ten minutes, and a voicemail was already waiting for us on his machine. I pulled open the refrigerator door looking for something to eat while Clemens headed across the room to check on the message. He hit the Play button.

"Um, hello, you came by my house this morning on West Selden."

The woman's voice obviously belonged to Juanda Tillery even though she didn't say so. I stood still to listen.

"I want you to know I totally do not want to be involved with this story or anything that has to do with this Romero Taylor thing. Because that happened over ten years ago, and I was a minor at the time. It was very traumatic then, and I don't need it to be traumatic now. I do not want my name printed in your story."

The longer she spoke, the more worked up she got.

"If you do, I'm gonna have to bring, I'm gonna have to sue or something. Because I don't want—I know about freedom of speech and freedom of press and all that. But no, this is my name and I'm going to keep it for me and I don't want it out there in the world for everybody else to see. I've moved on with my life."

Juanda Tillery took a moment, then continued. "I'm sorry what happened to that boy Romero, whatever, whatever," she said, "but I'm telling you, do *not* print my name and bother me or my family with this again."

There was a click, and then silence.

I walked over to where Clemens stood next to the phone.

"Wow," I said. "She's not happy."

Clemens had his head tilted down. I looked to see what he was looking at and saw he had caller ID on his phone. He was reading the screen to see where the message came from.

The screen read *Salon de Paris.*

Clemens seemed puzzled, but I wasn't.

"We drove past Salon de Paris," I said. "Just after Franklin Park, on the other side of Blue Hill. It was one of those new shops along there."

Clemens's eyes brightened. "It must be where she works."

We were both thinking the same thing.

When we walked into the salon, I spotted two women seated in chairs getting their hair done by stylists. The room was painted a deep red, and the fixtures were a shiny gold color. Behind a tiny counter, I saw a third worker writing in an appointment book. She had to be Juanda Tillery. I knew that because the moment we walked into the shop, she had looked up and her face flashed shock, then anger. The man behind the door on West Selden Street, besides telling her about our visit, must have said it had been a man and a girl who'd appeared on their front stoop.

Juanda, wearing heels, tight black slacks, and a matching short-sleeved black blouse, moved quickly from behind the counter. She met us before we were able to get any farther inside the long, narrow shop.

"I can't believe this," she seethed.

Clemens stayed calm. "We were hoping, if we could talk—"

"You cannot come to my place of business like this."

I tried to mimic Clemens. "We were hoping, if we could just—"

Juanda looked around quickly, at the customers and her coworkers. "Shhh," she hissed. She summoned us to follow her. She led us through the shop, into a back room, and then outside into a back alley. She turned on us.

"Didn't I make myself clear on the phone?" she said.

Seeing how upset she was, part of me felt bad. She'd already said in her message she didn't want anything to do with us. Now we'd surprised her at work. Messing up her day and making her so mad didn't make me feel very good. But I was also thinking about what Clemens had said about reporting, that it gets tough, that some people don't want to help, some people's feelings get hurt, but you got to stick with it if the story is important enough. No one could convince me that getting Daddy out of prison wasn't important enough. Persist, Clemens was always saying.

"When you were little, you knew my daddy," I said.

"Your daddy?" Juanda said.

"Romero Taylor is my daddy."

Juanda's face seemed to soften, but just a bit.

I wanted to keep her talking because I was remembering more information about her. Stuff from a Form 26 report police had given to Nora—a report about what Juanda had told a police detective when she was questioned the day after the shooting. I'd read the report when I did the filing for Nora, and Juanda's had stayed with me because I could tell from what she said that she liked Daddy. She said things like he was friendly to the little kids, always had a smile, and sometimes handed out treats. But the report also stayed with me for another reason—because at the trial later, Juanda said different things. Things that, along with what Monique Catron and Travis Golson testified, convicted Daddy.

I continued. "You were fourteen then, I think."

"Yes," Juanda said, "I was fourteen. I told you, I was a minor."

"Daddy, he was older, but you knew him?"

It was like Juanda, thinking about back then, couldn't help herself.

"I knew Romero. Everybody knew Romero. He was sweet to us kids."

"And the night of the shooting, you said you saw him beforehand?"

Juanda listened.

"Walking down the street? You ran into each other, and he

stopped and said hi to you. You guys talked. He even gave you a hug?"

She smiled at the thought. "I remember that. Like I said, he was good to us."

"The reason I know this is because I read it in one of the reports from the case. It was what you told a detective when he was asking you questions the day after the shooting."

"And?" Juanda said.

I looked at Clemens, then back at Juanda. "It's like, this is why we're wanting to talk to you. Because at the trial, the hug, the kindness, stuff like that, never came up. Instead, other things did. Something about another guy."

"There was another guy. Angelo, I think. Yeah, Angelo."

"In the report you said this other guy comes by, and you just say hello to each other, and the other guy leaves. But at the trial you said the guy stopped and has a real conversation with Daddy. He tries to get Daddy to go with him to some party somewheres, but Daddy won't go. You said Daddy told him, 'Naw, I got some business.'"

I had this part of the murder trial memorized, and it was like I could see the testimony scrolling in my head. "The prosecutor, Frank Flanagan, he stopped you there, and said, 'Say that again, slowly.'

"And you repeated for everyone to hear in the courtroom that Daddy told the other guy he can't go to a party. You quoted Daddy telling the guy, 'Can't go. I *got* to do this. It's business.'

Then, as everyone knows, a half hour later, Ruby Graham is dead, shot by mistake by someone looking to settle a score."

I paused, then added, "None of this part — what you testified to at the trial — was in your original report."

Juanda's face shook. "Maybe because it never happened that way."

Clemens interjected. "What do you mean?"

"I'm sayin' I don't recall Romero ever talking to Angelo about some business. In fact, they didn't talk about nothing, 'cause Angelo, he just passed us by."

"But it's what you said at the trial," I said. "It's in the transcript."

Juanda's hands went up. "I don't care what it says. I don't recall that." She was getting upset again. "Don't you get it? I was a weed smoker. Smoked so much they called me See-weed, 'cause my friends, whenever they see me, I had weed.

"I was scared, is why I testified. They were threatening to lock me up. I was just a kid. The day I went to court, I'm waiting in a room and the guy starts up, yellin' and screamin' at me."

"What guy?" Clemens asked.

"I don't know that white man's name," she said. "The one who was askin' all the questions. That man, he could have got me to say anything the way he was sticking his face into mine and yellin'. Because I don't remember Romero or Angelo or anyone that night talking about taking care of any business."

Clemens's voice had gone calm and measured. "So, is it

accurate to say you felt intimidated? Like you had to say what they wanted or else?"

"I don't care what you want to call it," she said. "All I know is they told me in no uncertain terms that if I didn't testify, my ass was gonna end up in jail."

I started to take my notebook out, and Juanda pounced.

"Don't you start takin' notes," she ordered. "I told you, no story."

Clemens said, "Juanda, this is the help we're after. It's like a pattern. It's what we're finding. Where witnesses—like you—were bullied into saying things that weren't true, but taken together, made Romero seem guilty."

"But he's not guilty," Juanda said. She spoke the words so casually, as if it was a matter of fact. "Everyone knows that."

"What do you mean everyone?" Clemens said.

"The street talks. The street knows Romero's no killer."

I was ready to burst.

"With your help, maybe there'd be justice," I said. "Don't you see, Ms. Tillery?"

"Justice!" It was like Juanda spit the word out. "C'mon, girl."

She folded her arms and turned to Clemens. "You probably'll never understand," she said. "But I have a new life, a new job. I have two kids, and I live here. I'm not gonna put my life or my family in danger." She turned to me. "I get you're trying to correct a wrong," she said, "and I'm sorry what happened to your daddy. But you do not quote me. You do not use my name. If it appears, maybe I get fired. Maybe I get shot taking my kids to the bus stop. It's too much stress, and I won't have it."

Juanda looked at her watch. "Now, I gotta get back inside. My next appointment is waiting." She marched toward the door. She turned suddenly and, with calm finality, said, "I'm not gonna be givin' any input to your story."

Juanda Tillery closed the door on us.

Clemens and I didn't move, just let things sink in.

"That's not good," I said after a couple of minutes.

"Not good," Clemens said.

He scratched his forehead. I looked down at my empty reporter's notebook.

"Sets us back," he said.

"What about reachin' critical mass?"

"I dunno," Clemens said. "What I do know: we gotta find Travis Golson."

CHAPTER 19
RICHIE BOYLE REDUX

Clemens sat in the kitchen at his laptop, working on his notes, while I was on the couch. He thought I was reading, but I was thinking about Juanda Tillery and her reaction to the fact that we were digging up the past. She didn't want any part of it. She was scared. You could see it on her face. She acted all mad, but you could see the fear behind it.

Made me think of Tracey and Boo, how they never stuck their neck out. Would never say Daddy had an alibi and was with them on Sonoma Street when the shooting went down. They'd been afraid, too. Even Miss Lola, the way she talked about police being in her home, pressuring Monique, she had the fear.

Juanda, Tracey, Boo, and Miss Lola. Everyone was so scared. The thing is, it was mainly fear of police, and that's what I couldn't stop thinking about on the couch while Clemens typed.

Police—you're supposed to trust them. They make you safe. But it's like Juanda and the others, they've seen too much. Seen police take Romero Taylor and arrest him for something he didn't do. Seen police pressure kids into lying so they can win a trial and put the wrong person in prison. Most people probably think police have solved a horrible murder by catching Daddy. But people in my neighborhood know different. The street knows, like Juanda said.

So they're afraid, a fear that turns everything on its head. Instead of trusting police, there's mistrust. Instead of feeling safe, there's fear. It's ironic when you think about it. Irony—when there's a difference between what you expect and what actually is. I learned about irony in school this year from my English teacher.

But this situation goes beyond being just ironic. Because when there's a shooting, the police chief goes on TV saying people with information need to come forward. Police can't do it alone, he says. The neighborhood's got to do its part. He's like blaming the neighborhood. It's unbelievable. Because he's leaving something really important out. People are only gonna come forward if they trust police. But people like Juanda, Tracey, Boo, and Miss Lola have seen police twist their words, or lie, or bully them. And no one ever seems to point this out when the chief starts complaining. Makes me so mad. You gotta be able to trust police—and you gotta fix that problem—before you get all huffy on TV about cooperation.

I looked across the room at Clemens. I was about to get up and go tell him what I was thinking, get these ideas off my chest. I was going to say it's the kind of thing a reporter could be pointing out to the chief at one of those press conferences when the chief is mainly dumping on the neighborhood. But before I could, the phone rang.

Clemens picked up. He nodded a few times, then put the phone down.

"It's Nora," he said to me. "She's got something."

When Clemens and I made it down the marble stairs to Nora's basement office, we found Nora leaning against the doorjamb, waiting for us. She was dangling a piece of paper at arm's length. The look on her face, and the way she held the paper away from her, it was like she was holding something rotten. She might as well have been pinching her nose.

She even said, as she waved the paper in our faces, "This stinks."

Nora turned and walked inside. We followed her. Nora flattened the document on a table. I recognized it at once as a Form 26 report from the Boston Police Department. And in the space at the top of the page to describe the subject of the report, someone had typed in: "Ruby Graham Shooting on August 20, 1988."

"I found this in the batch of Form 26s you got from your source," Nora said. "It was *not* in the original pile Boston Police gave me when I became Romero's attorney."

Clemens and I leaned forward. It was short, only a half page long, typewritten, and the police officer who prepared it began,

"I respectfully submit that I was in an unmarked cruiser in the Roxbury area when a description was broadcast to be on the lookout for a white Suzuki Samurai seen in the vicinity of a shooting on Humboldt. Said vehicle was described as containing an unknown black male."

I looked up. "I remember reading about a Suzuki in other reports. Some of the kids at the corner said they saw a Suzuki farther down Humboldt."

The officer's report continued. "I observed a Suzuki fitting the description and followed it along Blue Hill Ave toward Devon Street. Without blue lights, I followed the motor vehicle that took a right onto Devon. I turned my blue lights on, pulled out in front, and forced motor vehicle to the left side of street. Officer investigated and was able to identify the driver."

Clemens began rubbing his forehead. My eyes widened.

"Driver was identified as Lamar 'Thumper' Parish."

Clemens exhaled deeply. "Holy smokes."

"See what I mean?" Nora said.

The Form 26 had one more sentence. But it wasn't anything explaining why Thumper Parish was driving around Humboldt in a Suzuki Samurai. Instead, the Form 26 just ended abruptly: "After investigation, driver was able to leave scene."

"Just like that, 'able to leave scene,'" Nora said. "Gimme a break."

But that wasn't all. The name of the officer signing the report at the bottom of the page hit like a bolt of lightning: "Submitted by Det. Richard Boyle, Badge #9384."

"Richie Boyle," I said in disbelief.

"So many questions," Nora said. "So few answers."

"Clemens, what's going on?" I said.

Clemens was shaken. "I don't know."

I looked at Clemens, then at Nora. "Richie stops Thumper in a white Suzuki that police are looking for, then lets him go? What's that about? Why would Richie let Thumper go?"

Nora shrugged. She looked at Clemens. Clemens gritted his teeth.

Clemens squeezed a copy of the Form 26 in one hand as he gripped the steering wheel of his Volvo and drove to Richie Boyle's house. He was so intent and lost in thought, he didn't see what I saw—or thought I saw. We'd taken a turn, and, racing past a side street, I spotted a shiny black Mercedes at the intersection. I turned my head quickly to get a better look, but Clemens was driving too fast. Thumper? I felt a chill shoot up my neck, even if I couldn't tell for sure.

"You see that?" I said.

"What?" Clemens said.

"The Mercedes back there. The black Mercedes."

"No."

I wondered if I'd imagined it. Clemens was no help. In the time I'd known him and we'd become friends, I'd never seen him like this. I didn't know if the anger came from feeling our story was maybe slipping away. Juanda Tillery had shut us down,

Tracey Dailey wasn't fully on board, and we still had no idea where Travis Golson was. Or if it was because of Richie, and Clemens was feeling like he'd been betrayed. I just couldn't tell. I only knew Clemens was not happy about the way things were going.

Clemens wasn't the only one. Retired Detective Boyle was not too happy to see it was us pounding on his front door. No bear hug this time for Clemens—way past that. No invitation to come inside, either. But Clemens didn't wait for one. He brushed past Richie and stepped into the living room. Before I followed, I looked up and down the street. No sign of the black Mercedes.

Inside Richie's, things looked different. The big picture on the wall was gone. The picture of Richie, Frank Flanagan, and other police receiving a public service award for taking down George "G-man" Whigham and his drug operation. Now there was only a shadowy outline where it had once hung. There were other changes, too. Some cardboard boxes were scattered around, some of which were partly filled.

Even the police radio, which was blaring last time, was turned off.

"Goin' somewhere?" Clemens said.

"Thinkin' 'bout it," Richie said. "Maybe someplace the sun always shines."

I pointed to the wall. "What happened to G-man?"

Richie frowned. "Huh?"

"Your big award—the one you got for arresting George Whigham?"

He ignored me. Nothing had changed much from our first visit.

Clemens said, "That was a big one, Richie, a career highlight — the G-man bust. Thing is, I don't think you ever told me the whole drama. Told me plenty of other stories. You loved talking about your war stories. But the G-man bust, never heard much about that one, how you guys figured out where G-man was holed up with what turned out to be an arsenal of guns and a new shipment of drugs."

Richie wasn't in a hospitable mood.

"Okay, Clemens. You and your junior reporter here, whad-dya want?"

Clemens gently placed the Form 26 on the table.

"Where'd you get that?" Richie said.

"Richie, c'mon. I got sources."

Richie shot Clemens a look.

Clemens said, "You never told us you knew Thumper Parish."

"What's to tell?"

I had a hard time keeping still. "Really?"

Richie kept his calm. "My job was to know the street players, talk 'em up, try to establish some kind of rapport. Thumper's a player. Big deal."

"Thumper's not just any player," I said.

Richie glared at me.

Clemens said, "Says here you stopped Thumper in a Suzuki."

Richie acted like he was reading the document. "Yeah."

"Says you let him go 'after investigation.'"

"Yeah."

"Richie, what's that mean?"

Richie tilted his head, rubbed his chin.

"Richie?"

"It means I conferred with Flanagan."

"Conferred?"

"Yeah, conferred. You know, talked!" Richie looked agitated. "Christ, Clemens, we were responding to a shooting—god-awful shooting of a little girl. It was chaos. All hands on deck. Flanagan was coordinating. So, yeah, I called in—I *conferred*."

"How come none of that's in your Form 26?"

Richie shook his head. "Clemens, it's just a summary, not *War and Peace*."

Clemens would have none of it.

"Why did you let Thumper go, Richie?"

Richie stared at Clemens. "No comment."

"Was it Flanagan? He tell you to let him go?"

"I'm not gonna answer that."

"Well, you just did," Clemens said. He looked at Richie. "You stop Lamar Parish, let him go? Your Form 26 gets buried? You never tell us any of this?"

Clemens's voice was filled more with disappointment than anger.

He continued. "You know, Richie, right off you made it clear you didn't like me and Trell digging around on this thing. Then you-know-who starts popping up, makin' it clear he doesn't like it either. Something's going on, Richie."

"Whaddya talkin' about?"

Clemens told him about Thumper Parish bursting into Tracey Dailey's place looking for me, and, before that, Thumper doing a drive-by in his shiny black Mercedes past my house when we were leaving for the prison to see Daddy. He told him about two of Thumper's guys going after Daddy in the prison cafeteria.

I jumped in. "I think I saw the Mercedes on the way over here."

Richie began pacing in circles. A pained look came over his face. The veins in his neck pulsed, and he began rubbing his hands. It was like he wanted to tell us something, but all he said was, "You two gotta go."

Clemens bowed his head. I picked the Form 26 off the table, and we headed for the door. Clemens stopped suddenly and blurted out, "Travis Golson."

"That's a name I haven't heard in a while," Richie said. Maybe Richie was caught off guard, or maybe he wanted to somehow make nice.

"Know where he might be, Richie?" Clemens said. "Can you tell us that?"

Richie shrugged. "Naw. Last time I saw him, I think, was in Roxbury District Court. He'd caught a bunch of cases, faced some serious stuff. Not pretty."

"Ohh" is all Clemens said.

* * *

When Clemens basically went mute, I knew his mind was already spinning off in a new direction. I knew that because my mind took off, too. I'd learned a lot in the past month and was starting to think I had a knack for this. Court files include a ton of personal information. I'd learned that from reading Daddy's records. So, when Richie said Travis Golson had cases in Roxbury court, I knew our next move.

"We head to Roxbury District, find Travis's files, maybe get a lead?" I said.

"Maybe an address, maybe a relative's name," Clemens said as we drove away from Richie Boyle's house. "Something we can use to break this sucker open."

The clerk's office inside Roxbury District Court was cramped and busy. There were no windows and the air was stale. People were bunched at the counter, asking the clerks on duty questions about court cases or paying fines for minor crimes and traffic violations. We squeezed into the lobby and had been standing there for only a few minutes when one of the clerks took notice.

"Oh, my. Look who's here."

Behind the counter, a woman stood up at one of the desks along a side wall. She was tall, with straight black hair cut short, and black skin so shiny it seemed to reflect the overhead fluorescent lights. "Clemens Bittner," she said as she reached the counter. "I thought maybe you'd moved away, or retired. It's been years."

"Yeah, took a bit of a hiatus, I guess. How you doin', Toni?"

The two chatted a bit. Clemens asked about Toni's family, and she told him about her son, now away at college in Providence, and a daughter, who had finished school and was a social worker for the state. Toni turned to me. "He's such a doll. Most reporters come in here, always in such a rush, wanting this record or that. Clemens, he's good people. Takes the time, treats you like a human being."

Clemens introduced me, without going into Daddy's situation, and then said, "Toni, we're hoping to pull some cases, old ones. From the late 1980s."

Toni stepped to a computer screen at the counter. "Name?"

"Golson," I said. "Travis Golson."

She looked at me and smiled. "You the apprentice?" she said.

"Kinda," I said.

"Date of birth?" Toni said.

I looked at Clemens. He said, "We don't have one. In 1988 Travis Golson was sixteen or seventeen. My guess is he was born in the early 1970s."

"Okay, let's see what we find with just the name." Toni worked the keyboard and then waited. I could see her eyes reading information popping up on the screen. "Yep," she said. "This looks like your Travis Golson. Busy boy, he was. He's got a handful of cases in the system, and none are active. They're all closed."

"You mind pulling the files, Toni?"

"They're back in the vault," Toni said. She nodded toward two coworkers who were dealing with the crush at the counter and said, "Gimme a minute so I can help out front here, and then I'll go back and get them."

Clemens and I stood off to the side as the three clerks got busy shortening the line that had formed at the counter. Then Toni gave Clemens a nod and disappeared. Five minutes later, she returned carrying a small stack of files.

"Here you go—Travis Golson," she said.

With the crowd thinned, we had room to use the small table against the wall. I realized my heart was racing, knowing we'd be getting clues to Travis Golson's whereabouts. We'd finally be able to locate him. I counted six files in all, meaning Travis had once had six separate criminal cases pending against him. The actual charges were typed onto each file's tab. I read them aloud: possession of marijuana with intent to sell, burglary, larceny (stolen car), trespassing, possession of cocaine, disorderly conduct (fighting). Travis had been in pretty big trouble.

I took the top file, Clemens took the next, and we began flipping through the pages, looking for the arrest forms and other paperwork that contained personal information, like home address, parents' names, and all that great stuff.

Except it wasn't there. We tried the next two files, and then the last two. Not one contained the key information we had expected to find. On every form where the person's address and parents were supposed to be filled in, the box was either left empty or filled in with UNK, which stands for *unknown.*

We tried flipping through the files a second time.

"Unknown, unknown, unknown," I said.

"The same," Clemens said. "Nothing."

"This Travis kid homeless, or what?"

"Maybe," Clemens said. "No address and no parents to speak of."

"Which equals no leads. Just another dead end."

Then Clemens said, "Wait a minute."

He opened one file, then another. Something had caught his eye. He stacked them together. "I'm going to go through each, read you a date. You write it down." Clemens flipped open the first file and found the form called a docket sheet, which is a time line for a criminal case as it makes its way through the court system. He ran his finger down the docket sheet, then said, "Okay. July 16, 1989."

I wrote the date down on a pad.

"July 16, 1989," he said, reading the docket in the second file. He read the third: "July 16, 1989." It was the same for the rest: July 16, 1989.

"What's that mean?" I said.

"It means that Travis Golson appeared in court that day, and that all six criminal charges pending against him were bundled together."

"Bundled?"

"Yes, combined together," Clemens said. "You see, it's not like he committed six crimes on the same day. Like the stolen car. Travis was charged in 1986 with stealing a red Chevy Camaro. The cocaine possession? The docket for that case says Travis was arrested in June 1987 with a bag of crack cocaine.

In all, the crimes occurred on six different occasions between 1986 and 1988."

"Okay, I get that," I said. "So, six criminal charges were pending against him, and on July 16, 1989, Travis went to court to face all of them at once."

"Exactly," he said. "But look what happens in court that day."

I read the docket sheets. Each docket said, "Continued to Nov. 16, 1989."

"What's that mean?"

Clemens said, "It means the cases were postponed until November 16. It means that in July, nothing really happened. Nothing was resolved for Travis one way or another — guilty, not guilty, whatever. Instead, the cases were continued until this new date in the middle of November. In the meantime, the six charges were still hanging over Travis Golson's head. He could be found guilty of one crime or all six of them, and as a punishment, he could be sent away to prison."

Clemens was on the edge of his seat. He hovered over the files.

"What else we know was happening in 1989?" he asked.

Something I'll never forget. "Daddy's murder trial. The trial started in October, and Daddy was convicted on November 11, 1989."

"Okay — and it was a trial where, as we already know, a teenager named Travis Golson was a star witness."

Clemens slid one of the docket sheets in front of me. "Now look at the date where Travis's cases were postponed to."

I ran my finger down the docket sheet until I found November 16.

"What's it say?" Clemens said.

I looked at the two words filled in for that date. "Forget it," I said. "No way."

Clemens actually chuckled. "C'mon."

I squinted. The words were *nolle* and *prosequi.* "Nawllie prawskey?"

"Close," Clemens said. "It's Latin, a legal term meaning 'do not prosecute.'"

Clemens flipped through each of the six docket sheets to show me that on November 16, each charge against Travis Golson was nolle prosequi — all six.

"It means they decided not to prosecute the charges," he said. "They dropped them. Travis left court free and clear."

"Wow. Travis's lucky day."

"You think?"

I let what Clemens had walked me through sink in. Bingo.

"I get it," I said.

"You do?"

"I do."

I recited the sequence of events: Travis was in court in July, and all six of his cases got postponed until November. Travis testified, and Daddy was convicted on November 11. Travis's cases came up again five days later, on November 16 — and they were dropped.

"Quid pro quo, it's called," Clemens said.

"No more Latin, please."

"Something for something," Clemens said. "It's like this: Travis testifies against Romero, and the six cases go away. You help me, and I'll help you. Something for something. But if Travis didn't testify like they wanted, the six cases would be waiting for him like a firing squad."

Clemens had more. "Look closer, the name penciled in the entry for November 16."

It read, "nolle prosequi per order of Frank Flanagan, District Attorney."

"Flanagan was the one asking the judge to drop the cases," Clemens said.

"Something for something," I repeated. "You help me; I'll help you."

We'd come to court looking for one thing—a lead to locate Travis Golson—and found another—a sweet deal for Travis in return for the testimony that was so damaging to Daddy. More than ever, we needed to find Travis Golson in the hope he'd tell us more.

CHAPTER 20
HOLD THE PRESSES

Except we couldn't find Travis. Ma had the church ladies trying some more, but they were truly stumped. Clemens contacted a source he had at the Department of Motor Vehicles to see if Travis Golson ever had a driver's license. If so, it would have an address listed on it. But no. Travis apparently never drove, at least not legally.

No one had a clue. When it came to the star witness Frank Flanagan had used against Daddy at his trial, the entire neighborhood of Roxbury was left scratching its head.

The summer days dragged into August. I fell into a pretty deep funk. We couldn't visit Daddy; he still had two more weeks in solitary before he got out. I tried tackling my summer reading, but that only reminded me I had to make up my mind one way or another about returning to the Weld.

Ma said she was getting letters from the school. She tried talking to me about it, but I wasn't ready. I was in a crazy kind of limbo, a limbo that seemed multiplied by two. I was in limbo about school, and we were in limbo about Travis Golson and our story. When Ma was talking about school, I talked about the case.

"Ma, you heard anything?" I'd say.

"From the Weld?" she'd ask.

"No, from your friends. Travis Golson?"

Ma would shake her head no.

Even my workout runs didn't help much. My whole life, running had been a way to clear my head. I still went out every day, but now the runs were sluggish. My legs felt heavy, and my head was more foggy than clear. That just put me in a deeper funk.

Then Paul Parish called. He asked what I was up to and if I wanted to see the new Spider-Man movie.

I told him, "I don't think so."

"C'mon, Trell, it's supposed to be great. Everyone says so."

I said I had stuff to do, even though that wasn't true.

Paul called back a few days later.

"What about *Men in Black II*?" he said. "My cousin says it freaks you out."

"I'm not in a movie mood." I didn't even thank him for asking.

I mostly wanted to stay home. I was doing a shut-in thing. Reading some poems, a bit of James Baldwin, and listening to music. One song got stuck in my head, Shaggy's "Angel," which featured Rayvon singing the hook.

Girl, you're my angel, you're my darlin' angel.
Closer than my peeps you are to me, baby.
Shorty, you're my angel, you're my darlin' angel.
Girl, you're my friend when I'm in need, lady.

The lyrics made me think of my parents, made me imagine when they were young and first got together. If Daddy could carry a tune, it could have been him singing instead of Shaggy.

Life is one big party when you're still young.
But who's gonna have your back when it's all done.
It's all good when you're little, you have pure fun.
Can't be a fool, son, what about the long run.
Looking back Shorty always mention.
Said me not giving her much attention.
She was there through my incarceration.
I wanna show the nation my appreciation.

I liked the lyrics enough, but it was more the reggae beat that stayed with me, a rhythm breaking like a gentle wave, mixed with sadness. It sounded like how I was feeling. The song played over and over in my head.

Each day during my run, I swung by Clemens's apartment and checked in. I always found him at his laptop. He said he was going over his memos and roughing out what he called a foundation for the story.

"What about Travis Golson?" I asked. "Don't we need him?"

"I know, I know. But I'm trying to see if we can work around the Travis problem."

Then, one Saturday morning, I was getting ready to head out for a run when Clemens met me at the door. "Get changed," he said. "We're going to the *Globe*."

"The *Globe*?"

"Yep," he said. "We have a meeting. It's at eleven, so we better hurry."

"Meeting?"

"With Jack Morin. The editor."

"The editor? You mean the editor of the whole entire newspaper?"

"That's who. I wrote a draft, he's read it, and he called. He wants to talk."

Being in a hurry, Clemens pulled into a parking space in front of the *Globe*, not bothering with the employee lot on the roof deck in back. It meant we entered the building through the front lobby, which meant going through security. Tommy O'Donahue was the guard on duty. He looked up from behind the security desk as we hustled up the granite steps. His eyes popped open once he saw me, and his mouth dropped. I hurried alongside Clemens and made sure to give Tommy O'Donahue the widest grin I could summon, as if to say, *No stopping me now.* Wordless, Mr. O'Donahue buzzed us through.

"I want to tell you about Jack Morin," Clemens said as we

stepped onto the escalator to the second floor. He was talking fast, like we didn't have much time.

"He might seem—well, it's hard to put a finger on it exactly, but he might seem mean. Or maybe unfriendly is better. Or cold. You know, remote."

"That's confusing."

"Yeah." Clemens frowned. "You're probably right. Let me see . . . It's a personality thing—he's a flat line, if you know what I mean."

"Not really."

"The way he talks, for example—a monotone. No feeling, no emotion. He's not into small talk, either. Nothing like, 'How's the family? What about those Sox? Celtics? Bruins?' Nothing. You just don't get much, whether anger, joy, whatever. The man sits at his desk, you wonder if he even has a pulse. For him, it's all business."

"Like a computer."

"That's what I'm getting at—it's how most of us reporters regard him. Desktop computer. It's like he's built from the neck up. The joke is you could situate his head on a stand on his desk and there you'd have it, Jack Morin."

"Creepy."

"Well, maybe a little. But he knows his stuff, and he's really smart. I just don't want it to surprise you, the way he seems so detached, almost not human."

On the second floor, we walked down a long corridor to the newsroom—a sprawling open space filled with desks for reporters and copyeditors. Glassed-in offices lined one wall. They were for top editors. We stopped at the counter where telephone operators worked. I recognized Rose seated at one station.

"Hello, girl," she called out as she took off a headset.

I smiled. Clemens craned his neck, looking across the room to the largest glassed-in office in the far corner. It was Editor in Chief Jack Morin's office.

"He's waiting for you," Rose told Clemens.

Clemens thanked her. He began to head across the newsroom.

Rose turned to me. "Looks like you two have made some headway?"

"I think we got it, Rose. I really do."

The words rushed out—and caught me by surprise as they did. I hadn't felt any excitement when Clemens came by to get me and said we were meeting the editor to go over the story. It was like I wouldn't let myself go there. But now, suddenly, I felt it. I was really pumped up. I think seeing Rose did it. She reminded me of earlier in the summer—and how far we'd come since then. The funk I'd been in all week, I could feel it passing. I had an urge to tell Rose everything we had uncovered, but I knew we didn't have time.

Instead I told her, "We're gonna do it, Rose. We're gonna do it."

She squeezed my shoulders and said, "I knew you would."

Clemens was weaving his way among the reporters' desks.

"Trell," he called, waving to me. "This way."

I caught up to Clemens. "Jack Morin, he's got the largest glass house," he said, nodding toward the corner office that we were fast approaching.

"Glass house?"

"Yeah, it's what we call the editors' offices, glass houses."

I looked through the glass into other offices we passed, catching glimpses of editors working behind their desks. Some noticed us, and looked up. Others never stirred. "Fishbowls," I said. "More like fishbowls."

"That works, too," Clemens said.

Jack Morin's office was big enough to hold a large oak desk on one side, a sitting area with a couch and chairs, and also a round conference table. The office looked out onto the rear parking deck, and to the Southeast Expressway beyond it. Jack Morin and another person, a woman, were seated together at the conference table. I guessed she was one of the paper's editors, too.

"Clemens," Jack Morin called out when he saw us. "Come right in."

Jack Morin stayed in his seat, but the woman stood up.

"Hi, Clemens," she said. The two shook hands. The woman was dressed in green khaki slacks and a matching gray top that perfectly fit her tall, lean build. I thought she looked pretty cool and wondered if she was a runner. Then she turned to me and put her hand out. "I'm Helen Mulvoy," she said.

I took her hand.

"Helen's the managing editor," Clemens explained.

"I'm Trell," I said. "Van Trell Taylor."

"Nice to meet you," Helen Mulvoy said.

Jack Morin said, "I thought it would be good if Helen joined us." He lowered his head so he could look over the top of his thick-framed reading glasses. He was looking right at me, and his brow furrowed. "Clemens?" he said.

"Trell's been helping me," Clemens said. "Her father's Romero Taylor."

Jack Morin cleared his throat. "That's a tad unusual."

"She's been instrumental in digging up new information."

I liked the sound of that—*instrumental.*

Jack Morin sat there. Clemens was right. The editor in chief's voice was flat, and he hadn't moved more than an inch since we'd arrived. He wore a crisp white shirt and a navy-blue tie, and his skin was a pasty white, as if he never went outdoors.

"I think we're okay," Helen Mulvoy said.

Jack Morin sat still for a few more moments and finally shifted in his chair. "Well, then." He cleared his throat again. "Clemens, first off, let me say how happy I am to see you back working the big story. Back from the grave, so to speak."

Back from the grave? I almost gasped. Jack Morin was actually smiling. It was a strained, thin smile, but a smile. He thought he'd been clever, playing off slang for the overnight shift Clemens was no longer working. As if he was cracking a joke to get everyone relaxed. But so totally clueless, missing the reason entirely why Clemens was buried on the graveyard shift in the first place: his son.

I looked at Clemens. His face had twisted into a grimace.

"Jack," he said. "I know you probably thought that was funny. It wasn't. But, it's true—about being back." Clemens turned to look at me. "Trell here, she's been instrumental with that, too."

The room fell silent. Jack Morin had a blank look, like he didn't know what to say next. I looked around and noticed the office was filled with newspaper awards, commendations, and plaques honoring the *Globe*. Framed on one wall was a poster-size replica of the First Amendment, written in the fancy script they used in colonial times. Important front pages from the *Globe* lined another wall, and I spotted the one featuring Clemens's story that set Tony Rosario free. I couldn't help but wonder if there would be enough space for my daddy's front page.

The silence grew uncomfortable, and ended only when Helen Mulvoy began shuffling the papers she was reading when we'd first entered. "Jack?" she said.

"Yes, let's get started." Jack Morin adjusted his glasses and looked at the papers in front of him. It was Clemens's draft. "Clemens," he began. Then he paused, and added, "and Van Trell." The moment Jack Morin began to talk about the story he was different. Nothing awkward like before. With the copy in hand, he took charge, talking expertly about words, sentences, paragraphs, and overall content.

"You're on to something, no question," he said. "You've got good information—new information—to challenge the validity of Romero Taylor's murder conviction. The new alibi information, for example, is real good. Two women saying they were with Romero when the little girl was shot—that's compelling." Jack Morin used his finger to run down the page. "Tracey Dailey and—"

"Boo," I said.

Jack Morin nodded slowly. "Yes, Boo. Tracey and Boo. But, reading the draft, it's not clear to me whether you plan to use their names. Can you?"

"We're working on it," Clemens said.

"We'll get them to go on the record," I said reassuringly.

Jack Morin studied me. On purpose I'd used the newspaper term Clemens had taught me. I wanted to show the editor in chief I knew what I was doing. When people are quoted by name in the newspaper, it means they are on the record. Clemens taught me that a story is stronger when people are identified by name. It's more believable that way, a point I got right away: a story quoting Tracey Dailey saying she was with Daddy when Ruby was shot on Humboldt was way better than having it come from "a Roxbury woman who wished to remain anonymous."

"Let's do that, then," Jack Morin said. "Get them on the record." He made a checkmark in the margin of his copy. Then he flipped to the next page, and I could see that some words in the middle of the page were circled with a red pencil.

"Now, in the section here where you summarize the heart of the prosecutor's case against Mr. Taylor—and, before I get to that, let me say, Clemens, the writing is terrific. Clear and concise—a truly readable account of a complicated case."

Clemens nodded his appreciation.

"In the summary then, you explain to the reader that it was testimony from three witnesses—all teenagers at the time, in 1989—that proved crucial to Frank Flanagan being able to win a murder conviction against Mr. Taylor."

Jack Morin looked at the copy and read their names. "Monique Catron, Juanda Tillery, and Travis Golson. Do I have that right?"

"That's right," Clemens said. He shifted in his seat.

"The new information about Monique Catron's brain cancer is certainly revelatory," Jack Morin said. "Casts doubt on whether her testimony at the trial was reliable. The jury should have known her condition. That's strong stuff."

Jack Morin put the copy down. "But my question for you: What about the other two? Why aren't they in the story? According to your reporting, you have determined that all three teenagers were crucial. So, Juanda Tillery, where's she?"

"We had a great interview with her," Clemens said. Calmly, he described Juanda telling us about how she was pressured into saying things at the trial to make Daddy look guilty. "She said she lied, said she was so scared at the time she would have said anything the prosecutor and police wanted her to say."

Jack Morin looked straight at Clemens. "That's good, real good," he said. "But I don't see it here in the story, where it belongs. Why not?"

"Because she insisted everything she told us was *off* the record."

"It needs to be in the story," Jack Morin said, his voice flat and firm.

I was beginning to feel like I was in the principal's office getting bad news.

"Travis Golson?" Jack Morin said. "What about him?"

Clemens said, "We haven't been able to locate him."

"Not yet," I added quickly. "But we will."

Jack Morin and Helen Mulvoy exchanged looks.

Clemens sat forward. "Okay, the draft's got some gaps—I get that. But hear me out. Of course we want to get Juanda Tillery to go on the record. Find Travis Golson. Sometimes, in stories like this, you get lucky and hit all the bases in a single shot. But here's my strategy for this story—we start off with a first installment revealing the alibi and Monique Catron's cancer as big new developments, and then we keep working to get Juanda and Travis, and we use them in follow-up stories."

Jack Morin listened. He was unmoved.

"Jack, it's strong stuff as it is—you already said so," Clemens argued. "We get the ball rolling, and then we leverage the first story to spring loose the rest."

"I hear you," the editor said, "and sometimes we do use an approach like that in an ongoing investigative story, publish each major piece of news as we get it."

"So?" Clemens said.

"But not on a story of this scale," the editor ruled. "Ruby Graham's murder is one of the most notorious in our lifetime, if not in Boston's history. She was so young, and it was a time of unprecedented drugs and violence. People thought the city was going to explode. When police arrested Romero Taylor, and when Frank Flanagan—the same Frank Flanagan who's running for mayor, I don't have to remind you—when Flanagan put Mr. Taylor away, people thought they'd saved the city and done God's work. My point is you don't challenge that legacy piecemeal. It's got to be airtight, and, from what I see here, you don't have critical mass."

Jack Morin pushed his chair back and began to stand up.

"We're going to hold the presses on this one—for now," he said. "But Clemens—and you too, Van Trell—as disappointing as this news is, I want you back out there. This kid Travis, he seems huge. Find him and it's a new ballgame."

As if we didn't already know Travis Golson was huge. We left the corner office, and the thought crossed my mind that there wasn't going to be a framed front page of the *Boston Globe* with Clemens's Romero Taylor story. Not ever.

Clemens and I barely said a word during the ride home. When he pulled up at my house, he turned off the car's engine. "Okay, Trell, we got our work cut out."

I was silent.

"He's a good editor," Clemens said. "Story like this, the stakes are huge. You're asking readers—the public—to correct their understanding of a major event: who killed Ruby Graham.

You don't want any gaps, give the police and Flanagan any opening to refute the story. I tried, but Jack's got a point."

I wasn't feeling any better. I wanted Daddy to come home.

"I'll start working the phones again. We keep going."

"I think I'll go for a run," I said.

"Then what?"

I got out of the car.

"Trell?"

"Yeah."

"I never said this was gonna be a sprint. It's a marathon."

"I know. It's just — with the draft, and with what we'd found, I thought we were there. In that office, I saw those framed front pages on the wall. I saw your story about Tony Rosario. I started to picture our story up there, too."

Clemens smiled. "That'd be nice. For now, though, let's have a plan."

We talked about Juanda Tillery and how best to go back at her. We decided going to the Salon de Paris again was not a good idea. Instead, I would write her a note asking her to reconsider. Not come on too strong, but start with the note, then ask her again to help us. I could drop the note off during my run.

I closed the car door and walked to my apartment. Clemens pulled away from the curb and beeped the horn a couple of times, in a cheerleading kind of way. Inside, I got a piece of paper and wrote Juanda Tillery something that was short and simple. I sealed it inside an envelope, and while changing quickly into my running clothes, I thought of something else. I thought of Paul

Parish. I felt bad for the way I'd treated him when all he wanted to do was hang out. I'd told him I'd get him the catalog for the Weld School, but then never did anything about it. I decided this was as good a time as any. I pulled together the school materials from my closet and stuffed them into a running backpack. I called Paul to make sure he was around.

"Yeah," Paul said. He seemed eager. "Come over, if you want."

"I don't think I should."

"Why not?"

"Your uncle."

"What about my uncle?"

"I'll tell you later," I said.

"That's kinda mysterious," he said. "But okay. You know the alley that runs next to the house? There's a gate in the wall my uncle built when he bought the place. Meet me there."

I pictured the massive ten-foot cement wall surrounding Thumper's fortress and knew where Paul meant. "That works," I said. "I got to do one errand, so let's say forty minutes or so."

"See you then."

I raced out the door. For the first time in days, I had a bounce in my step; I was on the run again. In twenty minutes, I reached West Selden Street and Juanda Tillery's front door. The dog inside began barking like crazy. I slipped the envelope through the mail slot and hoped for the best. Hoped the dog wouldn't eat it and that Juanda would find it. Then I took off for Castlegate Road. I started feeling shaky the closer I got. It had been two weeks since

Thumper had chased me from Tracey Dailey's place, and I'd been avoiding going anywhere near his turf. When I got close, I slowed way down and practically tiptoed to the alley alongside his house.

I was a few minutes early. Even though the wall was ten feet high, the house rose up tall on the other side. It really was gross, the way Thumper had painted the house a deep green with neon-orange trim and black iron bars in all the windows. Thumper wasn't very original, either. I could hear The Notorious B.I.G.'s "Ready to Die" blasting from a front room on the second floor. The album had been around forever. I'd grown up listening to Biggie's gangsta rap that so many boys in the neighborhood tried to imitate. "You better grab your guns 'cause I'm ready, ready, I'm ready to die!" Someone upstairs belted out the lyrics along with the song, and I figured it must be Thumper himself. Terrible voice.

I hugged the wall as I made my way down the alley, as if that would keep me hidden, until I reached the wooden door. I heard rustling on the other side, then Paul's voice. He was calming the guard dogs, the ones Thumper owned to roam the grounds. I could tell Paul was ushering them into a pen. Then I saw the latch move up and down. The door rattled, like it was stuck. It suddenly popped open.

"Trell," Paul said. He seemed surprised. "You're here already."

"Got the errand done faster than I thought."

I dug into my running pack and pulled out the school materials.

"Here," I said, handing him the Weld catalog.

"Thanks," Paul said. He looked around. "Hey, Trell."

"What?"

"Why you uptight about coming around?"

I had thought I'd make a quick drop and be off. Maybe plan to meet another time to talk about the Weld. Even if we were out of sight in the alley, I still felt jumpy.

"Trell, what's up?"

"Fine," I said, and I told him. I told him Clemens and I had been working on my daddy's conviction, uncovering new information to show his innocence. I told him his uncle had found out, and didn't like us poking around, though I didn't know why. I told him his uncle came looking for me at Tracey Dailey's, real angry.

"I barely got away. At least that's how it felt."

When I finished, Paul looked stunned, the words hitting his head like a wooden bat. He didn't say anything, and after a few seconds, he turned his head toward the second-floor window where the music was coming from. Then he looked back at me, but still didn't say a word. He just stared off into space.

"What?" I finally said.

"I'm thinking," Paul said.

"Thinking what?"

"Thinking maybe this has something to do with the way my uncle's been."

"Huh?"

"Lately my uncle's been really spazzing." Paul began to pace. "You remember that guy, works for my uncle, the one who rode in Vinnie's Van to Water Country with all us kids a few weeks ago? Remember him?"

"The one with the scar on his face?"

"Yeah, that's the one. The scar guy. My uncle's driver. Gofer. Errand boy. My uncle treats him like a slave."

"Working for your uncle — I'd sure hate doing that."

"Yeah, well, you'd hate it even more now. My uncle's been in this guy's face like never before. Won't let the guy go anywhere. Ordered him not to leave the grounds. Actually told the guy that for the 'foreseeable future,' he was not even supposed to talk to anyone. He's just stuck in his shack out back. It's like he's in lockdown."

My neck stiffened. "Yeah. Lockdown. That would really suck."

Paul tried to backpedal. "Trell, I didn't mean that."

"Well, thanks for reminding me. I got to go." I turned away.

"Trell." Paul reached out his arm. I kept walking.

"What Travis is dealing with isn't anything like your dad. I'm not an idiot."

"Travis?" I whipped around.

It was my turn to feel like I'd been hit in the head.

"Yeah," Paul said.

"You said his name's *Travis*?"

"Yeah, Travis."

"What's his last name?"

"I dunno. Goleman? Somethin' like that."

"Golson?"

"Yeah, that's it. Golson. Travis Golson."

Jeezus. I gulped.

CHAPTER 21

RUN, TRELL, RUN

Clemens kept up as best he could as we made our way from his place on Esmond Street to Castlegate Road. The late afternoon sun cast long shadows, and as we got closer to Castlegate, I tried to hide inside them. We turned down the alley and inched our way to the door in Thumper's wall.

The last thirty minutes had been a blur. When I got over the shock of finding out that the man with the scar was Travis Golson and that he was practically a prisoner on Thumper's back lot, I told Paul how Clemens and I had been searching for Travis for weeks.

"He's the most important witness," I said. "He was the one who testified he saw Daddy with a gun at the time of the shooting. He claimed he knew Daddy, but my daddy never saw him before the trial. It was like he just came out of nowhere and gave police the last piece of the puzzle they needed to get Daddy."

"What should we do?" Paul said.

"I'm not sure."

After the scare at Tracey Dailey's, I knew better than to try anything alone.

"Clemens," I said.

Paul promised he would wait at the door. I took off and made it to Clemens's apartment in record time. He was on the phone calling around.

"I found him!" I shouted between breaths. "I found him!"

Clemens put the phone down. "What? Who?"

"Travis Golson!" I shouted. "I know where he is." I explained everything as fast as I could. Clemens ran his hands through his hair, as if he was pulling on his brain. I'd never seen him so rattled.

"This is crazy." He was trying to take it all in. "Travis Golson's been at Thumper's all this time? Why? What's Thumper care?"

"I don't know," I said. "I just know Thumper keeps him out back in some shack."

Clemens quit asking questions. "We need to talk to him."

"How do we do that?"

"I don't know."

"Call the police?" I said.

"What would we tell them?"

Clemens was right. Travis might have been number one on our most-wanted list, but not the police's. So what if he lived at

Thumper's house? That's not a crime. Thumper's got him in a shack, but who knew for sure what that was all about?

Besides, *call the police?* What was I thinking? Since when had the police done right by my daddy? Everything we'd uncovered so far we'd done on our own.

I told Clemens that Paul Parish was waiting for me at the door in the alley. I needed to go back and tell him something. Paul was on our side, I said.

"That's our play." Clemens slapped the table. "We go in, get Travis."

Paul was waiting like he said he would. He opened the door, and Clemens stepped through, nodding to Paul and putting a finger up to his lips to keep quiet. Escaping from Tracey Dailey's might have been scary, but I was way more scared entering Thumper's fortress.

There was no more music blaring from upstairs, and the place was quiet in a spooky kind of way. The dogs—three of them—wagged their tails and whimpered at Paul as we neared the pen. Paul stopped to rub their noses through the fencing and shush them. Then we followed him toward the rear of the property. For Roxbury, Thumper's yard was big. It went back deep and was littered with empty barrels, boxes, tools, and all kinds of junk. Three big black Harley motorcycles stood on their kickstands in a row, engine parts scattered around them. Farther back, two cars without any wheels sat on cinder blocks.

"Isn't that one a Suzuki?" Clemens whispered.

I walked over to the SUV for a closer look. It was covered in gray grime. I ran my index finger across the front bumper. "It's white, too."

The shack actually looked like a makeshift mini-apartment, with a power line running to it from the house, a regular door, and even a window, although the shade was drawn. When we reached the entrance, I could hear a TV inside.

Paul tapped on the door, then opened it slowly.

"Travis?" he said. "It's Paul."

Looking into the room, I saw a man sprawled on a cot with his legs twisted in the bed sheets. The body stirred at the sound of Paul's voice, but very slowly. We stepped inside. I covered my mouth and nose. The air was stale and heavy, and the room stank, as though Travis hadn't showered in weeks. Clemens waved his hand in front of his face as if trying to clear the air. The room was empty except for the TV, which sat on a milk crate; a mini-fridge; and a small wooden table next to the cot.

"These people, they want to talk to you," Paul said.

Travis rolled over. I saw the scar on his right cheek. He was wearing a dirty T-shirt and sweatpants cut off at the knees. His face was slack, and his eyes were glassy. He seemed dazed. As he rolled over awkwardly, his arm hit the table next to the cot, and that's when I saw the pills. Not one bottle, but several. He knocked them over.

"Oh, jeez," he moaned at the spilled pills. "Thumper'll be pissed."

"Travis," Paul said. "I brought these people."

Travis pulled himself up to the edge of the cot. He moved in slow motion. He rubbed his face like he was scratching an itch, just kept moving his hands up and down fast.

"I'm Trell Taylor," I said.

The rubbing stopped. Travis let his hands drop to the mattress. I could see his eyes were bloodshot and blank. He struggled to keep his balance and stay seated on the cot.

Clemens said, "He's been drugged."

Travis opened his eyes wider. He turned his head, his eyes roaming the room like a spotlight. They found me and stopped. Looking my way, he slapped himself gently on the cheek. He squinted, trying to focus on me.

"That mean you Romero's daughter?" he asked.

"Yes."

"You at Water Country that day?"

"I was."

Travis hung his head, rolled it sideways, mumbling things we couldn't follow, but also saying things we could. "Didn't have no choice," he said. "No choice."

"What do you mean, no choice, Travis?" Clemens said.

Before Travis could say anything else, I heard the dogs. They were barking, low at first, then loudly—loud and nonstop, like gunfire.

It was too late to run.

Thumper Parish's tall, wide body filled the door.

"Who the hell put the dogs in the pen?"

Thumper was dressed in loose-fitting black linen pants with an unbuttoned short-sleeved shirt that revealed his flat, hard stomach. He was gripping a pistol in his right hand. His eyes—clear and cold—scanned the room. Then he smiled. "Go figure. I come out here to check on Travis, and look at what we got." His teeth were gold capped. "What a nice surprise."

His voice was a throaty snarl.

He turned his gaze to Paul. "This your idea of a playdate, Paulie?" He didn't wait for an answer, and the phony smile twisted into one of disgust. "Deal with you later." Then Thumper waved his gun hand in circles. "Into the house," he commanded. "Let's go. Paulie, you help Travis. Bring his medicine."

We fell in line. Clemens first. Then me. Then Paul and Travis. Paul had his arm looped under Travis's armpit to help him walk. Thumper was last. The march across the backyard seemed to take forever. The dogs had quieted again, and all I heard was the sound of my own breathing, short and shallow.

We had almost reached the rear porch when Travis staggered. Paul lowered him onto the rim of a big truck tire that was lying flat in the yard. Thumper waited as Travis's head rolled and he breathed heavily.

"My boy, Travis," Thumper sighed. He rubbed the stubble on his chin. "Not been his regular self lately." He turned to Clemens and me. "Figured he needed a break, is all, to ride *this thing* out." I could tell Thumper meant us, the way his voice bore down on those words. "I keep tellin' him, this, too, will pass."

He waved the handgun toward the house. "C'mon."

Paul helped Travis to his feet, and we climbed the rear stairs. There was a gas grill on the porch along with a wicker table and chairs. Leaning on the railing was a stack of campaign signs stapled to wooden stakes. FLANAGAN FOR MAYOR, the signs read, the lettering in white on a backing of red and blue.

Thumper used his foot to push open the rear door. The long hallway was unlit, and the floorboards creaked as we made our way inside. I could see light coming from the other end. Thumper shouted, "The room on the left."

We walked through French doors into a large rectangular space with high ceilings. It was apparently Thumper's game room. The floor was covered with a thick shag carpet. The far end had a pool table, a dartboard, and a corner bar with stools. Behind the bar was mirrored, with shelves stocked with bottles. Black leather chairs and a couch were arranged throughout. Nearer to us was a jukebox, with wires running to speakers on the wall on each end. Four large windows were covered with plywood. There was no natural light. The room was airtight.

Hanging from the wall directly across from the entrance was a life-size photo of Thumper. He stared straight into the camera, his eyes ablaze. He was wearing black, including a black cape, and was leaning against the bumper of his black Mercedes, his arms folded across his chest. Thumper Parish sure had one big ego, probably saw himself as a gangsta movie star. To me it was pretty strange. If we weren't in such a fix, I might have laughed.

Posters from actual movies also hung in the room, but the picture that caught my eye was a smaller one just inside the door.

It was the photograph taken to commemorate the bust of drug lord George "G-man" Whigham, the same picture that was in the living room at Richie Boyle's. In it, police officials flanked District Attorney Frank Flanagan and Detective Richie Boyle. I took a step for a closer look.

"What you lookin' at?" Thumper said.

Nodding at the photo, I said, "G-man. It was a big deal, his getting busted."

"Damn straight," Thumper said.

My mind was racing. Thumper had the same photo as Richie Boyle, and I remembered the block party Thumper had thrown after G-man was arrested. I realized: Flanagan, Richie, Thumper— they all got something from G-man's demise. Flanagan and Richie got themselves a headline-making bust. Thumper got control of the streets. They could all celebrate. One for all, all for one.

Thumper moved closer until his nose practically touched the glass.

"Looking for yourself?" Clemens said. He was connecting dots, same as me.

Thumper didn't answer, just grunted. He jabbed his finger at a spot in the middle of the row of men, right next to Frank Flanagan. "Right there is where I go," he said. Thumper was bragging; he couldn't help himself.

Clemens said, "Meaning?"

Thumper turned his head and eyed Clemens suspiciously, then allowed a smile to stretch across his face. "Let me just say, without Thumper, Flanagan got nothin'."

Travis moaned. He'd been leaning on Paul the whole time but was struggling to stay on his feet. Thumper pointed with his gun hand across the room. He barked at Paul. "Put my boy down on the couch there." Thumper stepped away from the photograph and began walking across the carpeted room.

Clemens wasn't done connecting dots. He said he had another question.

"The campaign signs on the porch. The ones for Flanagan."

"What of 'em?"

Thumper looked hard at Clemens.

Clemens was studying Thumper, his head tilted. He was in full reporter mode, and I could tell he'd paused for effect. He waited a few seconds before continuing.

"I'm thinking you two are close. I'm thinking you're Flanagan's guy."

Not a question, a statement.

Thumper didn't like it.

"He'd make a great mayor, is all," he said with a cold finality.

But Clemens continued. "I'm not talking politics. I mean the street. You're Flanagan's guy on the street. You're his informant."

It's what I'd been thinking too—Thumper was a snitch. It's how Flanagan and Richie were able to bust G-man. Thumper told them when and where to find G-man with his drugs and guns. But I was worried for Clemens the moment he put it to Thumper. Everyone knew being a snitch for police was the worst.

Instead, to my surprise, Thumper twirled the gun above his head and let loose a howl of laughter. "Flanagan's guy? That's nuts. I ain't nobody's fool." Thumper bent over in stitches. "You got it backwards, man. Flanagan's mine."

Thumper began to pace the room. "I'm gonna teach you somethin'," he said. "Gonna call it Life on the Streets 101. Either you beat the street or the street beats you." Yeah, he said, he gave Flanagan a piece of "street intel" once in a while, some tidbit of information to help Frank Flanagan solve a case. "But rule number one is this: the information I gave Flanagan was always something gonna help me. Take the G-man. Instead of me having to make a move against him — some act of violence — I whisper in Flanagan's ear. Boom, just like that, police move in, bust G-man, and he's gone. That outcome is good for Flanagan and surely good for me."

Thumper punched the air like an exclamation point. "That ain't snitchin', not in my book. It's smart business, and even smarter is what I got in return. The state police investigating me? Flanagan let me know. The FBI — yep, the big-time FBI — trying to hide a bug here in my home? Flanagan tips me off. Federal drug agents start following me, day and night? Flanagan tells me. You name it, anybody tries to move on me, Flanagan is there for me. Why? Because Frank Flanagan — Mr. Law and Order — needs me on the street to throw something his way, make him look good."

Thumper nodded with self-satisfaction.

Clemens broke the silence. "Richie Boyle? He part of this?"

"Richie?" Thumper said. "Naw. I talk only to Flanagan. Richie maybe suspected something, but he didn't want to know. He basically did what Flanagan told him."

"Ruby Graham?" Clemens said.

Everything changed the moment Clemens mentioned her name. Thumper shut down, as if a switch had gone off. Maybe he could brag about having Frank Flanagan on a string, talk like he was some kind of criminal genius. Made me sick, actually, especially thinking about Flanagan running for mayor. But Ruby Graham?

Thumper glared at Clemens, said only, "That one's complicated."

Everything clicked in that instant for me. I felt on fire all over. "It was you!" I didn't care if we were prisoners in Thumper's castle. I didn't care if Thumper had a gun. I didn't care about anything but the truth. "It was you!" I was shouting.

Thumper snapped. He leaned into me, like a rattlesnake coiled and ready to strike. "You listen, you punk," his words hard and louder than mine. "Humboldt hurt my boys. Robbed 'em. Cut 'em. Can't let them be gettin' away with that."

"You killed Ruby Graham," I charged.

I met Thumper's eyes straight on. I saw only bottomless darkness, and it sent a chill down my spine. He didn't waver, said matter-of-factly, "Humboldt boys duck behind the blue mailbox, it's their fault the little girl got in the way."

I seethed with anger. "You killed her."

Thumper said no more.

"And you put it on Daddy."

He didn't blink.

Clemens pulled me to him.

"Here's what I think," Clemens said. "I think the city's in an uproar, Flanagan needs to solve this fast, and you tell him the word on the street is Romero Taylor was the shooter. You even get Flanagan the names of a couple of girls who might know something, and Flanagan instructs Richie to round them up."

Thumper looked at us blankly. He would neither confirm nor deny.

"I'm also thinking you had something to do with Travis Golson magically appearing right before the trial starts. I'm thinking maybe Flanagan was saying the girls weren't enough, that he needed a witness to tie it all together, put a gun in Romero's hand. Lo and behold, you produce Travis Golson — icing on the cake."

Thumper still didn't budge.

Clemens paused. "It's actually kind of brilliant," he said.

I couldn't believe it. Clemens flattering him? I shot Clemens a look.

Clemens continued admiringly. "How'd you *ever* come up with Travis?"

That's when I realized what Clemens was up to — and it worked.

"Found him on the street," Thumper said, walking over to Travis on the couch. "No family. Homeless. Just a kid. In trouble big time — a bunch of arrests."

"Perfect," Clemens said.

Thumper continued. "Took him in, fed him, got him pocket money. Treated him like a prince. Told Flanagan that Travis Golson was the witness he'd been looking for. Flanagan was over the moon. So, in return for his new testimony, Flanagan took care of the criminal cases—poof, all gone—and I promised to take care of Travis."

Thumper looked down at Travis. "Worked out great? No complaints?" He turned to us. "Until lately. You two poking around, stirring up trouble," he said. "I figured you'd get nowhere, whole thing'd go away quick. But no, you surprised me, tracking down Monique's mother, then Tracey Dailey. It's why I been keeping Travis on the down low, for safekeeping. And now, 'cause you two keep messin' things up, I gotta figure out my next move."

"You're always figuring every angle," Clemens said.

"I'm Thumper Parish. I play chess; everyone else is playin' checkers."

In the silence that followed, Travis dropped off into a deep sleep on the couch. Paul slumped into one of the chairs, his arms folded, his face crunched in frustration. Thumper made Clemens and me stand against a side wall, beneath a poster for a movie called *Hoodlum*, starring Laurence Fishburne and Vanessa Williams. Then he stormed off to the pool table at the far end of the room. He slammed his gun down, picked up a stick and set up a rack of balls.

He broke the balls and took a shot. Then he crouched for another. He studied the cue ball, moved the stick back and forth, but before taking the shot, he abruptly stood straight up and slammed the pool stick against the table. The stick flew off the green felt, hit the shag carpet, and bounced away.

Thumper marched across the room, rubbing his neck while staring at us.

"There's a room in the basement," he announced. "Gonna get you settled down there, get me some more time to figure this thing out."

I didn't like the sound of that. Locked up in Thumper's basement. Thumper Parish, who had killed in the past and wouldn't hesitate to kill again — and who could count on Frank Flanagan for protection. Couldn't get any worse than that.

Thumper began waving his gun like a lasso, herding us toward the door. "Paulie, you tend to Travis." I looked at Clemens. His eyes flickered toward the two French doors for a second, and his jaw tightened. "That the right move, Thumper?" he chided. I could tell Clemens was trying to distract Thumper.

Thumper turned on Clemens. "I'm not worried," he snarled.

"Just asking," Clemens said.

I watched Clemens's eyes flicker again, in a way that meant he wanted me to go first. I started walking. Clemens fell in line behind me. Thumper was behind Clemens, while Paulie worked on getting Travis to his feet. I made it three steps into the hallway, Clemens right behind me, when all of a sudden I could feel Clemens spinning around. I looked in time to see him kick the French door.

The door smacked Thumper, knocking him off balance.

Clemens screamed, "Run, Trell, run!"

In the same instant, the gun fired, and I heard Clemens howl in pain. I turned to see Clemens gripping his shoulder as he leaned hard against the door, blocking Thumper. I saw the pistol fly from Thumper's hand as he pushed his way past Clemens. Clemens crumpled to the floor.

"Run!" he ordered, his voice weaker.

I took off. I ran down the dark hall toward the back. Right away, I knew Thumper was after me. I could hear him snarling, his long legs pounding the wood floor. I didn't want to think what he'd do if he caught me. I never felt so scared.

I raced out the door and leaped off the porch, running straight for the door in the cement wall. There was a stretch of open space and I pumped faster, increasing my leg turnover the way I would to sprint to the finish line of a race. It made a big difference. Thumper fell behind. He swore at me, then I heard him stumble and gasp. He had tripped on something, but I didn't dare look.

I flew through the door and into the alley. It was pitch-black. Night had fallen. I ran up the alley faster than my mind could think. I didn't know what to do. I just ran. I reached the street, and for the first time stole a look back. Thumper had not made it through the alley door yet. I turned left onto Castlegate and began a deep breath of relief when I ran blindly into someone's arms.

I squealed as I was lifted off the ground and my legs ran in place. I felt like a spider caught in a web. I couldn't see who it was, and my first thought was, *Thumper?* I wondered how could Thumper have gotten here. I squirmed harder.

"Trell, slow down."

The voice belonged to Richie Boyle.

"Let me go! Let me go!"

"Cut it out, Trell," he said.

But I wouldn't. I kept kicking and screaming.

"I'm here to help," he said.

Help? My mind raced.

"Where's Clemens?" he asked. "Where is he, Trell?"

His voice was urgent, like it mattered. He was looking past me, down the alley.

So I said, "Thumper's got him. Travis Golson, too."

"Travis Golson?" His eyes lit up.

"Clemens is hurt, I think."

Richie dropped me like a rock. He took off down the alley. I followed. The workouts Richie did at home, the chin-up bar and weights, they'd all paid off, because he moved quickly and with ferocity. He pushed his way through the door and headed toward the house. I spotted Thumper. He was lumbering up the stairs to the rear porch, not yet back inside.

Richie Boyle hit the stairs running and threw himself at Thumper as Thumper reached the top step. Richie climbed onto Thumper's back, tackling him. Thumper roared. The two rolled into the hallway, and I lost sight of them. I heard shouting and punching until, suddenly, the two of them, a tangle of arms and legs, came exploding outside. They tumbled down the stairs into the yard, where Richie somehow managed to get a grip on Thumper's shoulders. Richie cocked his arms and hurled Thumper into a post. It knocked Thumper out cold.

The whole thing was over in seconds. I'd never seen anything like it. Richie staggered over to Thumper, who lay unconscious on the ground. He grabbed Thumper by the collar and scanned the backyard. Richie gulped air as he dragged Thumper a few feet to the closest empty vehicle that sat on cinder blocks. Richie hoisted Thumper by his arms and threw him into the front seat.

I crossed the yard. Richie was using a piece of rope he'd found on the ground to tie Thumper in. I could see Richie's face was scratched badly, and a steady trickle of blood oozed from one of his nostrils.

"It's the Suzuki," I blurted out.

"What?" Richie said. His chest heaved as he finished the knot.

"The white Suzuki," I said. "Thumper's white Suzuki from that night."

Richie lifted his head to study the SUV more closely. He grunted, then looked at Thumper. "Let you go once, when I shouldn't have. Not gonna do it twice."

We both turned toward the house.

Richie said, "Trell, there's a radio in my car, parked back on the street. I'm going inside, get Clemens and the rest. I need you to go to the car, call the police."

Call the police?

"Can you do that?"

"Yeah," I said. "I can do that."

CHAPTER 22
THE HOMECOMING

I did it. I called the police, I mean. I was nervous because in my experience police did more wrong than right. But Richie Boyle had come out of the blue and surprised me to no end, so when he ran inside Thumper's house to find Clemens and shouted, "Call the police," I did it. I ran to his car and called for help. We needed it.

I heard the sirens first, then saw blue lights crisscrossing the night sky. Within minutes, a whole bunch of noisy, angry police cruisers roared down Castlegate Road and screeched to a stop in front of Thumper's castle.

I joined Paul on the sidewalk to watch everything. The police came in force, and they did their job. Thumper Parish, in handcuffs, was hauled out of the backyard. He was still woozy from being knocked out, but he wasn't completely out of it — he glared at me and Paul while police put him into the back of a cruiser. Other police searched the house from top to bottom. They began removing Thumper's supply of handguns, rifles, ammunition, and even an Uzi machine gun. We learned later that one of the pistols matched the handgun used to kill Ruby Graham. It seemed crazy that Thumper had held on to the murder weapon, but Paul said he actually wasn't surprised. "He probably figured he was smarter than everybody else—better to hold on to the gun than take the chance of someone finding it if he tossed it."

Richie Boyle, holding a white cloth to his nose until the bleeding stopped, seemed to be everywhere, like he was directing traffic. He talked to the stream of police officials who kept showing up and also worked the phone. He was apparently attending to us, because when a couple of social workers arrived to be with Paul, Richie came over to make sure Paul was okay with that. Paul was. Even if the police had let him, he said he never wanted to spend another night in Thumper's house. His life was about to change forever, but Paul didn't seem to mind.

I spotted Ma rushing down the sidewalk from the direction of where we lived. I ran into her arms. We hugged tight. "Trell, oh, Trell," she kept saying. She said Richie Boyle had called her at home. I felt my whole body go soft in her arms and realized it was like I'd been holding my breath the whole time. "We found Travis," I said. Richie Boyle came over, told Ma, "Trell did great work tonight."

Travis was totally out of it when ambulance workers wheeled him from the house on a stretcher, placed him in the back of a white ambulance van, and left for Boston City Hospital. I was worried most about Clemens. I was on the sidewalk with Ma, her arm around me, when we finally saw him. He appeared at Thumper's front door, on his feet, which was a relief. He was helped by an ambulance worker, and together they walked gingerly down the front toward another ambulance. Clemens had his right arm tucked close against his chest. I could see bandages where his shirt had been cut away.

"Clemens," I called.

"Trell!" he yelled. He veered toward us. "I'm okay. It grazed me."

We hugged awkwardly, me and Ma and Clemens. Clemens looked at me. "You okay, Trell?" I told him I was—scared, but okay. In a rush of words, I told him about running into Richie Boyle in the alley, the biggest surprise ever.

"Knocked my socks off, too," Clemens said. "I was leaning against the doorjamb bleeding when I see Richie running down the hall." Clemens said Richie had filled him in while they were inside. "He had us under surveillance. No kidding." He said Richie had started keeping an eye on us after we were asking about Travis. "He was worried. Said he realized he'd made a ton of bad choices years ago while working for Flanagan. Said he never knew the whole truth about Flanagan and Thumper, but he wasn't trying to know, either—like that saying, 'see no evil.' Said he was focused only on getting convictions, no matter what it took. Especially in Ruby Graham's case. But his suspicions had been eating away at him for years. It was why he quit—and why he wasn't supporting Flanagan for mayor. When we came calling, asking questions, he couldn't take it anymore. He wanted the truth, not just a conviction."

"About time, you ask me."

Clemens said, "*Just* in time."

The ambulance worker interrupted. "Mr. Bittner, please. We need to go."

"Okay, okay." Clemens looked at us quickly — a bright intensity in his eyes. "They're taking me to Boston City, get my arm looked at. But I won't be long. Shey, can you get Trell over to the paper, meet me there?"

Ma was flustered. "You mean the newspaper?"

Clemens nodded. "Yep, the *Globe.*"

Ma said, "But it's so late."

"I know," Clemens said, "but we got a story to finish, and I need Trell."

We holed up in Jack Morin's office, Clemens seated at the editor's desk, typing away on the computer, me standing by, either looking over Clemens's shoulder or grabbing some of our notes and documents spread out on the table. Clemens was slowed by the bullet wound, and he even had an arm sling. But he'd removed it and managed to peck away on the keyboard using both hands.

Luckily, since he'd done that first draft, the story was already pretty much organized and in shape. The main thing was writing up and inserting all the new information Jack Morin had wanted about Travis Golson and Travis's false testimony, plus the new drama at Thumper's castle with his arrest.

I peered at the computer screen as Clemens typed. "Don't forget when Thumper was bragging, 'Flanagan's mine.'" My head was full of things Thumper had said, quotes I'd memorized the way a reporter does, to use later in a story. "Or this quote, when Thumper said, 'Anybody tries to move on me, Flanagan is there for me. Why? Because Frank Flanagan — Mr. Law and Order — needs me.'"

"Slow down, Trell," Clemens said.

I couldn't. I wanted to be sure the story spelled out in detail how wrong Frank Flanagan had been in every way possible — for being in cahoots with Thumper Parish and for framing Daddy for Ruby's murder. It was unbelievably sickening, and I felt anger like I'd never felt. People needed to know. "Don't forget the line when Thumper's thumpin' his chest: 'I play chess; everyone else is playin' checkers.'" I slammed the desk. "Except now it's checkmate."

We were on deadline for the Sunday edition, the *Globe*'s biggest circulation day. Jack Morin paced the hall outside his office, not wanting to put any more pressure on Clemens but wanting him to hurry up so he could edit the story and oversee its layout. Ma and Rose made sure Clemens and I had plenty to eat, carrying a tray of sandwiches and drinks from the cafeteria.

With less than ten minutes to spare, Clemens hit the Send button. In Helen Mulvoy's office, Helen and Jack Morin gave the story a quick edit. I could see Jack Morin through the glass wall smiling as he read. He punched the sky.

"You nailed it," he shouted to us through the glass.

Within minutes the Sunday edition was rolling off the huge printing presses downstairs. The story was splashed across the front page, under a screaming headline, "DOUBT CAST OVER RUBY GRAHAM VERDICT." The story recapped Ruby's killing in 1988, Romero Taylor's conviction a year later, and then said, "But a *Globe* investigation has found a prosecution marred by corruption that included suppressing key evidence and intimidating witnesses into testifying falsely." It was all there—Monique's brain cancer, Tracey and Boo's new alibi information, and what Clemens termed "the unholy alliance between the prosecutor and a drug lord," meaning Frank Flanagan and Thumper Parish. In summarizing our findings, the story said, "The *Globe*'s investigation demonstrates that Romero Taylor, who has protested his innocence from the day of his arrest, was not the killer."

It felt unreal. I stared at the front page after Jack Morin had flattened it onto the conference table in his office—and almost stopped breathing when I saw the beginning of the article, where the name of the reporter goes:

"By Clemens Bittner, Globe Staff, and Van Trell Taylor, Globe Correspondent."

Things happened really fast after that. The story was a huge smash, the talk of the town all day Sunday on radio and TV. On

Monday morning the FBI and federal prosecutors announced that Frank Flanagan and the Suffolk County District Attorney's office were under investigation. Reporters descended on Flanagan's campaign headquarters on Tremont Street only to find it empty and locked up. During live TV newscasts from the sidewalk out front, reporters said that, according to a campaign spokesman, Flanagan was dropping out of the mayor's race. He also dropped out of sight. No reporter could find Frank Flanagan anywhere for comment.

First thing Tuesday morning, Ma and I found ourselves racing downtown to meet Nora and attend an emergency hearing Superior Court Judge Nancy Ball convened to examine the new information revealed in the *Globe*'s investigation. The courtroom was packed with reporters and spectators, and a line of people wanting to get inside snaked down the hallway, down the stairs, and into the front lobby. It was a real circus.

Right off, Nora, dressed in a summer suit and all fired up, urged the judge to throw out Daddy's conviction, citing the "toxic and corrupt conspiracy" that was exposed in the newspaper story "between the district attorney and a Roxbury crime boss," along with the "corrupt basis by which Mr. Frank Flanagan and his cohorts framed one Romero Taylor for the tragic slaying of young Ruby Graham."

Judge Ball listened intently but then cut Nora off, saying she would not base a ruling on a newspaper article alone. She wanted verification under oath. That's when the large wooden side door swung open, and all eyes turned to see Lola Catron enter the courtroom. She was escorted to the witness stand, where she was sworn in and promised to tell the whole truth and nothing but the truth.

The judge had ordered officials to produce Miss Lola and the others to give testimony at the special session. I knew what Miss Lola was going to say, having heard it all before, but was still glued to my seat listening to her tell the whole world about her daughter's brain cancer and the pressure police put on her to lie. It was like watching our story come to life on a big stage. She was followed by Tracey Dailey and Boo, who spelled out the alibi. Even Juanda Tillery appeared, which was a surprise. Juanda was never mentioned in our story because of her demand that she not be, but on the witness stand, she told the judge that after reading the article in the newspaper, she'd had second thoughts. "I decided coming forward was the right thing to do." I also think she'd been watching the TV coverage and wanted a piece of the spotlight. She walked into court preening for the cameras, her hair and nails freshly done. She looked great. Nora, Clemens, and I sneaked looks and traded smiles while listening to her testify about how police had intimidated her to lie.

Travis Golson's testimony pulled on the heartstrings, as he described being young and homeless until Thumper Parish took him in. "Lying didn't seem like a big deal," he said. "I got food, money, a home, and when Mr. Flanagan nol-prossed my cases, I got a free pass in court, too." I nodded and half smiled when Travis tried using the Latin term for when a criminal case is dismissed. Travis went on to describe living at Thumper's and working for him, never really questioning any of it, even as Thumper "acted like I was his property." Travis figured he was in debt. But this summer he began to feel different, "first after hearing about that girl and the reporter snooping around," and then seeing me at Water Country. "Made me think about things," he told the judge. "Realize this girl's grown up with her daddy in prison, and I had somethin' big to do with that." It was like he awoke from a bad dream, but then Thumper got in his face, came down harder than ever on him. "I was torn," he said. "Seemed I owed Thumper, but I also felt rotten."

It was then Travis got choked up. "I'm sorry I lied," he said.

The hardest thing was watching Richie Boyle. He squirmed on the witness stand and looked so uncomfortable up there in front of everybody. Clemens said Richie knew he was a target of the new investigation but, unlike Flanagan, he didn't want to hide. He wanted to get out front, show he was cooperating and coming clean. He was in trouble and knew it, Clemens said, but had made peace with the idea that he was going to have to pay a price for the mistakes he made.

"He really is a good cop," Clemens whispered to me.

Under oath, Richie said he'd looked the other way when it came to Flanagan and Thumper, something he now regretted. "I never knew Thumper Parish had procured Travis Golson for us to testify falsely," he said. "I shoulda known, but I didn't." He admitted to berating other witnesses in the Ruby Graham case, driven to hold someone accountable for killing the girl on the blue mailbox.

The judge interrupted. "Even if the person was the wrong person?"

Richie lowered his head. "It was wrong," he said. "In hindsight, a lot was wrong."

Judge Nancy Ball took it all in, occasionally jotting notes. When Richie was done and had left the courtroom, she turned to Thumper Parish, handcuffed and slumped in a chair at one of the tables up front. He was dressed in an orange jumpsuit and wore a glum expression on his face. His lawyer sat with him.

"I've heard a lot this morning," the judge said, "and the thought keeps crossing my mind you could tell us more. I don't imagine you will."

But Thumper stood up, pushing aside his lawyer's effort to keep him still. "I got something," he grunted. He tried to spread his arms, like wings, to make the big, sweeping gesture that, coming from his tall and muscular frame, was so scary on the street. But in court, the handcuffs restricted him, and he looked smaller. He struggled against the restraints. "I don't belong here," he said angrily.

"Me and Flanagan, we had a deal," he said, his voice rising. Thumper began a rant, saying Frank Flanagan had "promised so long as I kept him appraised what was going down, he would watch my back, let me do my thing."

To me and everybody else who was listening, it sure was some kind of crazy argument he was making — claiming he could do whatever he wanted, commit any crime whatsoever, as long as he was snitching for Frank Flanagan.

"So you see, you can't arrest me," he said.

"No?" the judge said. "You're beyond the reach of the law?"

"It's how it is," Thumper insisted.

Heads began shaking, and murmurs spread through the audience.

"No," the judge said flatly. "No. Police and prosecutors do rely at times on criminal informants to assist them in an investigation, but no one in law enforcement—not District Attorney Frank Flanagan or anyone—has the authority to make a secret deal promising complete immunity."

Thumper couldn't do much with his hands, so he kicked the chair and anything else within reach. He shouted, "It was the deal. MY deal!" Court officers moved in quickly to remove him. Even after he was taken out through a side door, the shouting persisted briefly, then faded. Thumper was finished.

Following the disruption, it took the judge a few minutes to restore order, and as I sat there looking around, I realized that just about everyone Clemens and I had crossed paths with during the long summer had appeared in court—from Lola Catron to Travis Golson to Richie and, of course, Thumper Parish.

Except for one person. The one who mattered most. The one stuck in prison, where he didn't belong. Where he'd been my whole life. I felt a pit in my stomach. I repeated in my mind what I always used to say at the end of our prison visits. *Daddy, when you comin' home?*

That was when the judge surprised me and everybody else.

Using the gavel to restore quiet, she began her summation. I assumed she was going to explain that in the days and maybe weeks to come, she would consider the testimony she'd heard during the special hearing. That's what Nora had said was the most likely scenario for a legal hearing like this—the judge would take testimony, adjourn, take time to evaluate the evidence and then, finally, issue a ruling. It could take weeks, maybe even months, Nora said.

But as the judge kept talking, it dawned on me she was not waiting months, weeks, days, or even hours. Something was happening—*now*.

"Justice was not done in this case," she declared. "Of that, I am certain."

The judge paused to let the words sink in, and then continued. "The judicial system failed. The evidence has been cumulative and unambiguous. It failed Ruby Graham's family and Mr. Romero Taylor. Both, in their respective ways, have paid a huge price—and I am deeply sorry for that.

"Unfortunately, there is nothing I can do today regarding Ruby Graham's actual killer—that reckoning will have to wait until another day."

The judge surveyed the courtroom, her brow furrowed.

"But there is something I can do about the man who was wrongfully convicted fourteen years ago for the heinous murder of young Ruby."

The words were coming fast now. Nothing about an

adjournment or anything like that. Instead, the judge spoke with a force and pace that was dizzying.

"In the interests of justice," she proclaimed, "and exercising the powers granted to me under the laws of the Commonwealth of Massachusetts, I hereby order that the first-degree murder conviction of Romero Taylor be vacated."

The ruling exploded in my head: *I hereby order that the first-degree murder conviction of Romero Taylor be vacated.*

The courtroom erupted. Reporters scrambled out the exits to break the news. Ma and I turned to look at each other, our mouths gaping wide open.

Judge Nancy Ball wasn't finished. Pounding the gavel, she continued, "I further order that Mr. Taylor be released from the state penitentiary at Walpole by the close of business today — the 20th of August."

She looked down from the bench to her clerk and instructed, "I want confirmation of that." Then she turned back to address the courtroom.

"Not another day," she said.

I yelled. Many others did, too. I felt goose bumps all over.

Daddy was coming home.

Not another day, the judge had said. *Today.*

The 20th of August.

That's when it broke from the jumble of emotions — the date. I'd lost track of time during the past few days. But now it sank in, and I snapped to.

It was on this day, fourteen years ago, a girl on a blue mailbox was shot dead. The same day a rare disease killed a five-year-old boy named Peter Bittner.

In that moment I turned to Clemens. I saw a tiny tear forming on the cheek facing me. He saw me and smiled back. He wiped the tear, raised his hands, and like everyone else in the room, started whooping it up, cheering for justice.

Soon as we got untangled from the mash of people in the hall, Nora talked her way into one of the clerk's offices to call Daddy at the prison. She came out after and said Daddy went numb when she told him the news, kept saying, "Nora, is this real? Is this *real*?" She instructed Daddy to hurry and pack his things, give away what he didn't want. "The judge wants you out before nightfall."

Ma and I rushed home. I felt spazzed. There seemed so much to do to get ready. We began straightening up the apartment, but kept bumping into each other. Ma got on the phone, calling the ladies from church along with the other mothers who were family after all those years riding together to the prison. Everyone promised to bring something. I went into my room and changed into shorts and a green sleeveless top. I was fixing the birthday photos that ringed the mirror on my bureau when I caught my reflection. It stopped me cold. The eyes. The jawline. The mouth. I looked older. It was like in the two months since school got out, I'd grown. My eyes went around the photos of me and Daddy. No more, I thought. No more prison pictures. We were free to take the next one anywhere we wanted to.

Daddy was coming home.

Paul Parish arrived, wanting to help, and Ma got him busy right away pushing furniture against the walls to make room and setting up folding chairs from the basement. It was good to see him. When Paul and I had a chance to talk after everything that went down at Thumper's castle, I told him I would help him apply to the Weld School. Saying that made me realize that I was going to go back there. Part of it was that people from the school kept calling all day Monday, after the big article in the *Globe*. Ma took most of the calls, with the school people wanting to congratulate me and make sure we knew how much they wanted me to return. The only time I got on the phone was when my adviser called, and when he asked if there was anything he could do, an idea popped into my head. "I want to work on the *Weld News*. Maybe be an editor?"

"Done," he said.

The other big thing happening for Paul was Clemens. Paul never knew his own dad, and his ma—Thumper's sister—was long gone, maybe in New York City, or maybe Detroit. No one knew. But Clemens was talking to the social workers about being part of Paul's life—as some kind of big brother or guardian. It hadn't been sorted out completely, but something was definitely in the works.

Word spread fast, and our apartment soon filled up. The

crowd spilled onto the front porch. Everyone was laughing and happy, talking up the homecoming. We weren't used to something this big and good happening to people in our neighborhood. I took up a position by the front door, and was standing watch when we first heard the horn. Everyone looked to the left and saw Vinnie's Van turn sharply onto the street. Big Vinnie kept honking the horn and flashing his lights as the van came down Hutchings Street and screeched to a stop right out front.

My heart pounded. When the judge surprised everybody by ordering Daddy's release, we got freaked realizing we had no way to get him home. We didn't have a car. Nora didn't have one. Clemens wasn't allowed to drive because of his arm. Ma thought of Vinnie. When she called him in a panic, he cut her off.

"On my way," he said, making a show that he'd do the trip free of charge.

The door flew open and Daddy came down the steps. People cheered. Daddy was stunned, and shielded his eyes as if glaring into a bright sun. He wore baggy khaki pants and a Red Sox T-shirt that Vinnie had thought to bring along for him. I'd never seen Daddy dressed in anything other than a prison jumpsuit.

The moment his feet touched ground, Ma and I flew into his arms. I didn't know people could hug as hard as we did. "Daddy," I kept singing. "Daddy." He chanted quietly, "Shey-Shey, Trell. Shey-Shey, Trell." We hugged some more.

Then Daddy got swept away into the crowd. People wanted to greet him, be close, touch him. Clemens was off duty, hanging next to Nora, but other reporters had arrived. They circled and began firing questions at Daddy nonstop.

"My heart was pounding waiting for Vinnie to come— oh, yeah," he said. "I was nervous. Real nervous. But not anymore. I'm happy now, glad to be home."

The current pulled him toward the porch stairs. People had begun feasting on the barbecue chicken and hot dogs from Simco's the church ladies had supplied. Daddy stopped at the spread and looked it over.

"Any sweet cereal?" he asked. "Corn flakes is all there is where I been."

That got people laughing.

"I'm telling ya, I may want sweet cereal for supper."

"I'm on it!" shouted one of Ma's friends.

I stood back, just watching Daddy and soaking it all in. Clemens and Nora stood nearby, and I noticed Clemens's arm was around Nora. It looked good resting on her shoulder, and when Clemens caught me looking, he shrugged. Made me feel good inside.

One of the TV reporters squeezed her way near Daddy, a cameraman at her side. "Mr. Taylor, now that you're free, what do you want to do first?"

"Wow," Daddy said, his eyes wide. "My mind's running so fast." He scratched his head. "I know I wanna work. I'm ready to work, start my life over."

He smiled, added, "Maybe go shopping, too. I could use some sneakers."

I shouted, "I can help with that!"

Daddy looked at me. "I'm counting on that."

He was still looking at me. He turned calm. "If you'll excuse me," he said, making a T with his hands to signal a time-out. He left the reporters, took my elbow, and steered me away from the pack of people toward the front door.

"Gonna get a little fresh air with my girl," he said. "We'll be back."

Daddy and I walked together down Hutchings, leaving the party sounds behind. We took a left and headed toward Franklin Park. We didn't say anything at first, then Daddy said, "You done a lot, you and Clemens. I'm thankful, and proud. Very proud. You've come a long way. We've come a long way."

Daddy took a huge, huge breath of free air and looked around.

"Neighborhood's changed a lot," he said.

I couldn't believe it. Something as simple as a walk with my daddy was something I'd never done. I couldn't describe the feeling. It was like a dream. Or a fairy-tale wish come true. Or a science fiction story, where some person is brought back from the other side. Or all of those things combined. Except this was real. I felt funny, happy, strange all at once. I tingled all over.

"Where we going?" I asked. It was twilight, and the last light of day flickered through the tops of the park's trees up ahead.

Daddy kept walking. "In Vinnie's Van, I saw something. Just up ahead."

We turned the next corner onto Seaver Street and I saw what Daddy meant.

The tot lot — on Seaver along the side of Franklin Park.

The Ruby Graham Tot Lot.

I stopped in my tracks.

Daddy said, "C'mon."

I didn't budge.

He looked at me, puzzled.

He crossed to the gate and read the plaque out loud: "'In Memory of Ruby Graham.'" Daddy looked around at the swings, slides, and climbing equipment in their candy colors. "Looks like fun, Trell, having this in the neighborhood."

I didn't say anything.

"Nice way to remember her," he said.

I still didn't say a word.

"Trell?"

Finally, I said, "I never felt I could. Play here, I mean. Like I didn't belong."

"Oh," is all Daddy said. He nodded a few times, then reached for the gate and opened it. "Girl never should have been hurt."

"Too many people been hurt," I said.

There was a moment of silence. Then Daddy took off into the lot and jogged over to the swings. "Get over here," he yelled. "Let your daddy have the pleasure of pushing you in the swing."

That got a smile out of me.

"It's a toddler swing, Daddy! I'm too big."

"Naww," he said. "C'mon."

He came and got me, pushed and tickled me toward the swing set. The seat turned out to be bigger than it looked, and so I went along. I squeezed into it and Daddy began to push me, and once he did, I couldn't help but laugh, and so did Daddy. We laughed together. I felt the cool air rushing past me as he pushed me higher and higher, above the tops of the bushes into the blue sky, and for the first time in as long as I could remember, I felt I didn't have a care in the world.

Daddy was home.

Trell has its origins in one of Boston's most notorious murders — the shooting death of twelve-year-old Tiffany Moore on a hot summer night in 1988. Tiffany was seated on a blue mailbox on Humboldt Avenue in Roxbury, swinging her legs and socializing with friends, when masked gunmen approached. Their targets were boys in a competing street gang, but they hit Tiffany. She died instantly — the youngest victim of street gang violence in the city's history.

Tiffany became known as "the girl on the blue mailbox." Her murder instantly came to symbolize the cocaine-fueled lawlessness rocking Boston. Some officials even called for the deployment of the National Guard to cope with soaring violence. Police launched a massive investigation, and two weeks later, they arrested a young drug dealer named Shawn Drumgold. The next year, Drumgold was convicted of her murder. He was sentenced to life without the possibility of parole. The city breathed a sigh of relief. Tiffany's killer was in jail. Justice was served.

Except it wasn't. Fourteen years later, I reinvestigated Drumgold's conviction. I was a reporter at the *Boston Globe*, where I'd mostly served on its Spotlight Team. Contacts in the legal community had been telling me I should look into the case, saying police had rushed to judgment to quell public hysteria. In May 2003, the *Globe* published the results of that investigation, a story revealing prosecutorial wrongdoing. Special court hearings followed, where witnesses from the 1988 murder trial came forward and testified how officials had berated them and coerced their testimony. By summer's end, the Suffolk County District Attorney, who had previously opposed all of Drumgold's legal appeals, joined his lawyer in requesting that the hearing judge overturn his murder conviction "in the interests of justice." The judge did so, and Drumgold went home on November 7, 2003.

During my investigation, my focus was journalistic — exposing flaws in the murder case. Even so, I couldn't help but notice the women in Drumgold's life — his attorney, Rosemary Scapicchio; his mother, Juanda; his wife, Rachelle; and his daughter, Kiara. I learned Kiara was a newborn when Shawn was arrested in the summer of 1988. She'd grown up marking time with regular visits to see her father in prison. I learned that in saying good-bye, Kiara would always ask, "Daddy, when you coming home?"

It became the seed for this novel. I'd wonder periodically what it must be like to grow up with a parent wrongfully imprisoned. I'd also wonder about telling a story for a younger audience, a story showcasing the themes in the *Globe*'s stories — about gross injustice and the eventual search for justice, about journalism and the difference it can make. I began asking, what if the daughter were the central character? What if she possesses the true grit required to push for justice against a system that has failed? What if she convinces a reporter to help her, and together they uncover the truth? Therein came Trell and Clemens. The two of them took over, and the novel's story line began to take shape. It's a story intended to be inspirational. It's also intended to honor the memory of Tiffany Moore; the resolve of Shawn Drumgold; the tenacity of Rosemary Scapicchio; and the loyalty and love of Juanda, Rachelle, and Kiara Drumgold.

Dick Lehr
Boston, Massachusetts
2017

ACKNOWLEDGMENTS

Heartfelt thanks to Liz Bicknell, Carter Hasegawa, Katie Cunningham, Hannah Mahoney, Maya Myers, Jennifer Roberts, and all the folks at Candlewick Press; Micheal Flaherty of Epiphany Story Lab; Richard Abate, John Swomley, Josh Banville, Maggie O'Brien, Nathalie Hansen, and Julia and John Lehr. Most of all, thanks to Karin, Nick, Christian, Holly, and Dana for everything.

DISCUSSION QUESTIONS

1. Many families fall apart during hard times. How do the Taylors keep themselves together? How are they able to overcome the practical problems and emotional strains of Romero Taylor's long incarceration?

2. Trell lives in Roxbury, a largely poor and African-American section of Boston. Why is there so much distrust of the police in her neighborhood? Should there be? Are law enforcement officers trusted in your community? Why?

3. At home in Roxbury, Trell is friendly and talkative, but when she starts at the Weld, an exclusive private school, "I basically went mute," she says (page 8). Why? What does "To Certain Intellectuals," a poem by Langston Hughes, mean to her?

4. The murder of young Ruby Graham shocked the city of Boston in 1989. Why did it attract so much attention? How was the tragedy exploited by the media and by public officials? Is Trell another victim of the shooting? Why?

5. Trell's father didn't kill a little girl, but that doesn't mean that he's an innocent man. How does Trell react when she learns the extent of her father's past criminal activity? How does he explain his actions? Would you be able to forgive him if he were your father? Why?

6. "I'm Thumper Parish," the confident gangster brags. "I play chess; everyone else is playin' checkers" (page 283). What are the risks of believing that you're smarter than everyone else? How do Trell and Clemens prove Thumper wrong?

7. The press is sometimes called the fourth branch of government, as important to our democracy as the three official branches of government — the legislative, executive, and judicial. How does this novel validate the importance of a free press?

8. Dick Lehr, the author of *Trell,* is a journalist and a professor of journalism. What does this novel tell you about his profession? What skills does it require? What are the satisfactions of the work? What are the frustrations? Would you be a good reporter?